THE BEST FROM
FANTASY AND SCIENCE FICTION
Ninth Series

THE BEST FROM
FANTASY AND SCIENCE FICTION
Ninth Series

Edited by Robert P. Mills

DOUBLEDAY & COMPANY, INC., GARDEN CITY, NEW YORK

All of the characters in this book are fictitious, and any re-
semblance to actual persons, living or dead, is purely coin-
cidental.

Dedication

For Anthony Boucher and J. Francis McComas, who are truly responsible for this book's existence . . .

and for Anne, Alison, and Freddie, who contribute so much to the editor's.

Contents

Introduction

As THIS BOOK GOES TO PRESS, the public has been told of projects to put a man in orbit around Earth . . . to send a manned rocket to the moon . . . to land a missile on Venus. A surprising number of people have been heard to comment that such projects rather put science fiction behind the times—"So the scientists have caught up with you?" Which is, of course, altogether untrue.

In the first place, as Anthony Boucher remarked in a radio interview not long ago, scientists have so far done no more than stick their big toe in the ocean of the scientific achievement talked of in science fiction. As a quick, melodramatic example: Venus, the farthest away of the goals mentioned above, is somewhat less than three light minutes distant—as compared to the concept in the opening sentence of the Joel Townsley Rogers story herein, "I sighted the boundary of space-time with Henley ten billion light-years from Earth."

In the far more important second place, science fiction is, as the term clearly states, *fiction*—and to say that the scientists have caught up with science fiction because they have achieved some small smattering of the science it talks about is very nearly as absurd as it would be to say that the criminals had caught up with the crime writers when Cain slew Abel.

Not *quite* as absurd, however, because a science fiction story, by traditional definition, does concern itself with (in addition to its primary concern—human beings) at least one *something* which has not as yet been realized or accomplished by mankind. And it it is quite true that at least one story in this book—"A Different Purpose," by Kem Bennett, about the first man to be put into orbit around Earth—is measurably less solidly in the field of science fiction this year than it was last, and may well not qualify as science fiction at all before the end of 1960. This does not mean that the scientists are closing in on science fiction in general or Mr. Bennett in particular—to the contrary. Mr. Bennett was writing about man's next great frontier, and when the scientists make it possible for man to achieve that frontier, there will be another frontier beyond it for the science fiction writer to report and speculate on, and beyond that, another . . . and so on endlessly.

We have been speaking here by implication of purely physical frontiers, which are obvious and vast. The point also applies to the equally vast, if sometimes less obvious, frontiers of the mind (some of the immediate ones are considered in this book by Daniel Keyes, Lee Sutton, and R. M. McKenna). Both physical and mental matters are *theoretically* susceptible of scientific dissection and analysis—problems subject to being surrounded, overwhelmed, and unconditionally defeated. If that is true, then the imagination is susceptible to precisely the same fate—in a universe where everything is known, how can there be room for thought of what might possibly (though we are almost sure it couldn't conceivably) be? If science were ever to arrive at that point of completion, there would be no more fantasy stories, let alone science fiction stories.

In short, science fiction is limited only by the number of frontiers lying before mankind; and if mankind should ever run out of new frontiers, the question of a race between scientists and science fiction wouldn't much matter, because with no frontiers before it, mankind as we know it would surely die.

In this book, then, you will find stories of imagination. None of them, as far as anybody can prove, ever happened; some of them might happen, or might be proved as having happened, next week . . . or next year . . . or next century . . . or never. All of the stories have to do with mankind, however, and to that degree all of these stories *have* happened, and will happen again and again, as often as they are read. May you enjoy bringing them to life.

ROBERT P. MILLS

Norwalk, Conn.

DANIEL KEYES

Flowers for Algernon

progris riport 1—march 5 1965

DR. STRAUSS SAYS I SHUD RITE DOWN what I think and evrey thing that happins to me from now on. I dont know why but he says its importint so they will see if they will use me. I hope they use me. Miss Kinnian says maybe they can make me smart. I want to be smart. My name is Charlie Gordon. I am 37 years old and 2 weeks ago was my brithday. I have nuthing more to rite now so I will close for today.

progris riport 2—martch 6

I had a test today. I think I faled it. and I think that maybe now they wont use me. What happind is a nice young man was in the room and he had some white cards with ink spillled all over them. He sed Charlie what do you see on this card. I was very skared even tho I had my rabits foot in my pockit because when I was a kid I always faled tests in school and I spillled ink to.

I told him I saw a inkblot. He said yes and it made me feel good. I thot that was all but when I got up to go he stopped me. He said now sit down Charlie we are not thru yet. Then I dont remember so good but he wantid me to say what was in the ink. I dint see nuthing in the ink but he said there was picturs there other pepul saw some picturs. I coudnt see any picturs. I reely tryed to see. I held the card close up and then far away. Then I said if I had my glases I coud see better I usally only ware my glases in the movies or TV but I said they are in the closit in the hall. I got them. Then I said let me see that card agen I bet Ill find it now.

I tryed hard but I still coudnt find the picturs I only saw the ink. I told him maybe I need new glases. He rote somthing down on a paper and I got skared of faling the test. I told him it was a very nice inkblot with littel points all around the eges. He looked very sad so that wasnt it. I said please let me try agen. Ill get it in a few minits becaus Im not so fast somtimes. Im a slow reeder too in Miss Kinnians class for slow adults but I'm trying very hard.

He gave me a chance with another card that had 2 kinds of ink spillled on it red and blue.

He was very nice and talked slow like Miss Kinnian does and he explaned it to me that it was a *raw shok*. He said pepul see things in the ink. I said show me where. He said think. I told him I think a inkblot but that wasnt rite eather. He said what does it remind you—pretend something. I closd my eyes for a long time to pretend. I told him I pretned a fowntan pen with ink leeking all over a table cloth. Then he got up and went out.

I dont think I passd the *raw shok* test.

progris report 3—martch 7

Dr Strauss and Dr Nemur say it dont matter about the inkblots. I told them I dint spill the ink on the cards and I coudnt see anything in the ink. They said that maybe they will still use me. I said Miss Kinnian never gave me tests like that one only spelling and reading. They said Miss Kinnian told that I was her bestist pupil in the adult nite scool becaus I tryed the hardist and I reely wantid to lern. They said how come you went to the adult nite scool all by yourself Charlie. How did you find it. I said I askd pepul and sumbody told me where I shud go to lern to read and spell good. They said why did you want to. I told them becaus all my life I wantid to be smart and not dumb. But its very hard to be smart. They said you know it will probly be tempirery. I said yes. Miss Kinnian told me. I dont care if it herts.

Later I had more crazy tests today. The nice lady who gave it me told me the name and I asked her how do you spellit so I can rite it in my progris riport. THEMATIC APPERCEPTION TEST. I dont know the frist 2 words but I know what *test* means. You got to pass it or you get bad marks. This test lookd easy becaus I coud see the picturs. Only this time she dint want me to tell her the picturs. That mixd me up. I said the man yesterday said I shoud tell him what I saw in the ink she said that dont make no difrence. She said make up storys about the pepul in the picturs.

I told her how can you tell storys about pepul you never met. I said why shud I make up lies. I never tell lies any more becaus I always get caut.

She told me this test and the other one the raw-shok was for getting personalty. I laffed so hard. I said how can you get that thing from inkblots and fotos. She got sore and put her picturs away. I dont care. It was sily. I gess I faled that test too.

Later some men in white coats took me to a difernt part of the hospitil and gave me a game to play. It was like a race with a white mouse. They called the mouse Algernon. Algernon was in a box with a lot of twists and turns like all kinds of walls and they gave me a pencil and a paper with lines and lots of boxes. On one side it said START and on the other end it said FINISH. They said it was *amazed* and that Algernon and me had the same *amazed* to do. I dint see how we could have the same *amazed* if Algernon had a box and I had a paper but I dint say nothing. Anyway there wasnt time because the race started.

One of the men had a watch he was trying to hide so I woudnt see it so I tryed not to look and that made me nervus.

Anyway that test made me feel worser than all the others because they did it over 10 times with difernt *amazeds* and Algernon won every time. I dint know that mice were so smart. Maybe thats because Algernon is a white mouse. Maybe white mice are smarter then other mice.

progris riport 4—Mar 8

Their going to use me! Im so exited I can hardly write. Dr Nemur and Dr Strauss had a argament about it first. Dr Nemur was in the office when Dr Strauss brot me in. Dr Nemur was worryed about using me but Dr Strauss told him Miss Kinnian rekemmended me the best from all the people who she was teaching. I like Miss Kinnian becaus shes a very smart teacher. And she said Charlie your going to have a second chance. If you volenteer for this experament you mite get smart. They dont know if it will be perminint but theirs a chance. Thats why I said ok even when I was scared because she said it was an operashun. She said dont be scared Charlie you done so much with so little I think you deserv it most of all.

So I got scaird when Dr Nemur and Dr Strauss argud about it. Dr Strauss said I had something that was very good. He said I had a good *motor-vation*. I never even knew I had that. I felt proud when he said that not every body with an eye-q of 68 had that thing. I dont know what it is or where I got it but he said Algernon had it too. Algernons *motor-vation* is the cheese they put in his box. But it cant be that because I didnt eat any cheese this week.

Then he told Dr Nemur something I dint understand so while they were talking I wrote down some of the words.

He said Dr Nemur I know Charlie is not what you had in mind as the first of your new brede of intelek** (coudnt get the word) superman. But most people of his low ment** are host** and uncoop** they are usualy dull apath** and hard to reach. He has a good natcher hes intristed and eager to please.

Dr Nemur said remember he will be the first human beeng ever to have his intelijence trippled by surgicle meens.

Dr Strauss said exakly. Look at how well hes lerned to read and write for his low mentel age its as grate an acheve** as you and I lerning einstines therey of **vity without help. That shows the intenss motor-vation. Its comparat** a tremen** achev** I say we use Charlie.

I dint get all the words and they were talking to fast but it sounded like Dr Strauss was on my side and like the other one wasnt.

Then Dr Nemur nodded he said all right maybe your right. We will use Charlie. When he said that I got so exited I jumped up and shook his hand for being so good to me. I told him thank you doc you wont be sorry for giving me a second chance. And I mean it like I told him. After the operashun Im gonna try to be smart. Im gonna try awful hard.

progris ript 5—Mar 10

Im skared. Lots of people who work here and the nurses and the people who gave me the tests came to bring me candy and wish me luck. I hope I have luck. I got my rabits foot and my lucky penny and my horse shoe. Only a black cat crossed me when I was comming to the hospitil. Dr Strauss says dont be supersitis Charlie this is sience. Anyway Im keeping my rabits foot with me.

I asked Dr Strauss if Ill beat Algernon in the race after the operashun and he said maybe. If the operashun works Ill show that mouse I can be as smart as he is. Maybe smarter. Then Ill be abel to read better and spell the words good and know lots of things and be like other people. I want to be smart like other people. If it works perminint they will make everybody smart all over the wurld.

They dint give me anything to eat this morning. I dont know what that eating has to do with getting smart. Im very hungry and Dr Nemur took away my box of candy. That Dr Nemur is a grouch. Dr Strauss says I can have it back after the operashun. You cant eat befor a operashun . . .

Progress Report 6—Mar 15

The operashun dint hurt. He did it while I was sleeping. They took off the bandijis from my eyes and my head today so I can make a PROGRESS REPORT. Dr Nemur who looked at some of my other ones says I spell PROGRESS wrong and he told me how to spell it and REPORT too. I got to try and remember that.

I have a very bad memary for spelling. Dr Strauss says its ok to tell about all the things that happin to me but he says I shoud tell more about what I feel and what I think. When I told him I dont know how to think he said try. All the time when the bandijis were on my eyes I tryed to think. Nothing happened. I dont know what to think about. Maybe if I ask him he will tell me how I can think now that Im suppose to get smart. What do smart people think about. Fancy things I suppose. I wish I knew some fancy things alredy.

Progress Report 7—mar 19

Nothing is happining. I had lots of tests and different kinds of races with Algernon. I hate that mouse. He always beats me. Dr Strauss said I got to play those games. And he said some time I got to take those tests over again. Thse inkblots are stupid. And those pictures are stupid too. I like to draw a picture of a man and a woman but I wont make up lies about people.

I got a headache from trying to think so much. I thot Dr Strauss was my frend but he dont help me. He dont tell me what to think or when Ill get smart. Miss Kinnian dint come to see me. I think writing these progress reports are stupid too.

Progress Report 8—Mar 23

Im going back to work at the factery. They said it was better I shud go back to work but I cant tell anyone what the operashun was for and I have to come to the hospitil for an hour evry night after work. They are gonna pay me mony every month for lerning to be smart.

Im glad Im going back to work because I miss my job and all my frends and all the fun we have there.

Dr Strauss says I shud keep writing things down but I dont have to do it every day just when I think of something or some-

thing speshul happins. He says dont get discoridged because it
takes time and it happins slow. He says it took a long time with
Algernon before he got 3 times smarter then he was before.
Thats why Algernon beats me all the time because he had that
operashun too. That makes me feel better. I coud probly do that
amazed faster than a reglar mouse. Maybe some day Ill beat
Algernon. Boy that would be something. So far Algernon looks
like he mite be smart perminent.

Mar 25 (I dont have to write PROGRESS REPORT on top any more
just when I hand it in once a week for Dr Nemur to read. I just
have to put the date on. That saves time)

We had a lot of fun at the factery today. Joe Carp said hey
look where Charlie had his operashun what did they do Charlie
put some brains in. I was going to tell him but I remembered Dr
Strauss said no. Then Frank Reilly said what did you do Charlie
forget your key and open your door the hard way. That made me
laff. Their really my friends and they like me.

Sometimes somebody will say hey look at Joe or Frank or
George he really pulled a Charlie Gordon. I dont know why they
say that but they always laff. This morning Amos Borg who is
the 4 man at Donnegans used my name when he shouted at
Ernie the office boy. Ernie lost a packige. He said Ernie for god-
sake what are you trying to be a Charlie Gordon. I dont understand why he said that. I never lost any packiges.

Mar 28 Dr Strauss came to my room tonight to see why I dint
come in like I was suppose to. I told him I dont like to race with
Algernon any more. He said I dont have to for a while but I
shud come in. He had a present for me only it wasnt a present
but just for lend. I thot it was a little television but it wasnt.
He said I got to turn it on when I go to sleep. I said your kidding
why shud I turn it on when Im going to sleep. Who ever herd
of a thing like that. But he said if I want to get smart I got to do
what he says. I told him I dint think I was going to get smart

and he put his hand on my sholder and said Charlie you dont
know it yet but your getting smarter all the time. You wont
notice for a while. I think he was just being nice to make me
feel good because I dont look any smarter.

Oh yes I almost forgot. I asked him when I can go back to the
class at Miss Kinnians school. He said I wont go their. He said
that soon Miss Kinnian will come to the hospitil to start and
teach me speshul. I was mad at her for not comming to see me
when I got the operashun but I like her so maybe we will be
frends again.

Mar 29   That crazy TV kept me up all night. How can I sleep
with something yelling crazy things all night in my ears. And
the nutty pictures. Wow. I dont know what it says when Im up
so how am I going to know when Im sleeping.

Dr Strauss says its ok. He says my brains are lerning when I
sleep and that will help me when Miss Kinnian starts my lessons
in the hospitl (only I found out it isnt a hospitil its a labatory).
I think its all crazy. If you can get smart when your sleeping why
do people go to school. That thing I dont think will work. I
use to watch the late show and the late late show on TV all the
time and it never made me smart. Maybe you have to sleep while
you watch it.

PROGRESS REPORT 9–April 3

Dr Strauss showed me how to keep the TV turned low so now
I can sleep. I dont hear a thing. And I still dont understand what
it says. A few times I play it over in the morning to find out what
I lerned when I was sleeping and I dont think so. Miss Kinnian
says Maybe its another langwidge or something. But most times
it sounds american. It talks so fast faster then even Miss Gold
who was my teacher in 6 grade and I remember she talked so
fast I coudnt understand her.

I told Dr Strauss what good is it to get smart in my sleep. I want to be smart when Im awake. He says its the same thing and I have two minds. Theres the *subconscious* and the *conscious* (thats how you spell it). And one dont tell the other one what its doing. They dont even talk to each other. Thats why I dream. And boy have I been having crazy dreams. Wow. Ever since that night TV. The late late late late late show.

I forgot to ask him if it was only me or if everybody had those two minds.

(I just looked up the word in the dictionary Dr Strauss gave me. The word is *subconscious. adj. Of the nature of mental operations yet not present in consciousness; as, subconscious conflict of desires.*) Theres more but I still don't know what it means. This isnt a very good dictionary for dumb people like me.

Anyway the headache is from the party. My frends from the factery Joe Carp and Frank Reilly invited me to go with them to Muggsys Saloon for some drinks. I dont like to drink but they said we will have lots of fun. I had a good time.

Joe Carp said I shoud show the girls how I mop out the toilet in the factory and he got me a mop. I showed them and everyone laffed when I told that Mr Donnegan said I was the best janiter he ever had because I like my job and do it good and never come late or miss a day except for my operashun.

I said Miss Kinnian always said Charlie be proud of your job because you do it good.

Everybody laffed and we had a good time and they gave me lots of drinks and Joe said Charlie is a card when hes potted. I dont know what that means but everybody likes me and we have fun. I cant wait to be smart like my best frends Joe Carp and Frank Reilly.

I dont remember how the party was over but I think I went out to buy a newspaper and coffe for Joe and Frank and when I came back there was no one their. I looked for them all over till late. Then I dont remember so good but I think I got sleepy or sick. A nice cop brot me back home. Thats what my landlady Mrs Flynn says.

But I got a headache and a big lump on my head and black and blue all over. I think maybe I fell but Joe Carp says it was the cop they beat up drunks some times. I don't think so. Miss Kinnian says cops are to help people. Anyway I got a bad headache and Im sick and hurt all over. I dont think Ill drink anymore.

April 6 I beat Algernon! I dint even know I beat him until Burt the tester told me. Then the second time I lost because I got so exited I fell off the chair before I finished. But after that I beat him 8 more times. I must be getting smart to beat a smart mouse like Algernon. But I dont *feel* smarter.

I wanted to race Algernon some more but Burt said thats enough for one day. They let me hold him for a minit. Hes not so bad. Hes soft like a ball of cotton. He blinks and when he opens his eyes their black and pink on the eges.

I said can I feed him because I felt bad to beat him and I wanted to be nice and make frends. Burt said no Algernon is a very specshul mouse with an operashun like mine, and he was the first of all the animals to stay smart so long. He told me Algernon is so smart that every day he has to solve a test to get his food. Its a thing like a lock on a door that changes every time Algernon goes in to eat so he has to lern something new to get his food. That made me sad because if he coudnt lern he woud be hungry.

I dont think its right to make you pass a test to eat. How woud Dr Nemur like it to have to pass a test every time he wants to eat. I think Ill be frends with Algernon.

April 9 Tonight after work Miss Kinnian was at the laboratory. She looked like she was glad to see me but scared. I told her dont worry Miss Kinnian Im not smart yet and she laffed. She said I have confidence in you Charlie the way you struggled so hard to read and right better than all the others. At werst you will have it for a littel wile and your doing somthing for sience.

We are reading a very hard book. I never read such a hard book

before. Its called *Robinson Crusoe* about a man who gets mer-
ooned on a dessert Iland. Hes smart and figers out all kinds of
things so he can have a house and food and hes a good swimmer.
Only I feel sorry because hes all alone and has no frends. But I
think their must be somebody else on the iland because theres a
picture with his funny umbrella looking at footprints. I hope he
gets a frend and not be lonly.

April 10   Miss Kinnian teaches me to spell better. She says look
at a word and close your eyes and say it over and over until you
remember. I have lots of truble with *through* that you say *threw*
and *enough* and *tough* that you dont say *enew* and *tew*. You got
to say *enuff* and *tuff*. Thats how I use to write it before I started to
get smart. Im confused but Miss Kinnian says theres no reason
in spelling.

Apr 14   Finished *Robinson Crusoe*. I want to find out more about
what happens to him but Miss Kinnian says thats all there is. *Why*

Apr 15   Miss Kinnian says Im lerning fast. She read some of the
Progress Reports and she looked at me kind of funny. She says
Im a fine person and Ill show them all. I asked her why. She said
never mind but I shoudnt feel bad if I find out that everybody isnt
nice like I think. She said for a person who god gave so little to
you done more then a lot of people with brains they never even
used. I said all my frends are smart people but there good. They
like me and they never did anything that wasnt nice. Then she got
something in her eye and she had to run out to the ladys room.

Apr 16   Today, I lerned, the *comma*, this is a comma (,) a period,
with a tail, Miss Kinnian, says its importent, because, it makes
writing, better, she said, sombeody, coud lose, a lot of money, if a
comma, isnt, in the, right place, I dont have, any money, and I
dont see, how a comma, keeps you, from losing it,

   But she says, everybody, uses commas, so Ill use, them too,

Apr 17 I used the comma wrong. Its punctuation. Miss Kinnian told me to look up long words in the dictionary to lern to spell them. I said whats the difference if you can read it anyway. She said its part of your education so now on Ill look up all the words Im not sure how to spell. It takes a long time to write that way but I think Im remembering. I only have to look up once and after that I get it right. Anyway thats how come I got the word *punctuation* right. (Its that way in the dictionary). Miss Kinnian says a period is punctuation too, and there are lots of other marks to lern. I told her I thot all the periods had to have tails but she said no.

You got to mix them up, she showed? me" how. to mix! them(up,. and now; I can! mix up all kinds" of punctuation, in! my writing? There, are lots! of rules? to lern; but Im gettin'g them in my head.

One thing I? like about, Dear Miss Kinnian: (thats the way it goes in a business letter if I ever go into business) is she, always gives me' a reason" when—I ask. She's a gen'ius! I wish! I cou'd be smart" like, her;

(Punctuation, is; fun!)

April 18 What a dope I am! I didn't even understand what she was talking about. I read the grammar book last night and it explanes the whole thing. Then I saw it was the same way as Miss Kinnian was trying to tell me, but I didn't get it. I got up in the middle of the night, and the whole thing straightened out in my mind.

Miss Kinnian said that the TV working in my sleep helped out. She said I reached a plateau. Thats like the flat top of a hill.

After I figgered out how punctuation worked, I read over all my old Progress Reports from the beginning. Boy, did I have crazy spelling and punctuation! I told Miss Kinnian I ought to go over the pages and fix all the mistakes but she said, "No, Charlie, Dr. Nemur wants them just as they are. That's why he let you keep them after they were photostated, to see your own progress. You're coming along fast, Charlie."

That made me feel good. After the lesson I went down and played with Algernon. We don't race any more.

April 20 I feel sick inside. Not sick like for a doctor, but inside my chest it feels empty like getting punched and a heartburn at the same time.

I wasn't going to write about it, but I guess I got to, because it's important. Today was the first time I ever stayed home from work.

Last night Joe Carp and Frank Reilly invited me to a party. There were lots of girls and some men from the factory. I remembered how sick I got last time I drank too much, so I told Joe I didn't want anything to drink. He gave me a plain Coke instead. It tasted funny, but I thought it was just a bad taste in my mouth.

We had a lot of fun for a while. Joe said I should dance with Ellen and she would teach me the steps. I fell a few times and I couldn't understand why because no one else was dancing besides Ellen and me. And all the time I was tripping because somebody's foot was always sticking out.

Then when I got up I saw the look on Joe's face and it gave me a funny feeling in my stomack. "He's a scream," one of the girls said. Everybody was laughing.

Frank said, "I ain't laughed so much since we sent him off for the newspaper that night at Muggsy's and ditched him."

"Look at him. His face is red."

"He's blushing. Charlie is blushing."

"Hey, Ellen, what'd you do to Charlie? I never saw him act like that before."

I didn't know what to do or where to turn. Everyone was looking at me and laughing and I felt naked. I wanted to hide myself. I ran out into the street and I threw up. Then I walked home. It's a funny thing I never knew that Joe and Frank and the others liked to have me around all the time to make fun of me.

Now I know what it means when they say "to pull a Charlie
Gordon."

I'm ashamed.

PROGRESS REPORT 11

April 21 Still didn't go into the factory. I told Mrs. Flynn my
landlady to call and tell Mr. Donnegan I was sick. Mrs. Flynn
looks at me very funny lately like she's scared of me.

I think it's a good thing about finding out how everybody laughs
at me. I thought about it a lot. It's because I'm so dumb and I
don't even know when I'm doing something dumb. People think
it's funny when a dumb person can't do things the same way they
can.

Anyway, now I know I'm getting smarter every day. I know
punctuation and I can spell good. I like to look up all the hard
words in the dictionary and I remember them. I'm reading a lot
now, and Miss Kinnian says I read very fast. Sometimes I even
understand what I'm reading about, and it stays in my mind.
There are times when I can close my eyes and think of a page and
it all comes back like a picture.

Besides history, geography, and arithmetic, Miss Kinnian said
I should start to learn a few foreign languages. Dr. Strauss gave
me some more tapes to play while I sleep. I still don't understand
how that conscious and unconscious mind works, but Dr. Strauss
says not to worry yet. He asked me to promise that when I start
learning college subjects next week I wouldn't read any books on
psychology—that is, until he gives me permission.

I feel a lot better today, but I guess I'm still a little angry that
all the time people were laughing and making fun of me because I
wasn't so smart. When I become intelligent like Dr. Strauss says,
with three times my I.Q. of 68, then maybe I'll be like everyone
else and people will like me and be friendly.

I'm not sure what an I.Q. is. Dr. Nemur said it was something
that measured how intelligent you were—like a scale in the drug-
store weighs pounds. But Dr. Strauss had a big argument with

him and said an I.Q. didn't weigh intelligence at all. He said an I.Q. showed how much intelligence you could get, like the numbers on the outside of a measuring cup. You still had to fill the cup up with stuff.

Then when I asked Burt, who gives me my intelligence tests and works with Algernon, he said that both of them were wrong (only I had to promise not to tell them he said so). Burt says that the I.Q. measures a lot of different things including some of the things you learned already, and it really isn't any good at all.

So I still don't know what I.Q. is except that mine is going to be over 200 soon. I didn't want to say anything, but I don't see how if they don't know *what* it is, or *where* it is—— I don't see how they know *how much* of it you've got.

Dr. Nemur says I have to take a *Rorshach Test* tomorrow. I wonder what *that* is.

April 22   I found out what a *Rorshach* is. It's the test I took before the operation—the one with the inkblots on the pieces of cardboard. The man who gave me the test was the same one.

I was scared to death of those inkblots. I knew he was going to ask me to find the pictures and I knew I wouldn't be able to. I was thinking to myself, if only there was some way of knowing what kind of pictures were hidden there. Maybe there weren't any pictures at all. Maybe it was just a trick to see if I was dumb enough to look for something that wasn't there. Just thinking about that made me sore at him.

"All right, Charlie," he said, "you've seen these cards before, remember?"

"Of course I remember."

The way I said it, he knew I was angry, and he looked surprised. "Yes, of course. Now I want you to look at this one. What might this be? What do you see on this card? People see all sorts of things in these inkblots. Tell me what it might be for you—what it makes you think of."

I was shocked. That wasn't what I had expected him to say

at all. "You mean there are no pictures hidden in those inkblots?"

He frowned and took off his glasses. "What?"

"Pictures. Hidden in the inkblots. Last time you told me that everyone could see them and you wanted me to find them too."

He explained to me that the last time he had used almost the exact same words he was using now. I didn't believe it, and I still have the suspicion that he misled me at the time just for the fun of it. Unless—I don't know any more—could I have been *that* feeble-minded?

We went through the cards slowly. One of them looked like a pair of bats tugging at something. Another one looked like two men fencing with swords. I imagined all sorts of things. I guess I got carried away. But I didn't trust him any more, and I kept turning them around and even looking on the back to see if there was anything there I was supposed to catch. While he was making his notes, I peeked out of the corner of my eye to read it. But it was all in code that looked like this:

WF+A DdF-Ad orig. WF-A SF+obj

The test still doesn't make sense to me. It seems to me that any-one could make up lies about things that they didn't really see. How could he know I wasn't making a fool of him by mentioning things that I didn't really imagine? Maybe I'll understand it when Dr. Strauss lets me read up on psychology.

April 25 I figured out a new way to line up the machines in the factory, and Mr. Donnegan says it will save him ten thousand dollars a year in labor and increased production. He gave me a twenty-five-dollar bonus.

I wanted to take Joe Carp and Frank Reilly out to lunch to celebrate, but Joe said he had to buy some things for his wife, and Frank said he was meeting his cousin for lunch. I guess it'll take a little time for them to get used to the changes in me. Every-body seems to be frightened of me. When I went over to Amos Borg and tapped him on the shoulder, he jumped up in the air.

People don't talk to me much any more or kid around the way they used to. It makes the job kind of lonely.

April 27 I got up the nerve today to ask Miss Kinnian to have dinner with me tomorrow night to celebrate my bonus.

At first she wasn't sure it was right, but I asked Dr. Strauss and he said it was okay. Dr. Strauss and Dr. Nemur don't seem to be getting along so well. They're arguing all the time. This evening when I came in to ask Dr. Strauss about having dinner with Miss Kinnian, I heard them shouting. Dr. Nemur was saying that it was *his* experiment and *his* research, and Dr. Strauss was shouting back that he contributed just as much, because he found me through Miss Kinnian and he performed the operation. Dr. Strauss said that someday thousands of neurosurgeons might be using his technique all over the world.

Dr. Nemur wanted to publish the results of the experiment at the end of this month. Dr. Strauss wanted to wait a while longer to be sure. Dr. Strauss said that Dr. Nemur was more interested in the Chair of Psychology at Princeton than he was in the experiment. Dr. Nemur said that Dr. Strauss was nothing but an opportunist who was trying to ride to glory on *his* coattails.

When I left afterwards, I found myself trembling. I don't know why for sure, but it was as if I'd seen both men clearly for the first time. I remember hearing Burt say that Dr. Nemur had a shrew of a wife who was pushing him all the time to get things published so that he could become famous. Burt said that the dream of her life was to have a big-shot husband.

Was Dr. Strauss really trying to ride on his coattails?

April 28 I don't understand why I never noticed how beautiful Miss Kinnian really is. She has brown eyes and feathery brown hair that comes to the top of her neck. She's only thirty-four! I think from the beginning I had the feeling that she was an un-reachable genius—and very, very old. Now, every time I see her she grows younger and more lovely.

We had dinner and a long talk. When she said that I was coming along so fast that soon I'd be leaving her behind, I laughed.

"It's true, Charlie. You're already a better reader that I am. You can read a whole page at a glance while I can take in only a few lines at a time. And you remember every single thing you read. I'm lucky if I can recall the main thoughts and the general meaning."

"I don't feel intelligent. There are so many things I don't understand."

She took out a cigarette and I lit it for her. "You've got to be a *little* patient. You're accomplishing in days and weeks what it takes normal people to do in half a lifetime. That's what makes it so amazing. You're like a giant sponge now, soaking things in. Facts, figures, general knowledge. And soon you'll begin to connect them, too. You'll see how the different branches of learning are related. There are many levels, Charlie, like steps on a giant ladder that take you up higher and higher to see more and more of the world around you.

"I can see only a little bit of that, Charlie, and I won't go much higher than I am now, but you'll keep climbing up and up, and see more and more, and each step will open new worlds that you never even knew existed." She frowned. "I hope . . . I just hope to God—"

"What?"

"Never mind, Charles. I just hope I wasn't wrong to advise you to go into this in the first place."

I laughed. "How could that be? It worked, didn't it? Even Algernon is still smart."

We sat there silently for a while and I knew what she was thinking about as she watched me toying with the chain of my rabbit's foot and my keys. I didn't want to think of that possibility any more than elderly people want to think of death. I *knew* that this was only the beginning. I knew what she meant about levels because I'd seen some of them already. The thought of leaving her behind made me sad.

I'm in love with Miss Kinnian.

PROGRESS REPORT 12

April 30 I've quit my job with Donnegan's Plastic Box Company. Mr. Donnegan insisted that it would be better for all concerned if I left. What did I do to make them hate me so?

The first I knew of it was when Mr. Donnegan showed me the petition. Eight hundred and forty names, everyone connected with the factory, except Fanny Girden. Scanning the list quickly, I saw at once that hers was the only missing name. All the rest demanded that I be fired.

Joe Carp and Frank Reilly wouldn't talk to me about it. No one else would either, except Fanny. She was one of the few people I'd known who set her mind to something and believed it no matter what the rest of the world proved, said, or did—and Fanny did not believe that I should have been fired. She had been against the petition on principle and despite the pressure and threats she'd held out.

"Which don't mean to say," she remarked, "that I don't think there's something mighty strange about you, Charlie. Them changes. I don't know. You used to be a good, dependable, ordinary man—not too bright maybe, but honest. Who knows what you done to yourself to get so smart all of a sudden. Like everybody around here's been saying, Charlie, it's not right."

"But how can you say that, Fanny? What's wrong with a man becoming intelligent and wanting to acquire knowledge and understanding of the world around him?"

She stared down at her work and I turned to leave. Without looking at me, said: "It was evil when Eve listened to the snake and ate from the tree of knowledge. It was evil when she saw that she was naked. If not for that none of us would ever have to grow old and sick, and die."

Once again now I have the feeling of shame burning inside me. This intelligence has driven a wedge between me and all the people I once knew and loved. Before, they laughed at me and despised me for my ignorance and dullness; now, they hate me for my knowledge and understanding. What in God's name do they want of me?

They've driven me out of the factory. Now I'm more alone than ever before . . .

May 15   Dr. Strauss is very angry at me for not having written any progress reports in two weeks. He's justified because the lab is now paying me a regular salary. I told him I was too busy thinking and reading. When I pointed out that writing was such a slow process that it made me impatient with my poor handwriting, he suggested that I learn to type. It's much easier to write now because I can type nearly seventy-five words a minute. Dr. Strauss continually reminds me of the need to speak and write simply so that people will be able to understand me.

I'll try to review all the things that happened to me during the last two weeks. Algernon and I were presented to the American Psychological Association sitting in convention with the World Psychological Association last Tuesday. We created quite a sensation. Dr. Nemur and Dr. Strauss were proud of us.

I suspect that Dr. Nemur, who is sixty—ten years older than Dr. Strauss—finds it necessary to see tangible results of his work. Undoubtedly the result of pressure by Mrs. Nemur.

Contrary to my earlier impressions of him, I realize that Dr. Nemur is not at all a genius. He has a very good mind, but it struggles under the spectre of self-doubt. He wants people to take him for a genius. Therefore, it is important for him to feel that his work is accepted by the world. I believe that Dr. Nemur was afraid of further delay because he worried that someone else might make a discovery along these lines and take the credit from him.

Dr. Strauss on the other hand might be called a genius, although I feel that his areas of knowledge are too limited. He was educated in the tradition of narrow specialization; the broader aspects of background were neglected far more than necessary—even for a neurosurgeon.

I was shocked to learn that the only ancient languages he could

read were Latin, Greek, and Hebrew, and that he knows almost
nothing of mathematics beyond the elementary levels of the calculus of variations. When he admitted this to me, I found myself
almost annoyed. It was as if he'd hidden this part of himself in
order to deceive me, pretending—as do many people I've discovered—to be what he is not. No one I've ever known is what he
appears to be on the surface.

Dr. Nemur appears to be uncomfortable around me. Sometimes
when I try to talk to him, he just looks at me strangely and turns
away. I was angry at first when Dr. Strauss told me I was giving
Dr. Nemur an inferiority complex. I thought he was mocking me
and I'm oversensitive at being made fun of.

How was I to know that a highly respected psychoexperimen-
talist like Nemur was unacquainted with Hindustani and Chinese?
It's absurd when you consider the work that is being done in India
and China today in the very field of his study.

I asked Dr. Strauss how Nemur could refute Rahajamati's
attack on his method and results if Nemur couldn't even read them
in the first place. That strange look on Dr. Strauss' face can mean
only one of two things. Either he doesn't want to tell Nemur what
they're saying in India, or else—and this worries me—Dr. Strauss
doesn't know either. I must be careful to speak and write clearly
and simply so that people won't laugh.

May 18   I am very disturbed. I saw Miss Kinnian last night for the
first time in over a week. I tried to avoid all discussions of intellectual concepts and to keep the conversation on a simple, everyday level, but she just stared at me blankly and asked me what I
meant about the mathematical variance equivalent in Dorber-
mann's *Fifth Concerto*.

When I tried to explain she stopped me and laughed. I guess
I got angry, but I suspect I'm approaching her on the wrong level.
No matter what I try to discuss with her, I am unable to commu-
nicate. I must review Vrostadt's equations on *Levels of Semantic
Progression*. I find that I don't communicate with people much
any more. Thank God for books and music and things I can think

about. I am alone in my apartment at Mrs. Flynn's boardinghouse most of the time and seldom speak to anyone.

May 20   I would not have noticed the new dishwasher, a boy of about sixteen, at the corner diner where I take my evening meals if not for the incident of the broken dishes.

They crashed to the floor, shattering and sending bits of white china under the tables. The boy stood there, dazed and frightened, holding the empty tray in his hand. The whistles and catcalls from the customers (the cries of "hey, there go the profits!" . . . "*Mazeltov!*" . . . and "well, *he* didn't work here very long . . ." which invariably seems to follow the breaking of glass or dishware in a public restaurant) all seemed to confuse him.

When the owner came to see what the excitement was about, the boy cowered as if he expected to be struck and threw up his arms as if to ward off the blow.

"All right! All right, you dope," shouted the owner, "don't just stand there! Get the broom and sweep that mess up. A broom . . . a broom, you idiot! It's in the kitchen. Sweep up all the pieces."

The boy saw that he was not going to be punished. His frightened expression disappeared and he smiled and hummed as he came back with the broom to sweep the floor. A few of the rowdier customers kept up the remarks, amusing themselves at his expense.

"Here, sonny, over here there's a nice piece behind you . . ."

"C'mon, do it again . . ."

"He's not so dumb. It's easier to break 'em than to wash 'em . . ."

As his vacant eyes moved across the crowd of amused onlookers, he slowly mirrored their smiles and finally broke into an uncertain grin at the joke which he obviously did not understand.

I felt sick inside as I looked at his dull, vacuous smile, the wide, bright eyes of a child, uncertain but eager to please. They were laughing at him because he was mentally retarded.

And I had been laughing at him too.

Suddenly, I was furious at myself and all those who were smirking at him. I jumped up and shouted, "Shut up! Leave him alone! It's not his fault he can't understand! He can't help what he is! But for God's sake . . . he's still a human being!"

The room grew silent. I cursed myself for losing control and creating a scene. I tried not to look at the boy as I paid my check and walked out without touching my food. I felt ashamed for both of us.

How strange it is that people of honest feelings and sensibility, who would not take advantage of a man born without arms or legs or eyes—how such people think nothing of abusing a man born with low intelligence. It infuriated me to think that not too long ago I, like this boy, had foolishly played the clown.

And I had almost forgotten.

I'd hidden the picture of the old Charlie Gordon from myself because now that I was intelligent it was something that had to be pushed out of my mind. But today in looking at that boy, for the first time I saw what I had been. *I was just like him!*

Only a short time ago, I learned that people laughed at me. Now I can see that unknowingly I joined with them in laughing at myself. That hurts most of all.

I have often reread my progress reports and seen the illiteracy, the childish naïveté, the mind of low intelligence peering from a dark room, through the keyhole, at the dazzling light outside. I see that even in my dullness I knew that I was inferior, and that other people had something I lacked—something denied me. In my mental blindness, I thought that it was somehow connected with the ability to read and write, and I was sure that if I could get those skills I would automatically have intelligence too.

Even a feeble-minded man wants to be like other men.

A child may not know how to feed itself, or what to eat, yet it knows of hunger.

This then is what I was like, I never knew. Even with my gift of intellectual awareness, I never really knew.

This day was good for me. Seeing the past more clearly, I have decided to use my knowledge and skills to work in the field of increasing human intelligence levels. Who is better equipped for this work? Who else has lived in both worlds? These are my people. Let me use my gift to do something for them.

Tomorrow, I will discuss with Dr. Strauss the manner in which I can work in this area. I may be able to help him work out the problems of widespread use of the technique which was used on me. I have several good ideas of my own.

There is so much that might be done with this technique. If I could be made into a genius, what about thousands of others like myself? What fantastic levels might be achieved by using this technique on normal people? On *geniuses*?

There are so many doors to open. I am impatient to begin.

PROGRESS REPORT 13

May 23 It happened today. Algernon bit me. I visited the lab to see him as I do occasionally, and when I took him out of his cage, he snapped at my hand. I put him back and watched him for a while. He was unusually disturbed and vicious.

May 24 Burt, who is in charge of the experimental animals, tells me that Algernon is changing. He is less co-operative; he refuses to run the maze any more; general motivation has decreased. And he hasn't been eating. Everyone is upset about what this may mean.

May 25 They've been feeding Algernon, who now refuses to work the shifting-lock problem. Everyone identifies me with Algernon. In a way we're both the first of our kind. They're all pretending that Algernon's behavior is not necessarily significant for me. But it's hard to hide the fact that some of the other animals who were used in this experiment are showing strange behavior.

Dr. Strauss and Dr. Nemur have asked me not to come to the lab any more. I know what they're thinking but I can't accept it. I am going ahead with my plans to carry their research forward. With all due respect to both of these fine scientists, I am well aware of their limitations. If there is an answer, I'll have to find it out for myself. Suddenly, time has become very important to me.

May 29 I have been given a lab of my own and permission to go ahead with the research. I'm on to something. Working day and night. I've had a cot moved into the lab. Most of my writing time is spent on the notes which I keep in a separate folder, but from time to time I feel it necessary to put down my moods and my thoughts out of sheer habit.

I find the *calculus of intelligence* to be a fascinating study. Here is the place for the application of all the knowledge I have acquired. In a sense it's the problem I've been concerned with all my life.

May 31 Dr. Strauss thinks I'm working too hard. Dr. Nemur says I'm trying to cram a lifetime of research and thought into a few weeks. I know I should rest, but I'm driven on by something inside that won't let me stop. I've got to find the reason for the sharp regression in Algernon. I've got to know *if* and *when* it will happen to me.

June 4

LETTER TO DR. STRAUSS (*copy*)

Dear Dr. Strauss:

Under separate cover I am sending you a copy of my report entitled, "The Algernon-Gordon Effect: A Study of Structure and Function of Increased Intelligence," which I would like to have you read and have published.

As you see, my experiments are completed. I have included in my report all of my formulae, as well as mathematical analysis in the appendix. Of course, these should be verified.

Because of its importance to both you and Dr. Nemur (and need I say to myself, too?) I have checked and rechecked my results a dozen times in the hope of finding an error. I am sorry to say the results must stand. Yet for the sake of science, I am grateful for the little bit that I here add to the knowledge of the function of the human mind and of the laws governing the artificial increase of human intelligence.

I recall your once saying to me that an experimental *failure*

or the *disproving* of a theory was as important to the advance-
ment of learning as a success would be. I know now that this is
true. I am sorry, however, that my own contribution to the field
must rest upon the ashes of the work of two men I regard so
highly.

Yours truly,
Charles Gordon

encl.: rept.

June 5 I must not become emotional. The facts and the results of
my experiments are clear, and the more sensational aspects of my
own rapid climb cannot obscure the fact that the tripling of intelligence by the surgical technique developed by Drs. Strauss and
Nemur must be viewed as having little or no practical applicability
(at the present time) to the increase of human intelligence.

As I review the records and data on Algernon, I see that although he is still in his physical infancy, he has regressed mentally. Motor activity is impaired; there is a general reduction of
glandular activity; there is an accelerated loss of co-ordination.

There are also strong indications of progressive amnesia.

As will be seen by my report, these and other physical and mental deterioration syndromes can be predicted with statistically significant results by the application of my formula.

The surgical stimulus to which we were both subjected has re-
sulted in an intensification and acceleration of all mental proc-
esses. The unforeseen development, which I have taken the lib-
erty of calling the *Algernon-Gordon Effect,* is the logical extension
of the entire intelligence speed-up. The hypothesis here proven
may be described simply in the following terms: Artificially increased intelligence deteriorates at a rate of time directly pro-
portional to the quantity of the increase.

I feel that this, in itself, is an important discovery.

As long as I am able to write, I will continue to record my
thoughts in these progress reports. It is one of my few pleasures.
However, by all indications, my own mental deterioration will be
very rapid.

I have already begun to notice signs of emotional instability and forgetfulness, the first symptoms of the burnout.

June 10 Deterioration progressing. I have become absent-minded. Algernon died two days ago. Dissection shows my predictions were right. His brain had decreased in weight and there was a general smoothing out of cerebral convolutions as well as a deepening and broadening of brain fissures.

I guess the same thing is or will soon be happening to me. Now that it's definite, I don't want it to happen.

I put Algernon's body in a cheese box and buried him in the back yard. I cried.

June 15 Dr. Strauss came to see me again. I wouldn't open the door and I told him to go away. I want to be left to myself. I have become touchy and irritable. I feel the darkness closing in. It's hard to throw off thoughts of suicide. I keep telling myself how important this introspective journal will be.

It's a strange sensation to pick up a book that you've read and enjoyed just a few months ago and discover that you don't remember it. I remembered how great I thought John Milton was, but when I picked up *Paradise Lost* I couldn't understand it at all. I got so angry I threw the book across the room.

I've got to try to hold on to some of it. Some of the things I've learned. Oh, God, please don't take it all away.

June 19 Sometimes, at night, I go out for a walk. Last night I couldn't remember where I lived. A policeman took me home. I have the strange feeling that this has all happened to me before—a long time ago. I keep telling myself I'm the only person in the world who can describe what's happening to me.

June 21 Why can't I remember? I've got to fight. I lie in bed for days and I don't know who or where I am. Then it all comes back to me in a flash. Fugues of amnesia. Symptoms of senility—second childhood. I can watch them coming on. It's so cruelly logical. I learned so much and so fast. Now my mind is deteriorating rapidly. I won't let it happen. I'll fight it. I can't help thinking of the boy in the restaurant, the blank expression, the silly smile, the people laughing at him. No—please—not that again . . .

June 22   I'm forgetting things that I learned recently. It seems to be following the classic pattern—the last things learned are the first things forgotten. Or is that the pattern? I'd better look it up again. . . .

I reread my paper on the *Algernon-Gordon Effect* and I get the strange feeling that it was written by someone else. There are parts I don't even understand.

Motor activity impaired. I keep tripping over things, and it becomes increasingly difficult to type.

June 23   I've given up using the typewriter completely. My coordination is bad. I feel that I'm moving slower and slower. Had a terrible shock today. I picked up a copy of an article I used in my research, Krueger's *Uber psychische Ganzheit,* to see if it would help me understand what I had done. First I thought there was something wrong with my eyes. Then I realized I could no longer read German. I tested myself in other languages. All gone.

June 30   A week since I dared to write again. It's slipping away like sand through my fingers. Most of the books I have are too hard for me now. I get angry with them because I know that I read and understood them just a few weeks ago.

I keep telling myself I must keep writing these reports so that somebody will know what is happening to me. But it gets harder to form the words and remember spellings. I have to look up even simple words in the dictionary now and it makes me impatient with myself.

Dr. Strauss comes around almost every day, but I told him I wouldn't see or speak to anybody. He feels guilty. They all do. But I don't blame anyone. I knew what might happen. But how it hurts.

July 7   I don't know where the week went. Todays Sunday I know becuase I can see through my window people going to church. I think I stayed in bed all week but I remember Mrs. Flynn bringing food to me a few times. I keep saying over and over Ive got to do something but then I forget or maybe its just easier not to do what I say Im going to do.

I think of my mother and father a lot these days. I found a picture of them with me taken at a beach. My father has a big ball under his arm and my mother is holding me by the hand. I dont remember them the way they are in the picture. All I remember is my father drunk most of the time and arguing with mom about money.

He never shaved much and he used to scratch my face when he hugged me. My mother said he died but Cousin Miltie said he heard his mom and dad say that my father ran away with another woman. When I asked my mother she slapped my face and said my father was dead. I dont think I ever found out which was true but I don't care much. (He said he was going to take me to see cows on a farm once but he never did. He never kept his promises . . .)

July 10   My landlady Mrs Flynn is very worried about me. She says the way I lay around all day and dont do anything I remind her of her son before she threw him out of the house. She said she doesnt like loafers. If Im sick its one thing, but if Im a loafer thats another thing and she wont have it. I told her I think Im sick.

I try to read a little bit every day, mostly stories, but sometimes I have to read the same thing over and over again because I dont know what it means. And its hard to write. I know I should look up all the words in the dictionary but its so hard and Im so tired all the time.

Then I got the idea that I would only use the easy words instead of the long hard ones. That saves time. I put flowers on Algernons grave about once a week. Mrs Flynn thinks Im crazy to put flowers on a mouses grave but I told her that Algernon was special.

July 14   Its sunday again. I dont have anything to do to keep me busy now because my television set is broke and I dont have any money to get it fixed. (I think I lost this months check from the lab. I dont remember)

I get awful headaches and asperin doesnt help me much. Mrs Flynn knows Im really sick and she feels very sorry for me. Shes a wonderful woman whenever someone is sick.

July 22   Mrs Flynn called a strange doctor to see me. She was afraid I was going to die. I told the doctor I wasnt too sick and that I only forget sometimes. He asked me did I have any friends or relatives and I said no I dont have any. I told him I had a friend called Algernon once but he was a mouse and we used to run races together. He looked at me kind of funny like he thought I was crazy.

He smiled when I told him I used to be a genius. He talked to me like I was a baby and he winked at Mrs Flynn. I got mad and chased him out because he was making fun of me the way they all used to.

July 24   I have no more money and Mrs Flynn says I got to go to work somewhere and pay the rent because I havent paid for over two months. I dont know any work but the job I used to have at Donnegans Plastic Box Company. I dont want to go back there because they all knew me when I was smart and maybe theyll laugh at me. But I dont know what else to do to get money.

July 25   I was looking at some of my old progress reports and its very funny but I cant read what I wrote. I can make out some of the words but they dont make sense.

Miss Kinnian came to the door but I said go away I dont want to see you. She cried and I cried too but I wouldnt let her in because I didnt want her to laugh at me. I told her I didn't like her any more. I told her I didnt want to be smart any more. Thats not true. I still love her and I still want to be smart but I had to say

that so shed go away. She gave Mrs Flynn money to pay the rent.
I dont want that. I got to get a job.

Please . . . please let me not forget how to read and write . . .

July 27   Mr Donnegan was very nice when I came back and asked
him for my old job of janitor. First he was very suspicious but I
told him what happened to me then he looked very sad and put his
hand on my shoulder and said Charlie Gordon you got guts.

Everybody looked at me when I came downstairs and started
working in the toilet sweeping it out like I used to. I told myself
Charlie if they make fun of you dont get sore because you remember their not so smart as you once thot they were. And besides they
were once your friends and if they laughed at you that doesnt
mean anything because they liked you too.

One of the new men who came to work there after I went away
made a nasty crack he said hey Charlie I hear your a very smart
fella a real quiz kid. Say something intelligent. I felt bad but Joe
Carp came over and grabbed him by the shirt and said leave him
alone you lousy cracker or Ill break your neck. I didnt expect Joe
to take my part so I guess hes really my friend.

Later Frank Reilly came over and said Charlie if anybody
bothers you or trys to take advantage you call me or Joe and we
will set em straight. I said thanks Frank and I got choked up so I
had to turn around and go into the supply room so he wouldnt see
me cry. Its good to have friends.

July 28   I did a dumb thing today I forgot I wasnt in Miss Kinnians class at the adult center any more like I use to be. I went in
and sat down in my old seat in the back of the room and she
looked at me funny and she said Charles. I dint remember she
ever called me that before only Charlie so I said hello Miss Kinnian Im redy for my lesin today only I lost my reader that we was
using. She startid to cry and run out of the room and everybody
looked at me and I saw they wasnt the same pepul who used to be
in my class.

Then all of a suddin I rememberd some things about the opera-

shun and me getting smart and I said holy smoke I reely pulled a
Charlie Gordon that time. I went away before she come back to
the room.

Thats why Im going away from New York for good. I dont
want to do nothing like that agen. I dont want Miss Kinnian to feel
sorry for me. Evry body feels sorry at the factery and I dont want
that eather so Im going someplace where nobody knows that
Charlie Gordon was once a genus and now he cant even reed a
book or rite good.

Im taking a cuple of books along and even if I cant reed them
Ill practise hard and maybe I wont forget every thing I lerned.
If I try reel hard maybe Ill be a littel bit smarter then I was before the operashun. I got my rabits foot and my luky penny and
maybe they will help me.

If you ever reed this Miss Kinnian dont be sorry for me Im glad
I got a second chanse to be smart becaus I lerned a lot of things
that I never even new were in this world and Im grateful that I
saw it all for a littel bit. I dont know why Im dumb agen or what I
did wrong maybe its becaus I dint try hard enuff. But if I try and
practis very hard maybe Ill get a littl smarter and know what all
the words are. I remember a littel bit how nice I had a feeling with
the blue book that has the torn cover when I red it. Thats why
Im gonna keep trying to get smart so I can have that feeling agen.
Its a good feeling to know things and be smart. I wish I had it rite
now if I did I would sit down and reed all the time. Anyway I bet
Im the first dumb person in the world who ever found out somthing importent for sience. I remember I did somthing but I dont
remember what. So I gess its like I did it for all the dumb pepul
like me.

Good-by Miss Kinnian and Dr Strauss and evreybody. And P.S.
please tell Dr Nemur not to be such a grouch when pepul laff at
him and he woud have more frends. Its easy to make frends if
you let pepul laff at you. Im going to have lots of frends where
I go.

P.P.S. Please if you get a chanse put some flowrs on Algernons
grave in the bak yard . . .

ME

I think that I shall never see
A calculator made like me.
A me that likes Martinis dry
And on the rocks, a little rye.
A me that looks at girls and such,
But mostly girls, and very much.
A me that wears an overcoat
And likes a risky anecdote.
A me that taps a foot and grins
Whenever Dixieland begins.
They make computers for a fee,
But only moms can make a me.

HILBERT SCHENCK, JR.

KEM BENNETT

A Different Purpose

NOT FEELING IN THE LEAST LIKE a doomed man, Yourko Andropov ate a hearty breakfast. This was on the terrace of the Red Air Force villa at Alushta on the Crimean Riviera, and he was wearing pajamas. Below the terrace, at the foot of rocks falling a hundred feet, the Black Sea, belying its name, was a shining, breeze-ripped azure. The day promised to be pleasantly hot. It was May 1960.

After his breakfast Yourko lit a cigarette and contemplated the fact that the day was entirely his; until midnight he was free. Precisely what he intended to do with his day he had not yet decided, and, since it was an exceptional day, quite possibly his last, he was feeling that it would be wrong to be too casual about it. Yet somehow casualness of itself attracted him; certainly he wanted no drama.

Without having made any plans and not letting the fact disturb him, he decided to get dressed. He rose to his feet, flicking his half-smoked cigarette away so that it sailed over the balustrade of the terrace and down on to the rocks below. Then he turned and went into the villa. In his cool, clean, bare bedroom he dressed slowly and deliberately, choosing a light summer uniform of smock and baggy trousers and taking trouble over such things as the arrangement of the pleats under the belt and the medals he was entitled to wear on his chest. Watching himself as he made movements that were normally quite automatic and habitual, he felt very alive, very tranquil, and very content.

Yourko Andropov was of average height, fair, strong, and healthy—exceptionally healthy. He was thirty. He had blue eyes and a long scar across his forehead, acquired when he was thrown from a crashed aircraft in China six years previously. He was a Red Army flier, a major, and he had flown with the North Korean forces in the Korean War.

From the villa, long flights of rock-hewn steps made a short-cut down to one end of Alushta's main street. Yourko came down them slowly, taking his time, looking out over the white houses and the poplar trees of the public gardens. He made his way to a big café overlooking the beach. Here it was that he had a rendezvous with Olinka for midday. It was now just after ten. He sat down and ordered a *kvas*. After a quarter of an hour he was joined by an acquaintance, a convalescent government doctor from Smolensk, with whom he played a game of chess. He won.

At twelve, Olinka arrived. She was a girl of Yourko's own age, half Uzbek and dark in contrast with his fairness. She was a member of a troupe of Uzbek folk dancers, in Alushta on a rest-vacation as a reward for a successful tour of Hungary and Romania. Yourko had known her for six days. There was a strong bond of affection between them already and they pleased one another physically. Also, they made each other laugh.

They swam, Yourko taking a man's pride in the glances of admiration that Olinka's dancer's body earned from the onlookers. After swimming they went to the largest restaurant in Alushta and ate an expensive lunch. Then, before they had time to start feeling sleepy, they bought tickets for a motorboat trip along the coast which took them to Yalta and beyond, to botanical gardens and a bathing beach. They returned to Alushta in the evening in time to dine off caviar sandwiches and sweet Ukrainian champagne. Finally, after a walk in the sage-scented moonlight, they went back to the Air Force villa and let themselves quietly into Yourko's bedroom.

Two hours later, at midnight, Yourko kissed Olinka good-by. She did not know where he was going. She asked questions. Yourko said, "I will try to write, Olinichka," and she nodded, gazing at him. He left.

At the foot of the villa steps a Zis limousine was waiting. Yourko climbed in. A few hours later, in a military transport flying eastwards above the Caspian Sea, Yourko went over the day in his mind, taking it event by event and savoring it. It had been a strange day—a good day, he decided. And yet why strange, since he had done nothing in the least remarkable? The answer came with a sudden clarity; during the last few hours he had done all the things that a man could do—lived and breathed, seen, heard, and smelled, used his muscles and his mind, eaten, drunk, and made love—also, and this was the secret, he had done everything with the awareness that it was precious. That made the difference.

Presently, thinking of Olinka, he fell asleep.

The launching site was cleared and the count-down had started. *Dévyat, vósem, sem, shest, pyat, chetyre* . . .

With a sense of extraordinary detachment Yourko heard the measured words in his earphones, felt his pulses throbbing, felt himself swallowing in an effort to ease the dryness of his throat, recognized the voided feeling that intense apprehension brings to the pit of the stomach. He was watching himself be afraid.

Tri, dva, ODIN!

Watchers in the observation bunkers, although looking through tinted-glass panels, were dazzled, and half-deafened.

Inside the tall rocket, after a momentary hesitancy, a wavering that lasted a second in time and forever in Yourko Andropov's memory, he became aware of an upthrust, a surging, crushing, elevator-gone-mad feeling that made him groan and sweat and suffer.

By six that evening, less than twenty-four hours after Yourko had said good-by to Olinka in Alushta, the world knew that the Union of Soviet Socialist Republics had succeeded in establishing a man-carrying satellite, in a near-perfect orbit around the Earth. They called it 1960 Gamma.

Yourko had tilted his all-purpose contour couch into a seat and had turned himself round from a prone to a sitting position. This, in itself, had been a laborious process; his body and head and the special high-altitude suit that he was wearing were so encumbered with wires, tubes, and cables that he was capable of moving only with a slow, robotlike deliberation.

The chamber he was sitting in was cylindrical, six inches higher than his seated height and about five feet in diameter. Beside him, built into one arm of his seat, were controls for radio, tape recorder, temperature, television screen, and the shutters which would open and close his viewing portholes. On the other side of the seat, within easy reach of his right hand, were banks of instruments, dials, and gauges and, below them, serried ranks of switches. These controlled the manual or semiautomatic equipment that the satellite was carrying. Other equipment aboard her was fully automatic.

On Yourko's suit itself were controls by which he could feed himself, dose himself, if necessary, with pills, and to some degree regulate his oxygen supply.

He had been in space for just over six hours. He was feeling slightly sick and slightly dizzy, but quite unafraid. He was not overexcited or overawed; that had passed much earlier. For this experience he had been trained endlessly, week after week and month upon month. As a result he had brought familiarity with him into the empyrean, and that accomplished the rather sad miracle of making his situation seem ordinary.

He was now finishing the task of feeding a series of observations into an instrument that would transmit them in code to Earth. An hour earlier he had talked to the world over the radio; they had told him that his signals were being picked up, amplified and

rebroadcast by every radio network on the face of the Earth. He
had described for humanity Earth herself as he saw her, a brilliant,
shimmering immensity, swathed in cloud veils and patterned with
ocean and continent; still too big, even at his altitude, for him to
be able to see the whole of her at one time through the narrow observation windows. He had later described the stars, "Shining," he
had said, "with unimaginable brilliance," and yet, still only stars, re-
mote and splendidly unapproachable. He had tried to be lyrical,
in keeping with the occasion, but had found himself becoming
repetitive and adjectival, and had quickly returned to a correct
military matter-of-factness.

Now, for some hours, there was little or nothing for him to do.
The voice of a technician, making a periodical check, sounded in
his radio earphones: "*Allo, 1960 Gamma.*" The voice was filled
with a consciousness of the importance of the occasion. "*Allo,*
Comrade Major Andropov, is all well?"

"Fine," Yourko answered laconically. "Tell the doctors that the
gravity sickness is wearing off."

"Yes, Comrade Major."

Silence came down again.

Yourko noted that the dizziness he had been feeling, like the
gravity sickness, was decreasing. He was pleased. The dizziness
had brought with it a sense of mental impairment, as small but
as worrying as a slight headache, which he was glad to be rid of.
He still, of course, felt strange and weightless, but his human
adaptability, a small miracle in itself, was hard at work turning
the strange into the familiar. In a few hours, he felt sure, the
process would be completed and he would find himself acclima-
tized.

In a few hours . . . the thought recurred, this time with a very
different flavor. He saw hours stretching ahead of him, and days.
A sudden whiplash of panic struck at his heart and he felt
loneliness flood his whole being. The sensations took him by surprise, making him catch his breath. With an effort of will,
Yourko caught hold of himself, fighting down the panic, with-

drawing from the loneliness. There was danger in admitting to loneliness; he knew this well. He sought for a distraction.

Among the controls and selector switches at his left hand there was one with which he could project cinema films onto the screen of his television viewer; there was a second which would project in a similar way the pages of a selection of microphotographed books, and yet a third with which he could play recorded music to himself. The psychologists had thought of everything—or had tried to.

He moved a selector and pressed a button. The title page of a book appeared on the screen in front of him. It was a work on astronomy; the latest. It was neither abstruse nor condescendingly oversimplified, and Yourko had been looking forward to reading it for several months. The frontispiece consisted of a photograph of a spiral nebula, taken by the Americans with their giant telescope at the Mount Palomar observatory. Yourko leaned slightly forwards in order to see better. Admiration stirred in him, both for the nebula and for the American technology which had made the photograph possible. Presently he glanced up at his observation ports, now shuttered. He chuckled. If ever a man had been in the right place to read astronomy . . .

The satellite 1960 Gamma made a complete circuit of the Earth every ninety-seven minutes. For the scientists and technicians on watch below in the heart of the Kara-Kum Desert, a day and a night had gone by since the launching. The satellite, however, had passed from night to day nearly fifteen times during the same twenty-four hours. For some reason, which he did not attempt to analyze, this fact was one of the first things to get on Yourko's nerves.

Another was his enforced immobility. During his training he had spent longer and longer periods, culminating in a full week, strapped into just such a seat as he was sitting in now and wearing precisely the same equipment. But that had been training, make-believe—a tiresome endurance test and no more. This, the real thing, was turning out to be different. Already his body was yearning for movement, and already it was becoming more and more difficult to ignore its demands.

For a large part of each day he had plenty to do. In order to save weight, a great number of the satellite's instruments had been fitted with manual controls. Roughly every six hours, when he was within easy radio range of the launching site and research station in Turkmenistan, Yourko transmitted a series of coded observations which he had spent the previous two hours in taking and recording. His observations included measurements of the Earth's gravitational and magnetic fields and its electrical charges; they also included measurements and analyses of cosmic rays and solar radiation. They included meteor counts. In between taking readings from half a hundred dials and instruments, he also had to remember to take photographs with one or another of the several semiautomatic cameras which the satellite was carrying. These photographs were of the sun, the Earth and its cloud formations, the moon, the planets and the stars. Lastly, he had to take radar readings at stated intervals. Once in every twenty-four hours he was permitted to miss a transmission so that he could sleep.

In spite of being so fully occupied and in spite of the fact that his off-duty hours could be spent watching films or reading, Yourko, after he had been in space for less than two days, had to face the fact that he was becoming bored and restless to a degree that he had never known before. The recording of his observations, although they took time, made small demands upon his intellect; he was not a scientist and the routines had been intentionally simplified as far as possible. In many cases he did not know what purpose his readings would serve, nor what use they could be put to. He came to look upon them as chores, and from that moment they became flat and unexciting.

In the evening of his second day, trying to concentrate upon the projected image of his book on astronomy, he felt a sudden and powerful impulse to tear off his helmet, tear away the wires and tubes from his face and chest, and to drive his fist through the shining, shimmering glass of the television screen. He controlled

himself, lying back, closing his eyes, forcing himself to relax.
After a while he sat up, switched off the microbook projector and
turned on in its stead a recording of Prokoviev's Classical Sym-
phony. It was music that he loved. For a few minutes he enjoyed it,
but then found himself not listening, not caring, coming to think
of the sounds in his ears as noise—as something to be borne.
With a savage sideways sweep of his left hand he cut off the
recording.

Yourko lay back, panting slightly, staring fixedly at the green
metallic ceiling of his cell, not more than a foot and a half from
his nose. It seemed to press in and down upon him. What was
wrong? In training he had put up with even more than he was
putting up with now. Men had survived solitary imprisonment
in smaller cells and under far worse living conditions for months
running into years. Why, therefore, after a mere forty-eight hours,
was he feeling demoralized?

After ten minutes of intensive thought Yourko had to confess to
himself that he did not know. Ideas had come into his mind . . .
could it be the absence of a proper spacing of night and day?
Could it be the air he was breathing, used and reused, purified
and repurified until it was as flat in the nostrils as cotton wool?
Could it be his food, a diet perfected after hundreds of experiments by the doctors and yet now to his taste almost too insipid to
be swallowed? To each of these questions his logical mind answered no. But he knew that it was not he that was answering,
but the scientists, the theoreticians, answering through him.

Something was wrong. Something was dragging him down. He
knew it. It frightened him. He thought of plants taken from the
soil and slowly withering. Was that it? Must a man projected into
space, away from the Earth and away from his kind, wither like
an uprooted plant?

He found himself prepared to admit the possibility.

In the morning of the third day, Yourko was awakened from a
drugged sleep by the noise of his call-sign in his earphones. He
heaved himself into a sitting position and spoke in reply.

A voice that he recognized answered, "*Zdrasvuyté*, Yourko. How goes it?" It was Yumashev, the Head Psychiatrist and an old friend.

"*Zdrasvuyté*, Feodor," Yourko answered. "I am still alive. It goes as well as can be expected."

There was a short silence. Then Yumashev asked, "You sound depressed, Yourko—are you?"

"A little."

"Have you used any of the antidepressants in your drug supplies?"

"Yes," Yourko answered. The previous evening, to kill the fear that he had felt growing in him, he had taken two amphetamine tablets. Their effect had been three hours of frantic, uncontrollable mental activity. His brain had buzzed like a bluebottle in a cardboard box. "They upset me," he said. "I shall not be able to use them again."

"Have you other symptoms—apart from the depression?" Yumashev asked quietly.

"Yes, I feel a terrible restlessness some times, and other times a terrible dullness," Yourko said. "It is much worse than it ever was in training, Feodor."

Yumashev paused to think. Yourko could hear him breathing. He noted, but dully and without astonishment, that it was extraordinary that he should be in space, out of the Earth's atmosphere, and yet able to hear the breathing of a scientist in Russia. "Perhaps," Yumashev was saying with a tinge of reluctance in his voice, "perhaps we should be thinking of bringing you down, Yourko. What do you think?"

Trying to bring me down, Yourko thought. The loss of velocity and the fall back to Earth would be the high point of danger in the whole operation. Its prospect suddenly terrified him. "No," he said harshly. "Not yet." He knew that it was fear that had spoken, not judgment, and that he should have said yes.

"I shall ask again in six hours, Yourko," Yumashev said.

"Very well."

It was now that Yourko Andropov started to live by his pride.

During that day, his third in the satellite, a phonograph record in his brain reminded him over and over again that it was unthinkable that he should give up before six days had elapsed. Six days was the target; his batteries, food, and oxygen were sufficient for six days, and six days he had to endure. He reminded himself that he had been chosen for the task from thousands of others, that it had cost untold millions of rubles and the efforts of the best scientific brains in Russia to put him where he was, and that every hour he stayed in space increased the glory of the achievement. He was a patriot. Without being a fanatic, he believed in Soviet Russia, in science, and in progress, and he felt deeply that to betray the trust that had been put in him would be unthinkable. He was also an army officer.

The combination of pride and inbuilt discipline kept him going for that day.

During the fourth day Yourko realized that his body was weakening. Until then his troubles had been psychological; he had felt no loss of physical ability. Now the weakening had begun. Curiously enough, it had the effect of making him more comfortable, because, like a sick man, he relaxed instinctively and rested more.

He felt too apathetic and listless to make the usual readings for the second of his six-hourly transmissions, and he did not. Then, just before the transmission was due, pride faltered at last and he was able to think again with comparative clarity. It would not, he realized calmly, be either sensible or patriotic to endure beyond the bitter end. His experience had made him immensely valuable—alive. Dead he would be valueless.

He knew that he was dying—slowly, perhaps, but quite surely. When Yumashev came up to talk to him on the radio, he asked to be brought down.

Head Psychiatrist Yumashev tapped on the door of the Controller's office. "*Mozhno!*" Yumashev entered.

Neresenko, the Controller, a squat gray-haired man of fifty, sat at a big desk on which was placed a small gold model of a

satellite in orbit. It had been presented to him by the Academy of
Sciences for his achievement in launching Sputnik ahead of the
American Vanguard in 1957. Neresenko was not a scientist; he
was an enthusiast. Yumashev did not like him.

"Andropov has requested that he be brought down."

Neresenko rose from his chair. "Ah, so?" He had to look up to
talk to Yumashev, who was very tall, thin, and stooping. Neresenko
did not mind; his convictions of superiority and his self-confidence
were more than enough to compensate in him for the need to
look up at tall men. "Do we then have to bring him down?"

Yumashev said, "It is my professional opinion that we should."

Neresenko grunted. For some moments he paced the floor with
his hands clasped behind his back. When he turned to face Yumashev again, his eyes were shrewd and his face expressionless. "This
is confidential," he said. "It happens that Comrade Khrushchev
was told yesterday that we hoped to keep 1960 Gamma in orbit for
the full six days. Comrade Khrushchev was so delighted with the
news that he passed it on to the foreign press representatives. If
we bring Andropov down now, in the fourth day, much face will
be lost. Do you understand me, Feodor? Do you still think we
should bring him down?"

"I think that if you leave him up there for two more days he
will either die or go mad," Yumashev said. He kept emotion out
of his voice. Neresenko did not like emotion.

"How have you arrived at this opinion?"

"I have had many talks with Andropov. It has not been difficult
to detect the strain that he had been feeling; he has even con-
fessed it openly to me. I know him well. He is not a man to cry out
before he is hurt."

Neresenko shrugged. "Very well," he said. "I respect your
opinion. I think we should have a meeting. Will you please arrange it? I think the whole medical staff should attend."

There was a silence. Yumashev took a deep breath and raised his
head to speak. At the last moment he changed his mind. He knew
that it was useless to protest. Neresenko was covering up. Neresenko wanted unanimity. Well, he should have it. He, Yumashev,

knew that the other doctors would back him up. The trouble was
that it would take time . . .

He nodded. "In an hour, then?"

Neresenko said, "If you can arrange it so quickly. Remember
that I want all the doctors."

"You shall have them," Yumashev said and left the office.

In 1960 Gamma, Yourko Andropov was feeling better. They
were going to bring him down. The knowledge had acted in him
like a pain-killer. He felt appreciably weaker but did not mind.
It had not occurred to him that his request might not be granted.

He now felt little fear of the descent. Among his supplies of
drugs he had an anesthetic injection. He intended to use it. Hitherto pride might have restrained him, but Yourko's pride had been
battered by four days in space. He had come to understand many
things, the most important of which was that he, as an individual,
was very small in the scheme of things and almost powerless. Four
days earlier he had thought that he had chosen to be launched into
space. Now, without having had to think about it, he had realized
that the choice had never really been his. He had been asked if he
wished to volunteer. He had said "yes" because to have said "no"
would have been astonishing, a breaking of rules, a rejection of
glory. This, he now understood, had not been a choice.

And now, at this very moment, he was more powerless to change
his destiny, probably, than he had ever been. Whether he lived
or died depended entirely upon others—entirely! The knowledge
was a comfort; it absolved him from responsibility. He no longer
had to try.

Idly, without urgency, he wondered how he should spend the
rest of the time that remained to him in space. For a moment
he was tempted by the idea of music; he was too weak to read
and he suspected that any film, in his present mood, would irritate
him. His hand moved out to switch on the tape recorder.

Then he hesitated. A thought had come to him that had feeling
in it, and logic; ought he not to be looking at the stars? Ought
he not to be using, for the last time, the privilege that he shared

with no other human being—that of being able to see the full glory
of the heavens undimmed by atmosphere? Instead of switching on
music, he pressed the button controlling the opening of the shutters of the observation ports. The satellite was on the darkened
side of the Earth and all the shutters opened. Had it been on the
light side, those facing the sun would have remained closed, automatically locked to protect him from the unfiltered power of solar
radiation.

He turned his head. Across two of the portholes and half of a
third the Milky Way made a shimmering ribbon of light. A galaxy,
Yourko thought. He remembered what he had been reading in
the book of astronomy—while he had still been reading. Not only
were the stars innumerable, but the galaxies also—or so the book
had said. Galaxy upon galaxy . . . each at least as big as our own,
many far bigger. Galaxies being born, galaxies dying. Suns blazing, suns fading. Planets cooling. Atmospheres forming. Life
appearing, mosses and lichens on rocky outcrops, cells multiply-
ing in lava-warmed water . . .

This, Yourko thought, is what I am looking at now. All of it.

He singled out a brilliant star and watched it move across from
one side of a porthole to the other. It seemed to be moving, but
then, of course, it was he that was moving . . . Yet the star was
moving too, so the book said . . .

A computer ticked and clattered. Dvinski, the Head Astro-
physicist, crossed the room with a slip of paper which he passed
across to Neresenko. Dvinski was a scientist of brilliance, but as a
man he was nervous and given to unexpected outbursts of buf-
foonery. "That is the soonest we can get him down, Comrade Controller," he said. He snickered and pulled a funny face. "Needless
to say we don't want him to finish in North America—or in the
middle of the ocean."

Without looking at it, Neresenko passed the paper to Yumashev. He was fond of such gestures; disinterestedness indicated
aloofness and self-control, aloofness and self-control were the hall-
marks of the leader; ergo he, Neresenko, was a leader.

"Twenty-two forty-four," Yumashev said. "Two hours from now. If you will excuse me, Comrade Controller, I should like to radio the time to Yourko."

"I'll come with you," Neresenko said.

In the radio room, Feodor Yumashev sat down beside a microphone. Presently one of the technicians gave him a signal, a lifted thumb.

"*Allo!*" Yumashev said. "Yourko! This is Feodor. Can you hear me?"

There was no answer. Yumashev frowned. He tried again. "*Allo*, 1960 Gamma. Yourko! Yourko! *Allo*, Yourko! Are you all right, Yourko? Can you hear me?"

No answer. Yumashev turned to the man in charge. "He does not answer. Could his batteries have failed?"

"No, Comrade Doctor, we are receiving his automatic signals."

"Could his transmitter have broken down?"

"Yes, that is a possibility."

"Just read out the time to him," Neresenko said. "It is possible that he can hear but cannot answer."

"*Allo*, Yourko," Yumashev said, slowly and distinctly into the microphone. "We are bringing you down, Yourko. Do you hear me? We are bringing you down. You will start decelerating at ten forty-four. I repeat; you will start decelerating at ten forty-four."

Yourko's voice came suddenly from a loud-speaker. It was loud, but the loudness came by amplification, not from natural causes. Yumashev jumped.

"No," said Yourko's loud-soft, strong-weak voice. "No, Feodor. Not yet."

"Why not, Yourko?" Yumashev said into the microphone. "Tell me why not."

Neresenko was smiling. Yumashev had seen the smile begin and could feel it now, between his shoulder blades.

Silence.

Yumashev spoke again. "Yourko! Why should we not bring you down? You asked for it, Yourko. Do you not remember asking?"

"It is difficult to explain," Yourko answered. His voice was weaker, and strange. Yumashev scowled and cursed under his straggly mustache. . . . "I have something that I am doing," Yourko's voice continued. "I cannot explain. It is very important. It has to do with the universe, Feodor. It is very important. I cannot explain. Not now. Later. Later . . ."

Yumashev was on his feet, facing Neresenko. "He must still be brought down," he shouted. "Now more than ever. Did you not hear his voice? I insist. I invoke my authority as Head Psychiatrist."

"But he asked not to be, Feodor," Neresenko protested. "My friend, don't be unreasonable . . ."

"Will you have a sane man tonight or a madman tomorrow?" Yumashev's anger came through in his voice. "That is the choice, Neresenko! Which will give you the greater glory? Think!"

Neresenko thought. He frowned, pinching his upper lip. Then he shrugged. "I leave it to you, Yumashev," he said. "If you wish to take the responsibility . . ."

In space, 1960 Gamma's antennae folded. Jets of high-pressure gas turned her. She came round through a hundred-and-eighty degrees until her pointed nose was facing away from her direction of travel. In Turkmenistan a circuit was completed at the precise millisecond predetermined by the computers. Rockets flared from the satellite's square-cut tail.

In the Kara-Kum Desert, Yumashev was watching. He had his eye pressed against the eyepiece of a powerful telescope. Presently he straightened, and then abruptly turned away. This was the moment of crisis. If the satellite had been slowed down sufficiently, the chances were good. If not, it was all over; the great experiment would have failed and Yourko Andropov would be dead by incineration. Yumashev could not imagine why he had wanted to look. He took a cigarette from his overall pocket and lit it.

He waited.

Dvinski appeared in the open doorway of the computer room.

"So far so good, Feodor," Dvinski shouted. "He is now entering at-mosphere and we have detected no sign of overheating."

"Thank you!" Yumashev shouted. He turned and walked away toward a helicopter standing nearby, its engine already roaring.

Yourko was still unconscious when they took him out of the satellite. He had chosen to take the anesthetic. He came around in the helicopter that was taking him back to the experimental station. Yumashev was with him.

"Feodor!" Yourko's hand went out. Yumashev took it, smiling. At the same time he looked, narrowly and professionally, at the man on the stretcher. There were signs of weakness, but the eyes were bright—very bright. No insanity. Yumashev knew it, he was sure of it—he could feel insanity, smell it, detect it at a distance. His heart glowed.

"Feodor," Yourko said again, low-voiced but with urgency. "Listen! Something happened. I was looking at the stars. I began to understand. Are you listening?"

"Yes, but I think you should not talk now."

"I must talk. I . . . It is very difficult to explain. I began to un-derstand and I began to see, Feodor. I . . . I saw a unity." Yourko closed his eyes. He was sweating. Yumashev frowned. "It is all a unity," Yourko went on. "It is a being, Feodor. Everything fits. Everything conforms. All the parts work together. I saw that, Feodor. It was very clear. There was no doubt; there was not even room for doubt. Am I speaking intelligently?"

"Yes, Yourko."

"And I understand much—things that I have never even thought about before. I understand that neither time nor distance have their proper meaning—not in our minds. Have you ever thought of that?"

"No, Yourko," Yumashev said. "Won't you try to relax? It would be better for you to sleep now."

"Please," Yourko's voice was pleading. "Please listen, Feodor. Everything has its own time—can you understand that? Every-thing has its own time and its own space. For an electron its nucleus is distant; for us the sun is distant. Do you see what I mean? Can you see the importance of that?"

"No," Yumashev said gently. "There is time for everything, Yourko. You are seeing stars and I am seeing a man exhausted by a fantastic experience. Now, since you will not obey me, I am going to give you an injection."

"Feodor!" Yourko shouted. "Feodor, try! Please try to understand. Listen! I saw the universe, Feodor—as a whole, as an entity. It is a being—a living being! Everything is ordered. Everything has its place. We have our place. Don't you understand? I was seeing all, Feodor, all! I was beginning to understand what we, humanity, are here for. That's why I asked not to be brought down . . ."

The needle went in. Yumashev withdrew it from Yourko's arm and rolled back the blanket. "There," he said gently. "Now you will sleep, Yourko. It is better."

Yourko said nothing. He turned his head away from his friend and closed his eyes.

It was morning. Yourko was sitting up in bed. The room was air-conditioned and pleasantly cool—a hero's room, a room for a Hero of the Soviet Union. Through the window he could look out over an endless expanse of hostile, sun-parched Turkmani desert. He liked it better than a view of the satellite's instruments. He had a tray across his knees and he was eating boiled eggs out of a bowl.

Yumashev came in. "*Zdrasvuyté,* Yourko."

"*Zdrasvuyté,* Feodor."

"How are you feeling?"

"Good. I slept for twelve hours." Yourko smiled.

Yumashev sat down, folding his long body like the leg of a cricket. "Well," he said, "then I imagine you will be ready to tell. Start from the beginning."

Yourko frowned, laying down his spoon. He picked up his coffee cup and looked down into it. He might have been trying to read a fortune.

Yumashev said, "What was it that you were telling me in the

helicopter last night? I tried to listen, but I could not understand."

"Have you ever tried to remember a dream which you knew to be of the greatest importance," Yourko asked, "but which, however hard you tried, faded—faded irrevocably, piece by piece, until nothing remained but the knowledge that you had dreamed?"

Yumashev nodded.

"That is what I am doing now."

"But," Yumashev said, "I don't understand. This was not a dream, was it? You were not telling me of a dream, last night?"

"No. No, it was not a dream." Yourko put down his coffee cup. "Last night, Feodor, in the satellite, everything was clear—crystalline. I was not dreaming. If you like, I was having visions, but I was awake. I think I shall never be so much awake again. I seemed to see the universe, instantaneously, as an entirety . . . I would almost say solidly. Anyway, as a pattern. I . . ." Yourko stopped. He shook his head. "No, Feodor, I cannot explain."

"I think you are doing very well."

"No." Yourko shook his head again, more definitely, more decisively.

Yumashev was silent. Presently, diffidently—and his manner of speech was not normally diffident—he said, "I should have tried harder to listen last night, Yourko. I see now that you were right. You had something to say that would not keep. I am sorry I gave you that injection."

Yourko shrugged and smiled. "I don't think it made much difference," he said. "I don't think this can be told in words; that is perhaps the great secret and mystery of it."

Yumashev nodded. "That could be so," he said.

"Do you think I was a little mad?" Yourko asked. "Do you think that my visions were hallucinations, Feodor, and meaningless?"

Yumashev shook his head. "No, Yourko."

"Neither do I," Yourko said. "I am not a man for hallucinations—or for visions, for that matter. I am not even much of a thinker."

Yumashev rose to his feet. "You have made me wonder if I

should volunteer to go with the next satellite, Yourko," he said.
He was smiling, but there was no sarcasm in his smile, nor
mockery, unless it was directed at himself. "I'll leave you alone
now—to try to remember, perhaps. I have told the others that they
can have their questions ready for midday. Will that suit you?"

Yourko nodded. "Thank you, Feodor."

The psychiatrist left the room.

"Friends," Neresenko was saying at a high-level meeting a few
days later, "I think it can safely be said that we have the basic
problems of space travel defeated. Comrade Major Andropov suffered considerably during his journey in 1960 Gamma. Among
other things, he has told us that the sense of restlessness became
almost intolerable, and that it was almost impossible to fight off
the mental lethargy produced by the conditions in the satellite. He
has suggested that there may be undiscovered reasons for this.
However, it is my opinion that the obvious reasons are the right
reasons. I believe that he suffered from claustrophobia and the in-
ability to move, exaggerated by insecurity, loneliness, and the
strangeness of his surroundings. I think that we shall obtain quite
different results when we send men into space in twos and threes,
and when rocket development has permitted us to enlarge their
living quarters." Neresenko glanced round the room, taking in the
expressions on the faces of his listeners, and then, apparently satisfied, he looked down at his notes.

"Comrade Major Andropov," he went on, "also reports that he
suffered from delusions and hallucinations during the latter part
of his flight. This would be a disturbing matter did it not appear
that the symptoms were produced when he was already weakened
by his sufferings and after he had spent an overlong period staring
out into the heavens." Neresenko smiled. "It may emerge, com-
rades, that stargazing is bad for space fliers. If it does, I suggest
that we shall have a simple remedy. We shall only have to deny
space crews access to the viewing ports, or not provide viewing
ports at all, and the trouble will probably be cured. Radar can do

almost everything that the human eye can do, and many things it can do better . . ."

At the far end of the table, Feodor Yumashev, there more out of courtesy than because he was needed, stared down at the table top. He was remembering Yourko's eyes in the helicopter, and his voice, and the flavor and strangeness of the things that he had been trying to say and that he, Yumashev, had not even troubled to listen to. Why, Yumashev found himself thinking as Neresenko rumbled on, were they trying to get out into space at all? For knowledge, for minerals, for military advantage, in order to examine the structure of uninhabited planets . . . and so on and so on? Yumashev felt suddenly doubtful. Yourko's talk had given him a glimpse of a different purpose, one that none of them had known of . . .

Neresenko had finished. A round of clapping was sounding. Yumashev did not clap. Instead he scowled at the Controller. It had suddenly occurred to him that Neresenko, and all who thought like Neresenko, could be the Enemy.

A VAMPIRE'S SAGA

A particularly inoffensive and extremely helpful wraith I en-
Countered in a Carpathian
Mountain pass
Told my parents that the hunting grounds were better and the
    bloodsucking grass
Was greener, absolutely without peer,
In the western hemisphere.
So my mother and father packed and shipped two large Transyl-
    vanian-earth-filled coffins for themselves and my short bier
To a New York pier.
In America, Father got a job as a cupper and leecher in a Russian-
    type steam bath where he constantly amazes his employer by
    growing remarkably stout,
While he never brings his lunch and never eats out.
Mother's luck was rather slack
(Three anemic girls and a haemophiliac).
My own case, however, is unique,
And has been so for the better part of a week.
For, ever since I flew into an uptown hotel in the usual form of a
    bat and tapped this sleeping fellow's vena azygos major and/
    or
Minor, I've been staying up all day turning out more verses than
    George Gordon, Lord Byron, and Walter Savage Landor.
Where, you may well ask, did I find the compulsion to ride this
    poetic hobby horse?
Why, in the vein of Ogden Nash, of course.

NORMAN BELKIN

RON GOULART

Ralph Wollstonecraft Hedge: A Memoir

RALPH WOLLSTONECRAFT HEDGE was a particularly amiable recluse. However, because he spent his final years ducked down behind a discarded harmonium in the lumber room of his maternal aunt and, further, steadfastly refused to talk to interviewers, there is little biographical material available for the curious student who wishes to know more about the man many consider to be the logical successor to Charles Brockden Brown. To remedy this, I feel bound to set down my recollections of this writer I believe deserving the mantle of Poe.

In this paper I will deal chiefly with Hedge's mature years since nothing is known of his early life. He apparently was found on a doorstep in his twenty-first year, with no recollection of his past. The doorstep itself was found in a forest in Bristol, Rhode Island, where the Druids from the neighborhood held occasional outings up until the McKinley era. These early associations seemed to to have little effect on Hedge, although in the autumn he would turn a russet gold color and exhibit a tendency to drift gently to the ground.

For several years, interrupted only by a wedding trip to Providence in 1923, I served Hedge as secretary, and also saw to it that no squirrels, animals of which he had an exaggerated fear, got to the upper floors of his shuttered colonial house. Thus I feel I knew this master of the macabre better than most. Indeed, in 1926 and the early part of 1927, when Hedge had hidden himself among the living-room drapes, he spoke to no one but me, and that was only in a whisper.

Ralph Wollstonecraft Hedge spent a good deal of time behind things and so most of his tales were dictated. Usually to me, but several, especially in 1928, to a man named Collin A. Ruckersett. The stories Hedge wrote in his own crabbed hand were for the most part illegible. None of these latter were ever printed, except for a story called *At the Pits of Terror,* which appeared in *St. Nicholas Magazine* (I am not sure of the date, but I remember it was raining quite a lot that day). The version is, I contend, greatly garbled. I am sure Hedge did not include a character called Bunny Pitpat in the story. Nor was the tale meant to induce children to brush their teeth as frequently as possible, dealing as it did with the complex weird mythos Hedge had painstakingly built up.

After 1935 Hedge neither wrote nor dictated any further stories, except to ghostwrite three Big Little Books for the Whitman people. This task added not at all, in my opinion, to his stature as a master of the horror genre. When he ceased writing, RWH (as his circle called him) devoted himself to eating ice cream. He confided in me that he desired to do a major work in which he would compare and contrast all the existing flavors of ice cream, with an appendix covering sherbet and Popsicles. It was Hedge's intention to devote six months to each flavor, but his untimely end cut him off before he had gotten much beyond chocolate. I, for one, have always been sorry that this work did not see completion. I am sure it would have shown yet another side of the man who gained such renown with his stories of grave-robbing and lycanthropy.

Of course, RWH had a considerable influence, direct or otherwise, on the younger writers, George Worsnop Bangs, the youthful recluse of Paso Robles, California, was strongly influenced by Hedge's work, even to the point of signing Hedge's name to all his stories and tales. A circumstance, I might add, that has caused some amusing confusions in academic and scholarly circles. Rudyard Boland, the gifted assistant and macabrist of Yazoo, Mississippi, owed his early success to the kind literary advice and bundles of sandwiches that RWH sent him. And any but the most casual reader will see that Thomas Wolfe's *Of Time and the River* and Max Shulman's *Barefoot Boy with Cheek* are simply extended anagrams of Hedge's earlier *The Lurker in the Cabbage Patch*.

Unlike his weird stories Hedge was not weird at all. He was a small thin man with a round face and merry eyes, rather Dickensian in his speech. I believe he almost always wore a dark blue suit, but since he stood behind things so often, it is possible that he wore a blue coat and trousers of some other color. I cannot be sure. Hedge was not overly fond of animals, although in the spring of 1933 he took to carrying a manx cat around in a perforated shoe box, and sometime late in 1929 he dictated a fan letter to the artist of the comic-page strip *Barney Google*, expressing what I considered extravagant praise for the horse, Sparkplug. As I believe I have mentioned earlier, Hedge was violently afraid of squirrels. It is therefore somewhat ironic that during the Depression a great many squirrels took to hiding nuts all about the ground floor of Hedge's home. I have taken more than one nasty spill as a result of stepping unexpectedly on a cashew.

Ralph Wollstonecraft Hedge was married briefly in 1934 to a woman who had once driven a truck in St. Paul, Minnesota. I am not sure of her name because RWH was very shy in her presence and never introduced us. I have the feeling I heard somewhere that her name was Helen. She, whatever her name was, never understood Hedge's work and spent most of her time Indian wrestling with Collin A. Ruckersett. She moved away in 1935, taking two pounds of walnuts, and, outside of a Christmas card in 1937, we never heard of her again.

Only last year, while attending the jazz festival in Newport, I encountered several Hedge fans who asked me the familiar question about where RWH got his ideas. To the best of my knowledge, most of his best stories were the product of hallucinations. Many is the morning I would be sitting in the music room swatting squirrels only to have Hedge interrupt me by running in whooping. After I had locked the door and looked under everything, RWH would consent to dictate to me one of his famous yarns. It is in this way that his renowned *The Thing in the Dumbwaiter* and *The Shuffler Beyond the Transom* were composed. Readers who have noted a pronounced division in the middle of *The Peeper Round Corners* will be happy to learn that this story is the product of two separate hallucinations.

Most of Hedge's ideas were his own, but on rare occasions Collin A. Ruckersett would dress up in an old sheet and domino mask and scare RWH into a story. This method was only resorted to if RWH was behind in his work. To get him going on his novel, *The Straggler from the Moon Pit*, we had to buy quite a lot of Halloween masks and jump at him unexpectedly, which was hard to do with so many nut shells underfoot.

Most of RWH's better stories deal with the complicated mythos of the elder gods he created one day after reading the *American Weekly*. Essentially this mythos put forth the theory that beyond the gates of the universe lurked nameless, loathsome beings who were out to get Hedge. Most scholars agree that the best tales dealing with this mythos, especially *Here Comes the Vombis at the Door*, are worthy of Poe.

In late 1939, RWH was, as he had always feared would happen, carried off by the squirrels, and a career that added so much to American weird fiction came to a somewhat *outré* end. I will mention that I am again looking for a position as a confidential secretary, and close.

SPORTSMAN'S DIFFICULTY

To every man, his favorite hunting;
my game, the unicorn.
Never a thunder like his trumpet throat.
Never such lightning
as flames, all gold or lilac, from that eye.
I do not know how he can toss so proudly
his horse's head weighted with that vast horn.
He is the king
of all that tread on hooves;
his own are windshod,
and if you think wind is not hard like iron,
go lean against it in a city canyon.

I could have caught a herd of unicorns
were the bait easier
to find.

DORIS PITKIN BUCK

ROBERT A. HEINLEIN

"All You Zombies—"

2217 Time Zone V (EST) 7 Nov 1970 NYC—"Pop's Place": I was
polishing a brandy snifter when the Unmarried Mother came in.
I noted the time—10:17 P.M. zone five, or eastern time, November
7, 1970. Temporal agents always notice time & date; we must.

The Unmarried Mother was a man twenty-five years old, no
taller than I am, childish features and a touchy temper. I didn't
like his looks—I never had—but he was a lad I was here to recruit,
he was my boy. I gave him my best barkeep's smile.

Maybe I'm too critical. He wasn't swish; his nickname came
from what he always said when some nosy type asked him his
line: "I'm an unmarried mother." If he felt less than murderous he
would add: "—at four cents a word. I write confession stories."

If he felt nasty, he would wait for somebody to make something
of it. He had a lethal style of infighting, like a female cop—one
reason I wanted him. Not the only one.

He had a load on and his face showed that he despised people
more than usual. Silently I poured a double shot of Old Underwear and left the bottle. He drank it, poured another.

I wiped the bar top. "How's the 'Unmarried Mother' racket?"

His fingers tightened on the glass and he seemed about to throw it at me; I felt for the sap under the bar. In temporal manipulation you try to figure everything, but there are so many factors that you never take needless risks.

I saw him relax that tiny amount they teach you to watch for in the Bureau's training school. "Sorry," I said. "Just asking, 'How's business?' Make it 'How's the weather?' "

He looked sour. "Business is okay. I write 'em, they print 'em, I eat."

I poured myself one, leaned toward him. "Matter of fact," I said, "you write a nice stick—I've sampled a few. You have an amazingly sure touch with the woman's angle."

It was a slip I had to risk; he never admitted what pen names he used. But he was boiled enough to pick up only the last: " 'Woman's angle!' " he repeated with a snort. "Yeah, I know the woman's angle. I should."

"So?" I said doubtfully. "Sisters?"

"No. You wouldn't believe me if I told you."

"Now, now," I answered mildly, "bartenders and psychiatrists learn that nothing is stranger than truth. Why, son, if you heard the stories I do—well, you'd make yourself rich. Incredible."

"You don't know what 'incredible' means!"

"So? Nothing astonishes me. I've always heard worse."

He snorted again. "Want to bet the rest of the bottle?"

"I'll bet a full bottle." I placed one on the bar.

"Well——" I signaled my other bartender to handle the trade. We were at the far end, a single-stool space that I kept private by loading the bar top by it with jars of pickled eggs and other clutter. A few were at the other end watching the fights and somebody was playing the juke box—private as a bed where we were.

"Okay," he began, "to start with, I'm a bastard."

"No distinction around here," I said.

"I mean it," he snapped. "My parents weren't married."

"Still no distinction," I insisted. "Neither were mine."

"When——" He stopped, gave me the first warm look I ever saw on him. "You mean that?"

"I do. A one hundred per cent bastard. In fact," I added, "no one in my family ever marries. All bastards."

"Oh, that." I showed it to him. "It just looks like a wedding ring; I wear it to keep women off." It is an antique I bought in 1985 from a fellow operative—he had fetched it from pre-Christian Crete. "The Worm Ouroboros . . . The World Snake that eats its own tail, forever without end. A symbol of the Great Paradox."

He barely glanced at it. "If you're really a bastard, you know how it feels. When I was a little girl——"

"Wups!" I said. "Did I hear you correctly?"

"Who's telling this story? When I was a little girl—— Look, ever hear of Christine Jorgensen? Or Roberta Cowell?"

"Uh, sex-change cases? You're trying to tell me——"

"Don't interrupt or swelp me, I won't talk. I was a foundling, left at an orphanage in Cleveland in 1945 when I was a month old. When I was a little girl, I envied kids with parents. Then, when I learned about sex—and, believe me, Pop, you learn fast in an orphanage——"

"I know."

"—I made a solemn vow that any kid of mine would have both a pop and a mom. It kept me 'pure,' quite a feat in that vicinity—I had to learn to fight to manage it. Then I got older and realized I stood darn little chance of getting married—for the same reason I hadn't been adopted." He scowled. "I was horse-faced and buck-toothed, flat-chested and straight-haired."

"You don't look any worse than I do."

"Who cares how a barkeep looks? Or a writer? But people wanting to adopt pick little blue-eyed golden-haired morons. Later on, the boys want bulging breasts, a cute face, and an Oh-you-wonderful-male manner." He shrugged. "I couldn't compete. So I decided to join the W.E.N.C.H.E.S."

"Eh?"

"Women's Emergency National Corps, Hospitality & Entertainment Section, what they now call 'Space Angels'—Auxiliary Nursing Group, Extraterrestrial Legions."

I knew both terms, once I had them chronized. We use still a third name, it's that elite military service corps: Women's Hospitality Order Refortifying & Encouraging Spacemen. Vocabulary shift is the worst hurdle in time-jumps—did you know that "service station" once meant a dispensary for petroleum fractions? Once on an assignment in the Churchill Era, a woman said to me, "Meet me at the service station next door"—which is not what it sounds; a "service station" (then) wouldn't have a bed in it.

He went on: "It was when they first admitted you can't send men into space for months and years and not relieve the tension. You remember how the wowsers screamed? That improved my chance, since volunteers were scarce. A gal had to be respectable, preferably virgin (they liked to train them from scratch), above average mentally, and stable emotionally. But most volunteers were old hookers, or neurotics who would crack up ten days off Earth. So I didn't need looks; if they accepted me, they would fix my buck teeth, put a wave in my hair, teach me to walk and dance and how to listen to a man pleasingly, and everything else—plus training for the prime duties. They would even use plastic surgery if it would help—nothing too good for Our Boys.

"Best yet, they made sure you didn't get pregnant during your enlistment—and you were almost certain to marry at the end of your hitch. Same way today, A.N.G.E.L.S. marry spacers—they talk the language.

"When I was eighteen I was placed as a 'mother's helper.' This family simply wanted a cheap servant but I didn't mind as I couldn't enlist till I was twenty-one. I did housework and went to night school—pretending to continue my high-school typing and shorthand but going to a charm class instead, to better my chances for enlistment.

"Then I met this city slicker with his hundred-dollar bills." He scowled. "The no-good actually did have a wad of hundred-dollar bills. He showed me one night, told me to help myself.

"But I didn't. I liked him. He was the first man I ever met who was nice to me without trying games with me. I quit night school to see him oftener. It was the happiest time of my life.

"Then one night in the park the games began."

He stopped. I said, "And then?"

"And then *nothing!* I never saw him again. He walked me home and told me he loved me—and kissed me goodnight and never came back." He looked grim. "If I could find him, I'd kill him!"

"Well," I sympathized, "I know how you feel. But killing him—just for doing what comes naturally—hmm . . . Did you struggle?"

"Huh? What's that got to do with it?"

"Quite a bit. Maybe he deserves a couple of broken arms for running out on you, but——"

"He deserves worse than that! Wait till you hear. Somehow I kept anyone from suspecting and decided it was all for the best. I hadn't really loved him and probably would never love anybody —and I was more eager to join the W.E.N.C.H.E.S. than ever. I wasn't disqualified, they didn't insist on virgins. I cheered up.

"It wasn't until my skirts got tight that I realized."

"Pregnant?"

"He had me higher 'n a kite! Those skinflints I lived with ignored it as long as I could work—then kicked me out and the orphanage wouldn't take me back. I landed in a charity ward surrounded by other big bellies and trotted bedpans until my time came.

"One night I found myself on an operating table, with a nurse saying, 'Relax. Now breathe deeply.'

"I woke up in bed, numb from the chest down. My surgeon came in. 'How do you feel?' he says cheerfully.

" 'Like a mummy.'

" 'Naturally. You're wrapped like one and full of dope to keep you numb. You'll get well—but a Caesarean isn't a hangnail.'

" 'Caesarean,' I said. 'Doc—*did I lose the baby?*'

" 'Oh, no. Your baby's fine.'

" 'Oh. Boy or girl?'

" 'A healthy little girl. Five pounds, three ounces.'

"I relaxed. It's something, to have made a baby. I told myself I would go somewhere and tack 'Mrs.' on my name and let the kid think her papa was dead—no orphanage for *my* kid!

"But the surgeon was talking. 'Tell me, uh—' he avoided my name '—did you ever think your glandular setup was odd?'

"I said, 'Huh? Of course not. What are you driving at?'

"He hesitated. 'I'll give you this in one dose, then a hypo to let you sleep off your jitters. You'll have 'em.'

" 'Why?' I demanded.

" 'Ever hear of that Scottish physician who was female until she was thirty-five?—then had surgery and became legally and medically a man? Got married. All okay.'

" 'What's that got to do with me?'

" 'That's what I'm saying. You're a man.'

"I tried to sit up. 'What?'

" 'Take it easy. When I opened you, I found a mess. I sent for the Chief of Surgery while I got the baby out, then we held a consultation with you on the table—and worked for hours to salvage what we could. You had two full sets of organs, both immature, but with the female set well enough developed for you to have a baby. They could never be any use to you again, so we took them out and rearranged things so that you can develop properly as a man.' He put a hand on me. 'Don't worry. You're young, your bones will readjust, we'll watch your glandular balance—and make a fine young man out of you.'

"I started to cry. 'What about my *baby?*'

" 'Well, you can't nurse her, you haven't milk enough for a kitten. If I were you, I wouldn't see her—put her up for adoption.'

" '*No!*'

"He shrugged. 'The choice is yours; you're her mother—well, her parent. But don't worry now; we'll get you well first.'

"Next day they let me see the kid and I saw her daily—trying to get used to her. I had never seen a brand-new baby and had no idea how awful they look—my daughter looked like an orange monkey. My feeling changed to cold determination to do right by her. But four weeks later that didn't mean anything."

"Eh?"

"She was snatched."

" 'Snatched?' "

The Unmarried Mother almost knocked over the bottle we had bet. "Kidnaped—stolen from the hospital nursery!" He breathed hard. "How's that for taking the last a man's got to live for?"

"A bad deal," I agree. "Let's pour you another. No clues?"

"Nothing the police could trace. Somebody came to see her, claimed to be her uncle. While the nurse had her back turned, he walked out with her."

"Description?"

"Just a man, with a face-shaped face, like yours or mine." He frowned. "I think it was the baby's father. The nurse swore it was an older man but he probably used make-up. Who else would swipe my baby? Childless women pull such stunts—but whoever heard of a man doing it?"

"What happened to you then?"

"Eleven more months of that grim place and three operations. In four months I started to grow a beard; before I was out I was shaving regularly . . . and no longer doubted that I was male." He grinned wryly. "I was staring down nurses' necklines."

"Well," I said, "seems to me you came through okay. Here you are, a normal man, making good money, no real troubles. And the life of a female is not an easy one."

He glared at me. "A lot you know about it!"

"So?"

"Ever hear the expression 'a ruined woman'?"

"Mmm, years ago. Doesn't mean much today."

"I was as ruined as a woman can be; that bum *really* ruined me—I was no longer a woman . . . and I didn't know *how* to be a man."

"Takes getting used to, I suppose."

"You have no idea. I don't mean learning how to dress, or not walking into the wrong rest room; I learned those in the hospital. But how could I *live*? What job could I get? Hell, I couldn't even drive a car. I didn't know a trade; I couldn't do manual labor—too much scar tissue, too tender.

"I hated him for having ruined me for the W.E.N.C.H.E.S., too, but I didn't know how much until I tried to join the Space Corps instead. One look at my belly and I was marked unfit for military service. The medical officer spent time on me just from curiosity; he had read about my case.

"So I changed my name and came to New York. I got by as a fry cook, then rented a typewriter and set myself up as a public stenographer—what a laugh! In four months I typed four letters and one manuscript. The manuscript was for *Real Life Tales* and a waste of paper, but the goof who wrote it, sold it. Which gave me an idea; I bought a stack of confession magazines and studied them." He looked cynical. "Now you know how I get the authentic woman's angle on an unmarried-mother story . . . through the only version I haven't sold—the true one. Do I win the bottle?"

I pushed it toward him. I was upset myself, but there was work to do. I said, "Son, you still want to lay hands on that so-and-so?"

His eyes lighted up—a feral gleam.

"Hold it!" I said. "You wouldn't kill him?"

He chuckled nastily. "Try me."

"Take it easy. I know more about it than you think I do. I can help you. I know where he is."

He reached across the bar. "*Where is he?*"

I said softly, "Let go my shirt, sonny—or you'll land in the alley and we'll tell the cops you fainted." I showed him the sap.

He let go. "Sorry. But where is he?" He looked at me. "And how do you know so much?"

"All in good time. There are records—hospital records, orphanage records, medical records. The matron of your orphanage was Mrs. Fetherage—right? She was followed by Mrs. Gruenstein—right? Your name, as a girl, was 'Jane'—right? And you didn't tell me any of this—right?"

I had him baffled and a bit scared. "What's this? You trying to make trouble for me?"

"No indeed. I've your welfare at heart. I can put this character in your lap. You do to him as you see fit—and I guarantee that you'll get away with it. But I don't think you'll kill him. You'd be nuts to—and you aren't nuts. Not quite."

He brushed it aside. "Cut the noise. *Where is he?*"

I poured him a short one; he was drunk but anger was off-setting it. "Not so fast. I do something for you—you do something for me."

"Uh . . . what?"

"You don't like your work. What would you say to high pay, steady work, unlimited expense account, your own boss on the job, and lots of variety and adventure?"

He stared. "I'd say, 'Get those goddam reindeer off my roof!' Shove it, Pop—there's no such job."

"Okay, put it this way: I hand him to you, you settle with him, then try my job. If it's not all I claim—well, I can't hold you."

He was wavering; the last drink did it. "When d'yuh d'liver 'im?" he said thickly.

"If it's a deal—*right now!*"

He shoved out his hand. "It's a deal!"

I nodded to my assistant to watch both ends, noted the time— 2300—started to duck through the gate under the bar—when the juke box blared out: "*I'm My Own Granpaw!*" The service man had orders to load it with old Americana and classics because I couldn't stomach the "music" of 1970, but I hadn't known that tape was in it. I called out, "Shut that off! Give the customer his money back." I added, "Storeroom, back in a moment," and headed there with my Unmarried Mother following.

It was down the passage across from the johns, a steel door to which no one but my day manager and myself had a key; inside was a door to an inner room to which only I had a key. We went there.

He looked blearily around at windowless walls. "Where is 'e?"

"Right away." I opened a case, the only thing in the room; it was a U.S.F.F. Co-ordinates Transformer Field Kit, series 1992, Mod. II—a beauty, no moving parts, weight twenty-three kilos fully charged, and shaped to pass as a suitcase. I had adjusted it precisely earlier that day; all I had to do was to shake out the metal net which limits the transformation field.

Which I did. "Wha's that?" he demanded.

"Time machine," I said and tossed the net over us.

"Hey!" he yelled and stepped back. There is a technique to this; the net has to be thrown so that the subject will instinctively step back *onto* the metal mesh, then you close the net with both of you inside completely—else you might leave shoe soles behind or a piece of foot, or scoop up a slice of floor. But that's all the skill it takes. Some agents con a subject into the net; I tell the truth and use that instant of utter astonishment to flip the switch. Which I did.

1030-VI-3 April 1963-Cleveland, Ohio-Apex Bldg.: "Hey!" he repeated. "Take this damn thing off!"

"Sorry," I apologized and did so, stuffed the net into the case, closed it. "You said you wanted to find him."

"But—you said that was a time machine!"

I pointed out a window. "Does that look like November? Or New York?" While he was gawking at new buds and spring weather, I reopened the case, took out a packet of hundred-dollar bills, checked that the numbers and signatures were compatible with 1963. The Temporal Bureau doesn't care how much you spend (it costs nothing) but they don't like unnecessary anachronisms. Too many mistakes, and a general court-martial will exile you for a year in a nasty period, say 1974, with its strict rationing and forced labor. I never make such mistakes, the money was okay.

He turned around and said, "What happened?"

"He's here. Go outside and take him. Here's expense money." I shoved it at him and added, "Settle him, then I'll pick you up."

Hundred-dollar bills have a hypnotic effect on a person not used to them. He was thumbing them unbelievingly as I eased him into the hall, locked him out. The next jump was easy, a small shift in era.

7100-VI-10 March 1964-Cleveland-Apex Bldg.: There was a notice under the door saying that my lease expired next week; otherwise the room looked as it had a moment before. Outside, trees were bare and snow threatened; I hurried, stopping only for contemporary money and a coat, hat, and topcoat I had left there when I leased the room. I hired a car, went to the hospital. It took twenty minutes to bore the nursery attendant to the point where I could swipe the baby without being noticed. We went back to the Apex Building. This dial setting was more involved as the building did not yet exist in 1945. But I had precalculated it.

0010-VI-20 Sept 1945-Cleveland-Skyview Motel: Field kit, baby, and I arrived in a motel outside town. Earlier I had registered as "Gregory Johnson, Warren, Ohio," so we arrived in a room with curtains closed, windows locked, and doors bolted, and the floor cleared to allow for waver as the machine hunts. You can get a nasty bruise from a chair where it shouldn't be—not the chair of course, but backlash from the field.

No trouble. Jane was sleeping soundly; I carried her out, put her in a grocery box on the seat of a car I had provided earlier, drove to the orphanage, put her on the steps, drove two blocks to a "service station" (the petroleum products sort) and phoned the orphanage, drove back in time to see them taking the box inside, kept going and abandoned the car near the motel—walked to it and jumped forward to the Apex Building in 1963.

2200-VI-24 April 1963-Cleveland-Apex Bldg.: I had cut the time rather fine—temporal accuracy depends on span, except on return to zero. If I had it right, Jane was discovering, out in the park this balmy spring night, that she wasn't quite as "nice" a girl as she had thought. I grabbed a taxi to the home of those skin-flints, had the hackie wait around a corner while I lurked in shadows.

Presently I spotted them down the street, arms around each other. He took her up on the porch and made a long job of kissing her good night—longer than I thought. Then she went in and he came down the walk, turned away. I slid into step and hooked an arm in his. "That's all, son," I announced quietly. "I'm back to pick you up."

"*You!*" He gasped and caught his breath.

"Me. Now you know who *he* is—and after you think it over

you'll know who you are . . . and if you think hard enough, you'll figure out who the baby is . . . and who *I* am."

He didn't answer, he was badly shaken. It's a shock to have it proved to you that you can't resist seducing yourself. I took him to the Apex Building and we jumped again.

2300-VII-12 Aug 1985-Sub Rockies Base: I woke the duty sergeant, showed my I.D., told the sergeant to bed my companion down with a happy pill and recruit him in the morning. The sergeant looked sour, but rank is rank, regardless of era; he did what I said—thinking, no doubt, that the next time we met he might be the colonel and I the sergeant: which can happen in our corps. "What name?" he asked.

I wrote it out. He raised his eyebrows. "Like so, eh? *Hmm——*"

"You just do your job, Sergeant." I turned to my companion.

"Son, your troubles are over. You're about to start the best job a man ever held—and you'll do well. *I know.*"

"That you will!" agreed the sergeant. "Look at me—born in 1917—still around, still young, still enjoying life." I went back to the jump room, set everything on preselected zero.

2301-V-7 Nov 1970-NYC-"Pop's Place": I came out of the storeroom carrying a fifth of Drambuie to account for the minute I had been gone. My assistant was arguing with the customer who had been playing *"I'm My Own Granpaw!"* I said, "Oh, let him play it, then unplug it." I was very tired.

It's rough, but somebody must do it and it's very hard to recruit anyone in the later years, since the Mistake of 1972. Can you think of a better source than to pick people all fouled up where they are and give them well paid, interesting (even though dangerous) work in a necessary cause? Everybody knows now why the Fizzle War of 1963 fizzled. The bomb with New York's number on it didn't go off, a hundred other things didn't go as planned— all arranged by the likes of me.

But not the Mistake of '72; that one is not our fault—and can't be undone; there's no paradox to resolve. A thing either is, or it isn't, now and forever amen. But there won't be another like it; an order dated "1992" takes precedence any year.

I closed five minutes early, leaving a letter in the cash register telling my day manager that I was accepting his offer to buy me out, so see my lawyer as I was leaving on a long vacation. The Bureau might or might not pick up his payments, but they want things left tidy. I went to the room back of the storeroom and forward to 1993.

2200-VII-12 Jan 1993-Sub Rockies Annex-HQ Temporal DOL: I checked in with the duty officer and went to my quarters, intending to sleep for a week. I had fetched the bottle we bet (after all, I won it) and took a drink before I wrote my report. It tasted foul and I wondered why I had ever liked Old Underwear. But it was better than nothing; I don't like to be cold sober, I think too much. But I don't really hit the bottle either; other people have snakes—I have people.

I dictated my report; forty recruitments all okayed by the Psych Bureau—counting my own, which I knew would be okayed. I was here, wasn't I? Then I taped a request for assignment to operations; I was sick of recruiting. I dropped both in the slot and headed for bed.

My eye fell on "The By-laws of Time," over my bed:

> *Never Do Yesterday What Should Be Done Tomorrow.*
> *If At Last You Do Succeed, Never Try Again.*
> *A Stitch in Time Saves Nine Billion.*
> *A Paradox May Be Paradoctored.*
> *It Is Earlier When You Think.*
> *Ancestors Are Just People.*
> *Even Jove Nods.*

They didn't inspire me the way they had when I was a recruit; thirty subjective years of time-jumping wears you down. I undressed and when I got down to the hide I looked at my belly. A Caesarean leaves a big scar but I'm so hairy now that I don't notice it unless I look for it.

Then I glanced at the ring on my finger.

The Snake That Eats Its Own Tail, Forever and Ever . . . I *know* where *I* came from—but *where did all you zombies come from?*

I felt a headache coming on, but a headache powder is one thing I do not take. I did once—and you all went away.

So I crawled into bed and whistled out the light.

You aren't really there at all. There isn't anybody but me—Jane—here alone in the dark.

I miss you dreadfully!

AN EXPOSTULATION

(Against too many writers of science fiction)

Why did you lure us on like this,
Light-year on light-year, through the abyss,
Building (as though we cared for size!)
Empires that cover galaxies,
If at the journey's end we find
The same old stuff we left behind,
Well-worn Tellurian stories of
Crooks, spies, conspirators, or love,
Whose setting might as well have been
The Bronx, Montmartre, or Bethnel Green?

Why should I leave this green-floored cell,
Roofed with blue air, in which we dwell,
Unless, outside its guarded gates,
Long, long desired, the Unearthly waits,
Strangeness that moves us more than fear,
Beauty that stabs with tingling spear,
Or Wonder, laying on one's heart
That finger-tip at which we start
As if some thought too swift and shy
For reason's grasp had just gone by?

C. S. LEWIS

R. M. McKENNA

Casey Agonistes

YOU CAN'T JUST PLAIN DIE. You got to do it by the book.

That's how come I'm here in this TB ward with nine other recruits. Basic training to die.

You do it by stages. First a big ward, you walk around and go out and they call you mister. Then, if you got what it takes, a promotion to this isolation ward and they call you charles. You can't go nowhere, you meet the masks, and you get the feel of being dead.

Being dead is being weak and walled off. You hear car noises and see little doll-people down on the sidewalks, but when they come to visit you they wear white masks and nightgowns and talk past you in the wrong voices. They're scared you'll rub some off on them. You would, too, if you knew how.

Nobody ever visits me. I had practice being dead before I come here. Maybe that's how I got to be charles so quick.

It's easy, playing dead here. You eat your pills, make out to sleep in the quiet hours and drink your milk like a good little charles. You grin at their phony joshing about how healthy you look and feel. You all know better, but them's the rules.

Sick call is when they really make you know it. It's a parade—the head doctor and nurse, the floor nurse Mary Howard and two interns, all in masks and nightgowns. Mary pushes the wheeled rack with our fever charts on it. The doc is a tall skinhead with wooden eyes and pinch-nose glasses. The head nurse is fat, with little pig eyes and a deep voice.

The doc can't see, hear, smell, or touch you. He looks at your reflection in the chart and talks about you like you was real, but it's Mary that pulls down the cover and opens your pajama coat, and the interns poke and look and listen and tell the doc what they see and hear. He asks them questions for you to answer. You tell them how good you feel and they tell him.

He ain't supposed to get contaminated.

Mary's small, dark, and sweet and the head nurse gives her a bad time. One intern is small and dark like Mary, with soft black eyes and very gentle. The other one is pink and chubby.

The doc's voice is high and thin, like he ain't all there below decks. The head nurse snaps at Mary, snips at the interns, and puts a kind of dog wiggle in her voice when she talks to the doc.

I'm glad not to know what's under any of their masks, except maybe Mary's, because I can likely imagine better faces for them than God did.

The head nurse makes rounds, riding the book. When she catches us out of line, like smoking or being up in a quiet hour, she gives Mary hell.

She gives us hell too, like we was babies. She kind of hints that if we ain't respectful to her and obey rules maybe she won't let us die after all.

Christ, how I hate that hag! I hope I meet her in hell.

That's how it struck me, first day or two in isolation. I'd looked around for old shipmates, like a guy does, but didn't see any. On the third day one recognized me. I thought I knew that gravel voice, but even after he told me I couldn't hardly believe it was old Slop Chute Hewitt.

He was skin and bones and his blue eyes had a kind of puzzled look like I saw in them once years ago when a big limey sucker punched him in Nagasaki Joe's. When I remembered that, it made me know, all right.

He said glad to see me there and we both laughed. Some of the others shuffled over in striped bathrobes and all of a sudden I was in like Flynn, knowing Slop Chute. I found out they called the head doc Uncle Death. The fat nurse was Mama Death. The blond intern was Pink Waldo, the dark one Curly Waldo, and Mary was Mary. Knowing things like that is a kind of password.

They said Curly Waldo was sweet on Mary, but he was a poor Italian. Pink Waldo come of good family and was trying to beat him out. They were pulling for Curly Waldo.

When they left, Slop Chute and me talked over old times in China. I kept seeing him like he was on the *John D. Edwards,* sitting with a cup of coffee topside by the after fireroom hatch, while his snipes turned to down below. He wore bleached dungarees and shined shoes and he looked like a lord of the earth. His broad face and big belly. The way he stoked chow into himself in the guinea pullman—that's what give him his name. The way he took aboard beer and samshu in the Kongmoon Happiness Garden. The way he swung the little ne-sans dancing in the hotels on Skibby Hill. Now . . . Godalmighty! It made me know.

But he still had the big jack-o'-lantern grin.

"Remember little Connie that danced at the Palais?" he asked.

I remember her, half Portygee, cute as hell.

"You know, Charley, now I'm headed for scrap, the onliest one damn thing I'm sorry for is I didn't shack with her when I had the chance."

"She was nice," I said.

"She was green fire in the velvet, Charley. I had her a few times when I was on the *Monocacy.* She wanted to shack and I wouldn't never do it. Christ, Christ, I wish I did, now!"

"I ain't sorry for anything, that I can think of."

"You'll come to it, sailor. For every guy there's some one thing. Remember how Connie used to put her finger on her nose like a Jap girl?"

"Now Mr. Noble, you mustn't keep arthur awake in quiet hour. Lie down yourself, please."

It was Mama Death, sneaked up on us.

"Now rest like a good boy, charles, and we'll have you home before you know it," she told me on her way out.

I thought a thought at her.

The ward had green-gray linoleum, high, narrow windows, a spar-color overhead, and five bunks on a side. My bunk was at one end next to the solarium. Slop Chute was across from me in the middle. Six of us was sailors, three soldiers, and there was one marine.

We got mucho sack time, training for the long sleep. The marine bunked next to me and I saw a lot of him.

He was a strange guy. Name of Carnahan, with a pointed nose and a short upper lip and a go-to-hell stare. He most always wore his radio earphones and he was all the time grinning and chuckling like he was in a private world from the rest of us.

It wasn't the program that made him grin, either, like I thought first. He'd do it even if some housewife was yapping about how to didify the dumplings. He carried on worst during sick call. Sometimes Uncle Death looked across almost like he could hear it direct.

I asked him about it and he put me off, but finally he told me. Seems he could hypnotize himself to see a big ape and then make the ape clown around. He told me I might could get to see it too. I wanted to try, so we did.

"He's there," Carnahan would say. "Sag your eyes, look out the corners. He won't be plain at first."

"Just *expect* him, he'll come. Don't want him to do anything. You just *feel*. He'll do what's natural," he kept telling me.

I got where I could see the ape—Casey, Carnahan called him—in flashes. Then one day Mama Death was chewing out Mary and I saw him plain. He come up behind Mama and—I busted right out laughing.

He looked like a bowlegged man in an ape suit covered with red-brown hair. He grinned and made faces with a mouth full of

big yellow teeth and he was furnished like John Keeno himself.
I roared.

"Put on your phones so you'll have an excuse for laughing,"
Carnahan whispered. "Only you and me can see him, you know."

Fixing to be dead you're ready for God knows what, but Casey
was sure something.

"Hell no, he ain't real," Carnahan said. "We ain't so real ourselves any more. That's why we can see him."

Carnahan told me okay to try and let Slop Chute in on it. It
ended we cut the whole gang in, going slow so the masks wouldn't
get suspicious.

It bothered Casey at first, us all looking at him. It was like we
all had a string on him and he didn't know who to mind. He
backed and filled and tacked and yawed all over the ward not able
to steer himself. Only when Mama Death was there and Casey
went after her, then it was like all the strings pulled the same way.

The more we watched him the plainer and stronger he got till
finally he started being his own man. He came and went as he
pleased and we never knew what he'd do next except that there'd
be a laugh in it. Casey got more and more there for us, but he
never made a sound.

He made a big difference. We all wore our earphones and giggled like idiots. Slop Chute wore his big sideways grin more often.
Old Webster almost stopped griping.

There was a man filling in for a padre came to visitate us every
week. Casey would sit on his knee and wiggle and drool, with one
finger between those strong, yellow teeth. The man said the radio
was a godsend to us patient spirits in our hour of trial. He stopped
coming.

Casey made a real show out of sick call. He kissed Mama Death
smack on her mask, danced with her and bit her on the rump. He
rode piggy back on Uncle Death. He even took a hand in Mary's
romance.

One Waldo always went in on each side of a bunk to look,
listen, and feel for Uncle. Mary could go on either side. We kept

count of whose side she picked and how close she stood to him. That's how we figured Pink Waldo was ahead.

Well, Casey started to shoo her gently in by Curly Waldo and then crowd her closer to him. And, you know, the count began to change in Curly's favor. Casey had something.

If no masks were around to bedevil, Casey would dance and turn handsprings. He made us all feel good.

Uncle Death smelled a rat and had the radio turned off during sick call and quiet hours. But he couldn't cut off Casey.

Something went wrong with Roby, the cheerful black boy next to Slop Chute. The masks were all upset about it and finally Mary come told him on the sly. He wasn't going to make it. They were going to flunk him back to the big ward and maybe back to the world.

Mary's good that way. We never see her face, of course, but I always imagine for her a mouth like Venus has, in that picture you see her standing in the shell.

When Roby had to go, he come around to each bunk and said good-by. Casey stayed right behind him with his tongue stuck out. Roby kept looking around for Casey, but of course he couldn't see him.

He turned around, just before he left the ward, and all of a sudden Casey was back in the middle and scowling at him. Roby stood looking at Casey with the saddest face I ever saw him wear. Then Casey grinned and waved a hand. Roby grinned back and tears run down his black face. He waved and shoved off.

Casey took to sleeping in Roby's bunk till another recruit come in.

One day two masked orderlies loaded old Webster the whiner onto a go-to-Jesus cart and wheeled him off to X-ray. They said. But later one came back and wouldn't look at us and pushed Webster's locker out and we knew. The masks had him in a quiet room for the graduation exercises.

They always done that, Slop Chute told me, so's not to hurt the morale of the guys not able to make the grade yet. Trouble was, when a guy went to X-ray on a go-to-Jesus cart he never knew till he got back whether he was going to see the gang again.

Next morning when Uncle Death fell in for sick call Casey come bouncing down the ward and hit him a haymaker plumb on the mask.

I swear the bald-headed bastard staggered. I know his glasses fell off and Pink Waldo caught them. He said something about a moment of vertigo, and made a quick job of sick call. Casey stayed right behind him and kicked his stern post every step he took.

Mary favored Curly Waldo's side that day without any help from Casey.

After that Mama Death really got ugly. She slobbered loving care all over us to keep us knowing what we was there for. We got baths and back rubs we didn't want. Quiet hour had to start on the dot and be really quiet. She was always reading Mary off in whispers, like she knew it bothered us.

Casey followed her around aping her duck waddle and poking her behind now and again. We laughed and she thought it was at her and I guess it was. So she got Uncle Death to order the routine temperatures taken rectally, which she knew we hated. We stopped laughing and she knocked off the rectal temperatures. It was a kind of unspoken agreement. Casey give her a worse time than ever, but we saved our laughing till she was gone.

Poor Slop Chute couldn't do anything about his big, lopsided grin that was louder than a belly laugh. Mama give him a real bad time. She arthured the hell out of him.

He was coming along first rate, had another hemorrhage, and they started taking him to the clinic on a go-to-Jesus cart instead of in a chair. He was supposed to use ducks and a bedpan instead of going to the head, but he saved it up and after lights out we used to help him walk to the head. That made his reflection in the chart wrong and got him in deeper with Uncle Death.

I talked to him a lot, mostly about Connie. He said he dreamed about her pretty often now.

"I figure it means I'm near ready for the deep six, Charley."

"Figure you'll see Connie then?"

"No. Just hope I won't have to go on thinking about her then. I want it to be all night in and no reveille."

"Yeah," I said, "me too. What ever become of Connie?"

"I heard she ate poison right after the Reds took over Shanghai. I wonder if she ever dreamed about me?"

"I bet she did, Slop Chute," I said. "She likely used to wake up screaming and she ate the poison just to get rid of you."

He put on his big grin.

"You regret something too, Charley. You find it yet?"

"Well, maybe," I said. "Once on a stormy night at sea on the *Black Hawk* I had a chance to push King Brody over the side. I'm sorry now I didn't."

"Just come to you?"

"Hell, no, it come to me three days later when he give me a week's restriction in Tsingtao. I been sorry ever since."

"No. It'll smell you out, Charley. You wait."

Casey was shadowboxing down the middle of the ward as I shuffled back to my bunk.

It must've been spring because the days were longer. One night, right after the nurse come through, Casey and Carnahan and me helped Slop Chute walk to the head. While he was there he had another hemorrhage.

Carnahan started for help but Casey got in the way and motioned him back and we knew Slop Chute didn't want it.

We pulled Slop Chute's pajama top off and steadied him. He went on his knees in front of the bowl and the soft, bubbling cough went on for a long time. We kept flushing it. Casey opened the door and went out to keep away the nurse.

Finally it pretty well stopped. Slop Chute was too weak to stand. We cleaned him up and I put my pajama top on him, and we stood him up. If Casey hadn't took half the load, we'd'a never got him back to his bunk.

Godalmighty! I used to carry hundred-kilo sacks of cement like they was nothing.

We went back and cleaned up the head. I washed out the pajama top and draped it on the radiator. I was in a cold sweat and my face burned when I turned in.

Across the ward Casey was sitting like a statue beside Slop Chute's bunk.

Next day was Friday, because Pink Waldo made some crack about fish to Curly Waldo when they formed up for sick call. Mary moved closer to Curly Waldo and give Pink Waldo a cold look. That was good.

Slop Chute looked waxy, and Uncle Death seemed to see it because a gleam come into his wooden eyes. Both Waldoes listened all over Slop Chute and told Uncle what they heard in their secret language. Uncle nodded, and Casey thumbed his nose at him.

No doubt about it, the ways was greased for Slop Chute. Mama Death come back soon as she could and began to loosen the chocks. She slobbered arthurs all over Slop Chute and flittered around like women do when they smell a wedding. Casey give her extra special hell, and we all laughed right out and she hardly noticed.

That afternoon two orderly masks come with a go-to-Jesus cart and wanted to take Slop Chute to X-ray. Casey climbed on the cart and scowled at them.

Slop Chute told'em shove off, he wasn't going.

They got Mary and she told Slop Chute please go, it was doctor's orders.

Sorry, no, he said.

"Please, for me, Slop Chute," she begged.

She knows our right names—that's one reason we love her. But Slop Chute shook his head, and his big jawbone stuck out.

Mary—she had to then—called Mama Death. Mama waddled in, and Casey spit in her mask.

"Now arthur, what is this, arthur, you know we want to help

you get well and go home, arthur," she arthured at Slop Chute. "Be a good boy now, arthur, and go along to the clinic."

She motioned the orderlies to pick him up anyway. Casey hit one in the mask and Slop Chute growled, "Sheer off, you bastards!"

The orderlies hesitated.

Mama's little eyes squinted and she wiggled her hands at them. "Let's not be naughty, arthur. Doctor knows best, arthur."

The orderlies looked at Slop Chute and at each other. Casey wrapped his arms and legs around Mama Death and began chewing on her neck. He seemed to mix right into her, someway, and she broke and run out of the ward.

She come right back, though, trailing Uncle Death. Casey met him at the door and beat hell out of him all the way to Slop Chute's bunk. Mama sent Mary for the chart, and Uncle Death studied Slop Chute's reflection for a minute. He looked pale and swayed a little from Casey's beating.

He turned toward Slop Chute and breathed in deep and Casey was on him again. Casey wrapped his arms and legs around him and chewed at his mask with those big yellow teeth. Casey's hair bristled and his eyes were red as the flames of hell.

Uncle Death staggered back across the ward and fetched up against Carnahan's bunk. The other masks were scared spitless, looking all around, kind of knowing.

Casey pulled away, and Uncle Death said maybe he was wrong, schedule it for tomorrow. All the masks left in a hurry except Mary. She went back to Slop Chute and took his hand.

"I'm sorry, Slop Chute," she whispered.

"Bless you, Connie," he said, and grinned. It was the last thing I ever heard him say.

Slop Chute went to sleep, and Casey sat beside his bunk. He motioned me off when I wanted to help Slop Chute to the head after lights out. I turned in and went to sleep.

I don't know what woke me. Casey was moving around fidgety-like, but of course not making a sound. I could hear the others stirring and whispering in the dark too.

Then I heard a muffled noise—the bubbling cough again, and spitting. Slop Chute was having another hemorrhage and he had his head under the blankets to hide the sound. Carnahan started to get up. Casey waved him down.

I saw a deeper shadow high in the dark over Slop Chute's bunk. It came down ever so gently and Casey would push it back up again. The muffled coughing went on.

Casey had a harder time pushing back the shadow. Finally he climbed on the bunk straddle of Slop Chute and kept a steady push against it.

The blackness came down anyway, little by little. Casey strained and shifted his footing. I could hear him grunt and hear his joints crack.

I was breathing forced draft with my heart like to pull off its bed bolts. I heard other bedsprings creaking. Somebody across from me whimpered low, but it was sure never Slop Chute that done it.

Casey went to his knees, his hands forced almost level with his head. He swung his head back and forth and I saw his lips curled back from the big teeth clenched tight together. . . . Then he had the blackness on his shouders like the weight of the whole world.

Casey went down on hands and knees with his back arched like a bridge. Almost I thought I heard him grunt . . . and he gained a little.

Then the blackness settled heavier, and I heard Casey's tendons pull out and his bones snap. Casey and Slop Chute disappeared under the blackness, and it overflowed from there over the whole bed . . . and more . . . and it seemed to fill the whole ward.

It wasn't like going to sleep, but I don't know anything it was like.

The masks must've towed off Slop Chute's hulk in the night, because it was gone when I woke up.

So was Casey.

Casey didn't show up for sick call and I knew then how much he meant to me. With him around to fight back I didn't feel as

dead as they wanted me to. Without him I felt deader than ever.
I even almost liked Mama Death when she charlesed me.

Mary came on duty that morning with a diamond on her third
finger and a brighter sparkle in her eye. It was a little diamond,
but it was Curly Waldo's and it kind of made up for Slop Chute.

I wished Casey was there to see it. He would've danced all
around her and kissed her nice, the way he often did. Casey loved
Mary.

It was Saturday, I know, because Mama Death come in and
told some of us we could be wheeled to a special church hooraw
before breakfast next morning if we wanted. We said no thanks.
But it was a hell of a Saturday without Casey. Sharkey Brown said
it for all of us: "With Casey gone, this place is like a morgue
again."

Not even Carnahan could call him up.

"Sometimes I think I feel him stir, and then again I ain't sure,"
he said. "It beats hell where he's went to."

Going to sleep that night was as much like dying as it could be
for men already dead.

Music from far off woke me up when it was just getting light. I
was going to try to cork off again, when I saw Carnahan was
awake.

"Casey's around somewhere," he whispered.

"Where?" I asked, looking around. "I don't see him."

"I feel him," Carnahan said. "He's around."

The others began to wake up and look around. It was like the
night Casey and Slop Chute went under. Then something moved
in the solarium. . . .

It was Casey.

He come in the ward slow and bashful-like, jerking his head all
around, with his eyes open wide, and looking scared we was going
to throw something at him. He stopped in the middle of the ward.

"Yea, Casey!" Carnahan said in a low, clear voice.

Casey looked at him sharp.

"Yea, Casey!" we all said. "Come aboard, you hairy old bastard!"

Casey shook hands with himself over his head and went into his dance. He grinned . . . and I swear to God it was Slop Chute's big, lopsided grin he had on.

For the first time in my whole damn life I wanted to cry.

THROUGH TIME AND SPACE
WITH FERDINAND FEGHOOT

THE ISMAILI INSTITUTE OF HIGHER STUDIES always rewarded the annual Hayworth Memorial Lecturer with his weight in diamonds —but only if he withstood the attacks of the faculty.

Ferdinand Feghoot, lecturing on "Space Colonization and the Human Emotions," ran this gantlet successfully in 2883. "Everywhere man has gone," he declared, "and no matter how he has changed, you always find some small, homey, nostalgic reminder of old Mother Earth."

At once he was challenged. "What about the planet *Candide?*" a professor demanded. "They are infidels, cannibals! How could anything there remind one of Earth?"

For an instant, Feghoot was taken aback. Then he smiled. "I would have said you were right," he replied, "if it hadn't been for one thing. As you know, the Candideans especially relish the plump juicy buttocks of slaves raised on large farms for the purpose. And it was on one of these farms that I saw something which took me right back to my boyhood, and brought tears to my eyes."

"What was it?" everyone asked.

"It stood on a shelf in the kitchen," sighed Ferdinand Feghoot. "It was just an old *Fanny Farmer's Cook Book.*"

GRENDEL BRIARTON

WILLIAM TENN

Eastward Ho!

THE NEW JERSEY TURNPIKE had been hard on the horses. South of New Brunswick the potholes had been so deep, the scattered boulders so plentiful, that the two men had been forced to move at a slow trot, to avoid crippling their three precious animals. And, of course, this far south, farms were non-existent: they had been able to eat nothing but the dried provisions in the saddlebags, and last night they had slept in a roadside service station, suspending their hammocks between the tilted, rusty gas pumps.

But it was still the best, the most direct route, Jerry Franklin knew. The Turnpike was a government road: its rubble was cleared semiannually. They had made excellent time and come through without even developing a limp in the pack horse. As they swung out on the last lap, past the riven tree stump with the words TRENTON EXIT carved on its side, Jerry relaxed a bit. His father, his father's colleagues, would be proud of him. And he was proud of himself.

But the next moment, he was alert again. He roweled his horse, moved up alongside his companion, a young man of his own age.

"Protocol," he reminded. "I'm the leader here. You know better than to ride ahead of me this close to Trenton."

He hated to pull rank. But facts were facts, and if a subordinate got above himself he was asking to be set down. After all, he was the son—and the oldest son, at that—of the Senator from Idaho; Sam Rutherford's father was a mere Undersecretary of State and Sam's mother's family was pure post office clerk all the way back.

Sam nodded apologetically and reined his horse back the proper couple of feet. "Thought I saw something odd," he explained. "Looked like an advance party on the side of the road—and I could have sworn they were wearing buffalo robes."

"Seminole don't wear buffalo robes, Sammy. Don't you remember your sophomore political science?"

"I never had any political science, Mr. Franklin: I was an engineering major. Digging around in ruins has always been my dish. But, from the little I know, I didn't *think* buffalo robes went with the Seminole. That's why I was——"

"Concentrate on the pack horse," Jerry advised. "Negotiations are my job."

As he said this, he was unable to refrain from touching the pouch upon his breast with rippling fingertips. Inside it was his commission, carefully typed on one of the last precious sheets of official government stationery (and it was not one whit less official because the reverse side had been used years ago as a scribbled interoffice memo), and signed by the President himself. In ink!

The existence of such documents was important to a man in later life. He would have to hand it over, in all probability, during the conferences, but the commission to which it attested would be on file in the capitol up north. And, when his father died, and he took over one of the two hallowed Idaho seats, it would give him enough stature to make an attempt at membership on the Appropriations Committee. Or, for that matter, why not go the whole hog—the Rules Committee itself? No Senator Franklin had ever been a member of the Rules Committee. . . .

The two envoys knew they were on the outskirts of Trenton when they passed the first gangs of Jerseyites working to clear the road. Frightened faces glanced at them briefly, and quickly bent again to work. The gangs were working without any visible supervision. Evidently the Seminole felt that simple instructions were sufficient.

But as they rode into the blocks of neat ruins that was the city proper and still came across nobody more important than white men, another explanation began to occur to Jerry Franklin. This all had the look of a town still at war, but where were the combatants? Almost certainly on the other side of Trenton, defending the Delaware River—that was the direction from which the new rulers of Trenton might fear attack—not from the north where there was only the United States of America.

But if that were so, who in the world could they be defending against? Across the Delaware to the south there was nothing but more Seminole. Was it possible—was it possible that the Seminole had at last fallen to fighting among themselves?

Or was it possible that Sam Rutherford had been right? Fantastic. Buffalo robes in Trenton! There should be no buffalo robes closer than a hundred miles westward, in Harrisburg.

But when they turned onto State Street, Jerry bit his lip in chagrin. Sam had seen correctly, which made him one up.

Scattered over the wide lawn of the gutted state capitol were dozens of wigwams. And the tall, dark men who sat impassively, or strode proudly among the wigwams, all wore buffalo robes. There was no need even to associate the paint on their faces with a remembered lecture in political science: these were Sioux.

So the information that had come drifting up to the government about the identity of the invader was totally inaccurate—as usual. Well, you couldn't expect communication miracles over this long a distance. But that inaccuracy made things difficult. It might invalidate his commission for one thing: his commission was addressed directly to Osceola VII, Ruler of All the Seminoles. And if Sam Rutherford thought this gave him a right to preen himself——

He looked back dangerously. No, Sam would give no trouble. Sam knew better than to dare an I-told-you-so. At his leader's look, the son of the Undersecretary of State dropped his eyes groundwards to immediate humility.

Satisfied, Jerry searched his memory for relevant data on recent political relationships with the Sioux. He couldn't recall
much—just the provisions of the last two or three treaties. It would
have to do.

He drew up before an important-looking warrior and carefully
dismounted. You might get away with talking to a Seminole while
mounted, but not the Sioux. The Sioux were very tender on matters of protocol with white men.

"We come in peace," he said to the warrior standing as impassively straight as the spear he held, as stiff and hard as the rifle
on his back. "We come with a message of importance and many
gifts to your chief. We come from New York, the home of our
chief." He thought a moment, then added: "You know, the Great
White Father?"

Immediately, he was sorry for the addition. The warrior
chuckled briefly; his eyes lit up with a lightning-stroke of mirth.
Then his face was expressionless again, and serenely dignified as
befitted a man who had counted coup many times.

"Yes," he said. "I have heard of him. Who has not heard of the
wealth and power and far dominions of the Great White Father?
Come. I will take you to our chief. Walk behind me, white man."

Jerry motioned Sam Rutherford to wait.

At the entrance to a large, expensively decorated tent, the Indian stood aside and casually indicated that Jerry should enter.

It was dim inside, but the illumination was rich enough to take
Jerry's breath away. Oil lamps! Three of them! These people lived
well.

A century ago, before the whole world had gone smash in the
last big war, his people had owned plenty of oil lamps themselves.
Better than oil lamps, perhaps, if one could believe the stories the
engineers told around the evening fires. Such stories were pleasant
to hear, but they were glories of the distant past. Like the stories
of overflowing granaries and chock-full supermarkets, they made
you proud of the history of your people, but they did nothing for
you now. They made your mouth water, but they didn't feed you.

The Indians whose tribal organization had been the first to

adjust to the new conditions, in the all-important present, the Indians had the granaries, the Indians had the oil lamps. And the Indians . . .

There were two nervous white men serving food to the group squatting on the floor. An old man, the chief, with a carved, chunky body. Three warriors, one of them surprisingly young for council. And a middle-aged Negro, wearing the same bound-on rags as Franklin, except that they looked a little newer, a little cleaner.

Jerry bowed low before the chief, spreading his arms apart, palms down.

"I come from New York, from our chief," he mumbled. In spite of himself, he was more than a little frightened. He wished he knew their names so that he could relate them to specific events. Although he knew what their names would be like—approximately. The Sioux, the Seminole, all the Indian tribes renaissant in power and numbers, all bore names garlanded with anachronism. That queer mixture of several levels of the past, overlaid always with the cocky, expanding present. Like the rifles *and* the spears, one for the reality of fighting, the other for the symbol that was more important than reality. Like the use of wigwams on campaign, when, according to the rumors that drifted smokily across country, their slave artisans could now build the meanest Indian noble a damp-free, draftproof dwelling such as the President of the United States, lying on his special straw pallet, did not dream about. Like paint-spattered faces peering through newly reinvented, crude microscopes. What had microscopes been like? Jerry tried to remember the Engineering Survey Course he'd taken in his freshman year—and drew a blank. All the same, the Indians were so queer, *and* so awesome. Sometimes you thought that destiny had meant them to be conquerors, with a conqueror's careless inconsistency. Sometimes . . .

He noticed that they were waiting for him to continue. "From our chief," he repeated hurriedly. "I come with a message of importance and many gifts."

"Eat with us," the old man said. "Then you will give us your gifts and your message."

Gratefully, Jerry squatted on the ground a short distance from them. He was hungry, and among the fruit in the bowls he had seen something that must be an orange. He had heard so many arguments about what oranges tasted like!

After a while, the old man said, "I am Chief Three Hydrogen Bombs. This"—pointing to the young man—"is my son, Makes Much Radiation. And this"—pointing to the middle-aged Negro —"is a sort of compatriot of yours."

At Jerry's questioning look, and the chief's raised finger of permission, the Negro explained. "Sylvester Thomas. Ambassador to the Sioux from the Confederate States of America."

"The Confederacy? She's still alive? We heard ten years ago——"

"The Confederacy is very much alive, sir. The Western Confederacy that is, with its capital at Jackson, Mississippi. The Eastern Confederacy, the one centered at Richmond, Virginia, did go down under the Seminole. We have been more fortunate. The Arapahoe, the Cheyenne, and"—with a nod to the chief—"especially the Sioux; if I may say so, sir, have been very kind to us. They allow us to live in peace, so long as we till the soil quietly and pay our tithes."

"Then would you know, Mr. Thomas——" Jerry began eagerly. "That is . . . the Lone Star Republic—Texas—— Is it possible that Texas, too . . . ?"

Mr. Thomas looked at the door of the wigwam unhappily. "Alas, my good sir, the Republic of the Lone Star Flag fell before the Kiowa and the Comanche long years ago when I was still a small boy. I don't remember the exact date, but I do know it was before even the last of California was annexed by the Apache and the Navajo, and well before the nation of the Mormons under the august leadership of——"

Makes Much Radiation shifted his shoulders back and forth and flexed his arm muscles. "All this talk," he growled. "Paleface talk. Makes me tired."

"Mr. Thomas is not a paleface," his father told him sharply.

"Show respect! He's our guest and an accredited ambassador—you're not to use a word like paleface in his presence!"

One of the other, older warriors near the chief spoke up. "In the old days, in the days of the heroes, a boy of Makes Much Radiation's age would not dare raise his voice in council before his father. Certainly not to say the things he just has. I cite as reference, for those interested, Robert Lowie's definitive volume, *The Crow Indians,* and Lesser's fine piece of anthropological insight, *Three Types of Siouan Kinship.* Now, whereas we have not yet been able to reconstruct a Siouan kinship pattern on the classic model described by Lesser, we have developed a working arrangement that——"

"The trouble with you, Bright Book Jacket," the warrior on his left broke in, "is that you're too much of a classicist. You're always trying to live in the Golden Age instead of the present, and a Golden Age that really has little to do with the Sioux. Oh, I'll admit that we're as much Dakotan as the Crow, from the linguist's point of view at any rate, and that, superficially, what applies to the Crow should apply to us. But what happens when we quote Lowie in so many words and try to bring his precepts into daily life?"

"Enough," the chief announced. "Enough, Hangs A Tale. And you, too, Bright Book Jacket—enough, enough! These are private tribal matters. Though they do serve to remind us that the paleface was once great before he became sick and corrupt and frightened. These men whose holy books teach us the lost art of living like Sioux, men like Lesser, men like Robert H. Lowie, were not these men palefaces? And in memory of them should we not show tolerance?"

"A-ah!" said Makes Much Radiation impatiently. "As far as I'm concerned, the only good palefaces are dead. And that's that." He thought a bit. "Except their women. Paleface women are fun when you're a long way from home and feel like raising a little hell."

Chief Three Hydrogen Bombs glared his son into silence. Then he turned to Jerry Franklin. "Your message and your gifts. First your message."

"No, Chief," Bright Book Jacket told him respectfully but definitely. "First the gifts. *Then* the message. That's the way it was done."

"I'll have to get them. Be right back." Jerry walked out of the tent backwards and ran to where Sam Rutherford had tethered the horses. "The presents," he said urgently. "The presents for the chief."

The two of them tore at the pack straps. With his arms loaded, Jerry returned through the warriors who had assembled to watch their activity with quiet arrogance. He entered the tent, set the gifts on the ground and bowed low again.

"Bright beads for the chief," he said, handing over two star sapphires and a large white diamond, the best that the engineers had evacuated from the ruins of New York in the past ten years.

"Cloth for the chief," he said, handing over a bolt of linen and a bolt of wool, spun and loomed in New Hampshire especially for this occasion and painfully, expensively carted to New York.

"Pretty toys for the chief," he said, handing over a large, only slightly rusty alarm clock and a precious typewriter, both of them put in operating order by batteries of engineers and artisans working in tandem (the engineers interpreting the brittle old documents to the artisans) for two and a half months.

"Weapons for the chief," he said, handing over a beautifully decorated cavalry saber, the prized hereditary possession of the Chief of Staff of the United States Air Force, who had protested its requisitioning most bitterly ("Damn it all, Mr. President, do you expect me to fight these Indians with my bare hands?" "No, I don't, Johnny, but I'm sure you can pick up one just as good from one of your eager junior officers").

Three Hydrogen Bombs examined the gifts, particularly the typewriter, with some interest. Then he solemnly distributed them among the members of his council, keeping only the typewriter and one of the sapphires for himself. The sword he gave to his son.

Makes Much Radiation tapped the steel with his fingernail.

"Not so much," he stated. "Not-*so-much*. Mr. Thomas came up with better stuff than this from the Confederate States of America for my sister's puberty ceremony." He tossed the saber negligently to the ground. "But what can you expect from a bunch of lazy, good-for-nothing whiteskin stinkards?"

When he heard the last word, Jerry Franklin went rigid. That meant he'd have to fight Makes Much Radiation—and the prospect scared him right down to the wet hairs on his legs. The alternative was losing face completely among the Sioux.

"Stinkard" was a term from the Natchez system and was applied these days indiscriminately to all white men bound to field or factory under their aristocratic Indian overlords. A "stinkard" was something lower than a serf, whose one value was that his toil gave his masters the leisure to engage in the activities of full manhood: hunting, fighting, thinking.

If you let someone call you a stinkard and didn't kill him, why, then you *were* a stinkard—and that was all there was to it.

"I am an accredited representative of the United States of America," Jerry said slowly and distinctly, "and the oldest son of the Senator from Idaho. When my father dies, I will sit in the Senate in his place. I am a free-born man, high in the councils of my nation, and anyone who calls me a stinkard is a rotten, no-good, foul-mouthed liar!"

There—it was done. He waited as Makes Much Radiation rose to his feet. He noted with dismay the well-fed, well-muscled sleekness of the young warrior. He wouldn't have a chance against him. Not in hand-to-hand combat—which was the way it would be.

Makes Much Radiation picked up the sword and pointed it at Jerry Franklin. "I could chop you in half right now like a fat onion," he observed. "Or I could go into a ring with you knife to knife and cut your belly open. I've fought and killed Seminole, I've fought Apache, I've even fought and killed Comanche. But I've never dirtied my hands with paleface blood, and I don't intend to start now. I leave such simple butchery to the overseers of our estates. Father, I'll be outside until the lodge is clean again." Then he threw the sword ringingly at Jerry's feet and walked out.

Just before he left, he stopped, and remarked over his shoulder: "The oldest son of the Senator from Idaho! Idaho has been part of the estates of my mother's family for the past forty-five years! When will these romantic children stop playing games and start living in the world as it is now?"

"My son," the old chief murmured. "Younger generation. A bit wild. Highly intolerant. But he means well. Really does. Means well."

He signaled to the white serfs who brought over a large chest covered with great splashes of color.

While the chief rummanged in the chest, Jerry Franklin relaxed inch by inch. It was almost too good to be true: he wouldn't have to fight Makes Much Radiation, and he hadn't lost face. All things considered, the whole business had turned out very well indeed.

And as for that last comment—well, why expect an Indian to understand about things like tradition and the glory that could reside forever in a symbol? When his father stood up under the cracked roof of Madison Square Garden and roared across to the Vice-President of the United States: "The people of the sovereign state of Idaho will never and can never in all conscience consent to a tax on potatoes. From time immemorial, potatoes have been associated with Idaho, potatoes have been the pride of Idaho. The people of Boise say *no* to a tax on potatoes, the people of Pocatello say *no* to a tax on potatoes, the very rolling farmlands of the Gem of the Mountain say *no, never,* a thousand times *no,* to a tax on potatoes!"—when his father spoke like that, he *was* speaking for the people of Boise and Pocatello. Not the crushed Boise or desolate Pocatello of today, true, but the magnificent cities as they had been of yore . . . and the rich farms on either side of the Snake River. . . . And Sun Valley, Moscow, Idaho Falls, American Falls, Weiser, Grangeville, Twin Falls. . . .

"We did not expect you, so we have not many gifts to offer in return," Three Hydrogen Bombs was explaining. "However, there is this one small thing. For you."

Jerry gasped as he took it. It was a pistol, a real, brand-new pistol! And a small box of cartridges. Made in one of the Sioux slave workshops of the Middle West that he had heard about. But to hold it in his hand, and to know that it belonged to him!

It was a Crazy Horse forty-five, and, according to all reports, far superior to the Apache weapon that had so long dominated the West, the Geronimo thirty-two. This was a weapon a General of the Armies, a President of the United States, might never hope to own—and it was his!

"I don't know how—— Really, I—I——"

"That's all right," the chief told him genially. "Really it is. My son would not approve of giving firearms to palefaces, but I feel that palefaces are like other people—it's the individual that counts. You look like a responsible man for a paleface: I'm sure you'll use the pistol wisely. Now your message."

Jerry collected his faculties and opened the pouch that hung from his neck. Reverently, he extracted the precious document and presented it to the chief.

Three Hydrogen Bombs read it quickly and passed it to his warriors. The last one to get it, Bright Book Jacket, wadded it up into a ball and tossed it back at the white man.

"Bad penmanship," he said. "And 'receive' is spelled three different ways. The rule is: '*i* before *e*, except after *c*.' But what does it have to do with us? It's addressed to the Seminole chief, Osceola VII, requesting him to order his warriors back to the southern bank of the Delaware River, or to return the hostage given him by the Government of the United States as an earnest of good will and peaceful intentions. We're not Seminole: why show it to us?"

As Jerry Franklin smoothed out the wrinkles in the paper with painful care and replaced the document in his pouch, the confederate ambassador, Sylvester Thomas, spoke up. "I think I might explain," he suggested, glancing inquiringly from face to face. "If you gentlemen don't mind . . . ? It is obvious that the United States Government has heard that an Indian tribe finally crossed the Delaware at this point, and assumed it was the Seminole. The last movement of the Seminole, you will recall, was to Philadelphia, forcing the evacuation of the capital once more and its transfer to New York City. It was a natural mistake: the communications of the American States, whether Confederate or United"—a small, coughing, diplomatic laugh here—"have not been as good as might have been expected in recent years. It is quite evident that neither this young man nor the government he represents so ably and so well, had any idea that the Sioux had decided to steal a march on his majesty, Osceola VII, and cross the Delaware at Lambertville."

"That's right," Jerry broke in eagerly. "That's exactly right. And now, as the accredited emissary of the President of the United States, it is my duty formally to request that the Sioux nation honor the treaty of eleven years ago as well as the treaty of fifteen —I *think* it was fifteen—years ago, and retire once more behind the banks of the Susquehanna River. I must remind you that when we retired from Pittsburgh, Altoona, and Johnstown, you swore that the Sioux would take no more land from us and would protect us in the little we had left. I am certain that the Sioux want to be known as a nation that keeps its promises."

Three Hydrogen Bombs glanced questioningly at the faces of Bright Book Jacket and Hangs A Tale. Then he leaned forward and placed his elbows on his crossed legs. "You speak well, young man," he commented. "You are a credit to your chief. . . . Now, then. Of course the Sioux want to be known as a nation that honors its treaties and keeps its promises. And so forth and so forth. But we have an expanding population. You don't have an expanding population. We need more land. You don't use most of the land you have. Should we sit by and see the land go to waste—worse yet, should we see it acquired by the Seminole who already rule a domain stretching from Philadelphia to Key West? Be reasonable. You can retire—to other places. You have most of New England left and a large part of New York State. Surely you can afford to give up New Jersey."

In spite of himself, in spite of his ambassadorial position, Jerry Franklin began yelling. All of a sudden it was too much. It was one thing to shrug your shoulders unhappily back home in the

blunted ruins of New York, but here on the spot where the process was actually taking place—no, it was too much.

"What else can we afford to give up? Where else can we retire to? There's nothing left of the United States of America but
a handful of square miles, and still we're supposed to move back!
In the time of my forefathers, we were a great nation, we
stretched from ocean to ocean, so say the legends of my people,
and now we are huddled in a miserable corner of our land, starving, filthy, sick, dying, and ashamed. In the North, we are op-
pressed by the Ojibway and the Cree, we are pushed southward
relentlessly by the Montaignais; in the South, the Seminole
climb up our land yard by yard; and in the West, the Sioux take
a piece more of New Jersey, and the Cheyenne come up and
nibble yet another slice out of Elmira and Buffalo. When will it
stop—where are we to go?"

The old man shifted uncomfortably at the agony in his voice.
"It *is* hard; mind you, I don't deny that it *is* hard. But facts are
facts, and weaker peoples always go to the wall. . . . Now, as to
the rest of your mission. If we don't retire as you request, you're
supposed to ask for the return of your hostage. Sounds reasonable
to me. You ought to get something out of it. However, I can't for
the life of me remember a hostage. Do we have a hostage from
you people?"

His head hanging, his body exhausted, Jerry muttered in misery,
"Yes. All the Indian nations on our border have hostages. As
earnests of our good will and peaceful intentions."

Bright Book Jacket snapped his fingers. "That girl. Sarah Cam-
eron—Canton—what's-her-name."

Jerry looked up. "Calvin?" he asked. "Could it be *Calvin?* Sarah
Calvin? The daughter of the Chief Justice of the United States
Supreme Court?"

"Sarah Calvin. That's the one. Been with us for five, six years.
You remember, chief? The girl your son's been playing around
with?"

Three Hydrogen Bombs looked amazed. "Is *she* the hostage? I
thought she was some paleface female he had imported from his

plantations in southern Ohio. Well, well, well. Makes Much Radiation is just a chip off the old block, no doubt about it." He became suddenly serious. "But that girl will never go back. She rather goes for Indian loving. Goes for it all the way. And she has the idea that my son will eventually marry her. Or some such."

He looked Jerry Franklin over. "Tell you what, my boy. Why don't you wait outside while we talk this over? And take the saber. Take it back with you. My son doesn't seem to want it."

Jerry wearily picked up the saber and trudged out of the wigwam.

Dully, uninterestedly, he noticed the band of Sioux warriors around Sam Rutherford and his horses. Then the group parted for a moment, and he saw Sam with a bottle in his hand. Tequila! The damned fool had let the Indians give him tequila—he was drunk as a pig.

Didn't he know that white men couldn't drink, didn't dare drink? With every inch of their unthreatened arable land under cultivation for foodstuffs, they were all still on the edge of starvation. There was absolutely no room in their economy for such luxuries as intoxicating beverages—and no white man in the usual course of a lifetime got close to so much as a glassful of the stuff. Give him a whole bottle of tequila and he was a stinking mess.

As Sam was now. He staggered back and forth in dipping semicircles, holding the bottle by its neck and waving it idiotically. The Sioux chuckled, dug each other in the ribs and pointed. Sam vomited loosely down the rags upon his chest and belly, tried to take one more drink, and fell over backwards. The bottle continued to pour over his face until it was empty. He was snoring loudly. The Sioux shook their heads, made grimaces of distaste, and walked away.

Jerry looked on and nursed the pain in his heart. Where could they go? What could they do? And what difference did it make? Might as well be as drunk as Sammy there. At least you wouldn't be able to feel.

He looked at the saber in one hand, the bright new pistol in the other. Logically, he should throw them away. Wasn't it ridiculous when you came right down to it, wasn't it pathetic—a white man carrying weapons?

Sylvester Thomas came out of the tent. "Get your horses ready, my dear sir," he whispered. "Be prepared to ride as soon as I come back. Hurry!"

The young man slouched over to the horses and followed instructions—might as well do that as anything else. Ride where? Do what?

He lifted Sam Rutherford up and tied him upon his horse. Go back home? Back to the great, the powerful, the respected, capital of what had once been the United States of America?

Thomas came back with a bound-and-gagged girl in his grasp. She wriggled madly. Her eyes crackled with anger and rebellion. She kept trying to kick the Confederate Ambassador.

She wore the rich robes of an Indian princess. Her hair was braided in the style currently fashionable among Sioux women. And her face had been stained carefully with some darkish dye.

Sarah Calvin. The daughter of the Chief Justice. They tied her to the pack horse.

"Chief Three Hydrogen Bombs," the Negro explained. "He feels his son plays around too much with paleface females. He wants this one out of the way. The boy has to settle down, prepare for the responsibilities of chieftainship. This may help. And listen, the old man likes you. He told me to tell you something."

"I'm grateful. I'm grateful for every favor, no matter how small, how humiliating."

Sylvester Thomas shook his head decisively. "Don't be bitter, young sir. If you want to go on living you have to be alert. And you can't be alert and bitter at the same time. . . . The Chief wants you to know there's no point in your going home. He couldn't say it openly in council, but the reason the Sioux moved in on Trenton has nothing to do with the Seminole on the other side. It has to do with the Ojibway-Cree-Montaignais situation in the North. They've decided to take over the eastern seaboard—that includes what's left of your country. By this time, they're probably in Yonkers or the Bronx, somewhere inside New York

City. In a matter of hours, your government will no longer be in existence. The Chief had advance word of this and felt it necessary for the Sioux to establish some sort of bridgehead on the coast before matters were permanently stablized. By occupying New Jersey he is preventing an Ojibway-Seminole junction. But he likes you, as I said, and wants you warned against going home."

"Fine. But where *do* I go? Up a rain cloud? Down a well?"

"No," Thomas admitted without smiling. He hoisted Jerry up on his horse. "You might come back with me to the Confederacy——" He paused, and when Jerry's sullen expression did not change, he went on, "Well, then, may I suggest—and mind you, this is my advice, not the Chief's—head straight out to Asbury Park. It's not far away—you can make it in reasonable time if you ride hard. According to reports I've overheard, there should be units of the United States Navy there, the Tenth Fleet, to be exact."

"Tell me," Jerry asked, bending down. "Have you heard any other news? Anything about the rest of the world? How has it been with those people—the Russkies, the Sovietskis, whatever they were called—the ones the United States had so much to do with years ago?"

"According to several of the chief's councilors, the Soviet Russians were having a good deal of difficulty with people called Tatars. I *think* they were called Tatars. But, my good sir, you should be on your way."

Jerry leaned down farther and grasped his hand. "Thanks," he said. "You've gone to a lot of trouble for me. I'm grateful."

"That's quite all right," said Mr. Thomas earnestly. "After all, by the rocket's red glare, and all that. We were a single nation once."

Jerry moved off, leading the other two horses. He set a fast pace, exercising the minimum of caution made necessary by the condition of the road. By the time they reached Route 33, Sam Rutherford, though not altogether sober or well, was able to sit in his saddle. They could then untie Sarah Calvin and ride with her between them.

She cursed and wept. "Filthy paleface! Foul, ugly, stinking

whiteskins! I'm an Indian, can't you see I'm an Indian? My skin isn't white—it's brown, brown!"

They kept riding.

Asbury Park was a dismal clatter of rags and confusion and refugees. There were refugees from the north, from Perth Amboy, from as far as Newark. There were refugees from Princeton in the west, flying before the Sioux invasion. And from the south, from Atlantic City—even, unbelievably, from distant Camden—were still other refugees, with stories of a sudden Seminole attack, an attempt to flank the armies of Three Hydrogen Bombs.

The three horses were stared at enviously, even in their lathered, exhausted condition. They represented food to the hungry, the fastest transportation possible to the fearful. Jerry found the saber very useful. And the pistol was even better—it had only to be exhibited. Few of these people had ever seen a pistol in action: they had a mighty, superstitious fear of firearms. . . .

With this fact discovered, Jerry kept the pistol out nakedly in his right hand when he walked into the United States Naval Depot on the beach at Asbury Park. Sam Rutherford was at his side; Sarah Calvin walked sobbing behind.

He announced their family backgrounds to Admiral Milton Chester. The son of the Undersecretary of State. The daughter of the Chief Justice of the Supreme Court. The oldest son of the Senator from Idaho. "And now. Do you recognize the authority of this document?"

Admiral Chester read the wrinkled commission slowly, spelling out the harder words to himself. He twisted his head respectfully when he had finished, looking first at the seal of the United States on the paper before him, and then at the glittering pistol in Jerry's hand.

"Yes," he said at last. "I recognize its authority. Is that a real pistol?"

Jerry nodded. "A Crazy Horse forty-five. The latest. *How* do you recognize its authority?"

The admiral spread his hands. "Everything is confused out here. The latest word I've received is that there are Ojibway warriors in

Manhattan—that there is no longer any United States Government.
And yet this"—he bent over the document once more—"this is a
commission by the President himself, appointing you full pleni-
potentiary. To the Seminole, of course. But full plenipotentiary.
The last official appointment, to the best of my knowledge, of the
President of the United States of America."

He reached forward and touched the pistol in Jerry Franklin's hand curiously and inquiringly. He nodded to himself, as if
he'd come to a decision. He stood up, and saluted with a flourish.

"I hereby recognize you as the last legal authority of the United
States Government. And I place my fleet at your disposal."

"Good." Jerry stuck the pistol in his belt. He pointed with the
saber. "Do you have enough food and water for a long voyage?"

"No, sir," Admiral Chester said. "But that can be arranged in a
few hours at most. May I escort you aboard, sir?"

He gestured proudly down the beach and past the surf to where
the three, forty-five foot, gaff-rigged schooners rode at anchor.
"The United States Tenth Fleet, sir. Awaiting your orders."

Hours later when the three vessels were standing out to sea, the
admiral came to the cramped main cabin where Jerry Franklin
was resting. Sam Rutherford and Sarah Calvin were asleep in the
bunks above.

"And the orders, sir . . . ?"

Jerry Franklin walked out on the narrow deck, looked up at the
taut, patched sails. "Sail east."

"East, sir? *Due* east?"

"Due east all the way. To the fabled lands of Europe. To a place
where a white man can stand at last on his own two legs. Where
he need not fear persecution. Where he need not fear slavery.
Sail east, Admiral, until we discover a new and hopeful world—
a world of freedom!"

THROUGH TIME AND SPACE
WITH FERDINAND FEGHOOT: XIV

FERDINAND FEGHOOT was a close friend of the Very Reverend William Ralph Inge. His time shuttle was installed in a back bedroom of St. Paul's Deanery, and the Gloomy Dean knew perfectly well that he came from the future. (Indeed, his tale of coming events was largely responsible for the nickname.)

"My boy," the Dean said one day, "couldn't we take a jaunt in your time machine? I'd like to talk with John Donne, the great poet. He was Dean of St. Paul's too, you know."

Feghoot acceded. He rented Dean Inge an appropriate costume and took him back to 1624, where, after explaining the situation to Donne, who was vastly amused, he left them alone for a full day of discussion. The effect on Donne became obvious only a week later.

"fferdinand ffeghoote," demanded King James I, "what's awrv? There's not a merry word from Iohn Donne. Last night he read a Deuotion full only of funerals and death. He said, *Never send to ask for whom the bell tolls; it tolls for thee.* Aye, as gloomy as that! What makes him take such a subject?"

"Your Majesty," said Ferdinand Feghoot, "you know how these great poets are—give 'em an Inge and they take a knell."

GRENDEL BRIARTON

LEE SUTTON

Soul Mate

THE CHURCH WAS A JUMBLED DISORDER of towers, false buttresses and arches, reaching irrationally into nothing—but achieving peace. Quincy Summerfield rushed by it, down the stairs to the subway, intent only on his own kind of peace. He picked his way quickly through the crowds, avoiding the eyes that followed him. The chaos of people was an agony, but, because of the rain, he could have missed his train waiting for a taxi.

He settled himself behind a pillar near the tracks, looking cool and contained in his perfectly tailored covert coat and dark-blue homburg, but inside he was trembling. He had had these periods before, when every set of human eyes seemed to open into agony and even the order and control of his office could not allay his sense of disorder in the presence of his staff. Seven interviews in a row had done it today. He had played seven men like instruments and had hired the five best for his company at fifty thousand dollars a year less than any other personnel man could have gotten them for. It was for this that he was paid. But now he would need a day or so of isolation. It might even be better to send away Charlotte, the wife whom he had schooled into order and control.

Just then a girl's rich laugh floated to him down the tunnel and he glanced around the pillar. A girl with a long black ponytail squatted just past the turnstiles, art portfolios propped against her legs. With distaste he noticed the full breasts thrust out against an overbright blouse under an open, dirty trench coat. Her full mouth was deeply curved with laughter as she gathered up the miscellany of a spilled handbag; and she seemed to Quincy Summerfield the very essence of disorder.

He pulled his eyes away from her. He had to force his eyes away from her. He was seized with the shocking conviction that he had known her all his life; yet another part of his mind knew that he had never seen her before. She was like a fragment of a nightmare that had wandered into daylight. He prayed she wouldn't be on the same car with him. She was not; as he went through the sliding doors, he saw her enter the car ahead of him.

Inside the car, Quincy looked quickly around him, and sensing her monumental calm, sat down beside a gray-haired woman with light brown skin. Out of the crowd of the ramp he felt a little better. He seemed almost the embodiment of dignity as he sat there, erect, his long slender face, with its clipped graying mustache, composed and calm. The effect was achieved, however, only by considerable effort.

A guard pushed open the sliding door at the end of the car. The girl in the trench coat teetered through, rich lips in a teeth-flashing smile. Her sloppy good humor seemed to reach out to everyone in the car. For a moment even the guard's sullen face came alive. She sank gratefully into the seat directly opposite from Quincy Summerfield, dropping her load of portfolios helter-skelter.

Quincy Summerfield looked down, staring at the dull rain marks on his well-polished shoes. He felt her eyes on him. He began to shake inside again, and looked up. He looked deliberately away from her, as if in an attempt to ignore her so obviously she could not fail to notice the slight.

The sense of her presence was just too great. Even across the car he could feel the scent of her heavy perfume; it was deep with musk. His eyes were slowly drawn toward her: the pile of portfolios in disorder around her knees; the foolish, soaked ballet slippers on tiny feet. A squiggle of modernist jewelry, tied with a leather thong, nestled in the hollow of her throat. It was a distorted crucifix. All this messiness and the messiness of religion, too, he thought. But his eyes were drawn up to the curve of her lips. He was trembling even more; for no reason his feet ached with cold.

Then he met her clear, deep brown eyes; *lambent the word is. Such cool, gray eyes.*

He moved his feet. They were very cold. *That damned bra is much too tight . . .* His hand pushed up against his breasts. A drip from the homburg fell cool and sharp onto her nose. His breasts actually hurt. *A hot shower if the heater is fixed . . . Then I'll tell everyone about selling the picture . . . Charlotte will make me a warm drink . . . God, I'm feeling funny. I wonder if Arthur —would he believe? That's a distinguished disgusting-looking girl how aristocratic homburg mustache low class slut.*

My seeing's all wrong. That's me and there's no mirror. Who's Charlotte, Arthur, Quincy? I'm Quincy. I'm . . . That man. That girl. Jesus, Jesus. I'm thinking his her thoughts. Let me out. Let me out!

"Let me out!" The girl's rising scream brought everyone in the car to his feet. She stood there a moment, her eyes rolling and wild, then collapsed to the concrete floor in a faint.

Quincy Summerfield was shaking from head to foot, his hands over his face, fingers digging into his eyes. He had been conscious of the lifting of a great weight as the world had whirled into darkness and the girl collapsed onto the floor. She was going to throw up. He knew. He could feel every sensation she had as she lay there in the half faint. He could feel his own gorge rising. People were lifting her up. He felt her eyelids flutter. The mirror, mirror, mirror of her being conscious of his being conscious of her being conscious of the colored woman with the sculptured calm taking her into her arms. Then the girl threw up horribly and his throat ached with the agony of her embarrassment.

The train came screeching to a stop. Quincy jumped up and ran blindly headlong through the sliding door. He all but knocked down an old lady entering. She hit after him with her umbrella.

"Young pup!" The words followed him down the ramp as he

ran, his leather heels echoing through the noisy underground. His face was wild. People stopped in their tracks and stared after him, but he did not care. His hat fell off. He stumbled, almost fell. His head was awhirl with her seeing and his seeing, her thoughts and his thoughts. The turnstiles were just ahead. Soon he would be away, outside, away from all the people, away from the girl, into the open air.

The colored woman—she'll help me. She was picking up his pictures.

He pushed down a scream, and plunged through the tangled vision. He hardly knew how he got there, but finally, hatless, his trousers torn from a fall on the stairs, he was standing out in the street, flailing his arm at taxis.

Blessedly one stopped.

"Where to, buster?"

"Grand Central. Hurry, for God's sake!"

Through images of her seeing, he looked at his watch. He had smashed the crystal in some way and his wrist was numb. He sank back into the slick upholstery, breathing hard. Exhausted, he closed his eyes and gave himself up to single vision.

His bra was too tight; he reached around, letting out the hooks and eyes and breathed more easily.

"Now, honey," a soft voice was saying, "you be fine. You just got something now to tell your husband." The brown face was smiling. "You do got a husband?"

"But I'm not pregnant!" He burst out, speaking as the girl spoke.

"What's that, buster?" the taxi driver tossed over his shoulder. "You're not what?"

Quincy Summerfield opened his eyes and sat bolt upright. "Just thinking over some dialogue for a radio play," he said desperately.

With a grunt, the taxi driver went on driving.

Summerfield looked around him. It was a taxi, like any taxi. A small sign announced the driver was Barney Cohen. Outside it was raining. People leaned into the rain as they always did. He tried to push away the other images.

But he could not.

When he closed his eyes, he was in a dirty white, tiled lavatory, a vague stench of vomit and the scent of a musky perfume surrounding him. A women's lavatory. He was looking into the mirror at his white, shaking face, a woman's face with frightened brown eyes. He was putting on lipstick. *SHE is putting on lipstick,* he forced his mind to say. She shook her head and closed her eyes.

You're still here, she thought.

Yes.

What's happened, for God's sake? There was the same desperate fear in her mind that he felt in his.

Fear. They shared their fear for a long moment.

Then he fought to bring his thoughts into order again. *Nothing to fear. Nothing. Just the same as I always was. Just the same. She, you just the same. She. Me. Just the same.*

Christ, Christ her mind intruded. *Our Father . . .* The prayer distorted into a jumble of religious images.

The depth of her superstitious outcry shocked him into steel-bright control, and he fought for domination. *There is nothing to fear.* He forced the thought through the images. *I am just the same. You are just the same. Somehow . . .* and for a second he slid out of control . . . *we have made total mental contact. I know what you think, feel what you feel, and you know my thoughts, my feelings.*

Under his controlling thought she calmed and contemplated his ideas for a moment. He could feel her mind reach out for the sensations of his body, his male body and he allowed himself to become fully conscious of hers, the femaleness of her.

A deep wave of erotic feeling took them both: him in the taxi, her a quarter of a mile away before the mirror. He could feel her breath quicken.

"But fabulous," she breathed aloud as her images of Arthur and Fred interlaced with his imaged memories of Charlotte.

Revulsion. He stamped down on the images as if they were pale, dangerous worms.

"Stop it!" he shouted.

"For Christ's sake, buster, we got three blocks yet," the taxi driver growled, but swung toward the curb.

"Sorry. Thinking aloud again."

"Nuts," the taxi driver muttered. "A stooge for nuts, that's all I am," and cut back into traffic.

You're a cold, terrible man, thought the girl, swept by feelings of shame and hurt that were alien to her. *Things were just getting . . .* she searched for a word which meant good, but which would not betray her to his disapproval.

You're a slut, he thought savagely. He was deeply shaken, as by a nightmare. *I've wandered into a nightmare. Just like the nightmares I started having at fourteen. Are they connected? Were they reflections out of the mind of this terrible slut of a girl?*

Christ, you're a prig! the girl thought. She was very angry at him and at herself. Very deliberately she brought up an image of Arthur, a hairy young man with . . .

Setting his teeth, Quincy tried to force her thoughts away from the image forming in her mind and thus in his, but it was like trying to push back water—a deluge that was sweeping over him. He opened his eyes, almost to the breaking point, almost ready to scream. His mental pain hurt her into submission.

All right, all right, I'll stop. But you'll have to stop being nasty, too. After all, I didn't do this. I didn't try to bring us together this way. She was trembling with his pain.

"Okay, buster. Grand Central."

Summerfield thrust a five-dollar bill into the man's hand and rushed off into the crowd.

Five dollars! You gave that man five dollars! Why . . . ?

Couldn't wait. Got to get my train. Get away. Far away. Then maybe I'll be rid of you.

Pushing through the people, her thoughts went on steadily through his mind. *Am I so terrible?* they came, touched with wistfulness.

Yes, he thought. *You are so terrible. Everything I cannot stand. Wretchedly superstitious. Involved in a messy affair with two men. Disorderly.*

Images of her apartment flashed into his mind: modern pictures askew, undusted. Garbage in the sink. *Everything I cannot stand.*

Then, for the first time, he really knew her deep hurt as his own, as if he were committing violence upon himself. It was as if some rich and various part of himself, long suppressed, were alive again and in pain. For a fraction of a moment his mind reached out hesitantly toward her with compassion.

In spite of everything, she thought, *I rather admire you. Why, now we're practically soul mates.*

His revulsion at the idea was too deep to be stopped by any consideration of her or of himself.

I hope I can get rid of you, she thought, trying desperately to withdraw from him as from the violent touch of cruel hands.

But I'm afraid. I'm afraid. Those ESP men at Duke . . . Her mind sought wildly for a shadowy memory. *Didn't they shield their people with lead, separate them miles and miles?* And he got tangled pictures of men in white robes, separating "sensitive" people, shielding them in a variety of ways, but with no effect on their abilities to read each other's minds. He let his contempt slap at her at believing such nonsense.

But she was right. The edges of perception sharpened; they did not fade. There was no shutting her off. And there was always the continuing and horrible sense of familiarity. It was almost as if the eyes of his mind were being drawn against his will toward a disgusting part of himself held up in a mirror.

Going down the walk to his home he was conscious of her in her apartment. But he concentrated on holding his own line of thought. His home, its barbered lawns and well-trimmed hedges, the whiteness and neatness of it, the pattern of twigs in the single tree was bringing him, momentarily, a pool of quiet.

Spare . . . bare . . . such crude design. The house was suddenly mirrored back at him from her mind. Suddenly he saw: *Petty bourgeois cheapness. All richness and complexity sacrificed to achieve a banal balance.*

Damn you.

Sorry. I didn't mean to hurt. But her laughter and scorn were still there under the surface.

And he couldn't help being infected by her thoughts. The landscape he owned and loved: *Poor stuff. Deliberately manufactured by a second-rate artist for people with third-rate taste.*

And Charlotte, so calm and sweet. Suddenly he saw how lost she was, the lines of frustration around her mouth.

Poor thing, the girl thought. *No children. No love. Then came* more than scorn. *You needed release and you've used her—just like the men you work with. You——*

There was no escaping her. Her scorn or shame or teasing laughter was omnipresent.

He didn't dare go back to work, for his confusion would have been noticed, and that was something he could not have borne. Luckily his post was high enough that he could make his own schedule, and could remain at home for a few days.

But the days were torture. There was not one flicker of his thought, one twinge of emotion the girl did not reflect. Worse, he caught all of hers. Not one of his her secret shabbinesses she he did not know. The tangled days ended only in nights where their tangled dreams were all nightmares to him. It was as if his whole life were being immersed in deep deep seas where nothing swam but strangeness which came echoing and re-echoing through caverns of mirrors.

He lasted three days at home. During those three days he sought desperately for some reasonable explanation of the sudden, shocking contact that they had made. He half believed now that the knowledge of her had always been there, just below the surface, fended off, forcing itself up to his attention only when his defenses were down in sleep—the source of his strange nightmares. That day on the subway his defenses had been all but worn away by his work; and her defenses, were they ever up? Besides, she had just sold one of her silly pictures and was in love with the entire world of people. By the most fantastic of bad luck they had to meet just at that time. It was their eyes meeting that finally pierced the thin shells holding them apart. Maybe there was something to the Old Wives' Tales about the magic meeting of eyes, windows of souls. But all that was superstitious nonsense; he couldn't believe it.

He sought out one of the books by Rhine, but couldn't believe that either. He would have rather believed he was insane. Particularly he wouldn't believe that distance would make no difference. He decided to put a continent between them to see if that couldn't break the contact. He had Charlotte drive him to La Guardia field and he took the first plane west.

It was a bad mistake, for on the plane there were no distractions, and her presence remained as clear as it had always been. He could not move around. He found he could not force himself to concentrate on a book. Having been lucky enough to find a seat to himself, he couldn't engage anyone in conversation. There was nothing to do but lean back and close his eyes and live her life with her. That evening on the plane he became convinced that since he could not get rid of her, he must dominate her.

It was her peculiar religious notions which finally convinced him. She was walking through a tiny park at evening; it was spring and the trees were just beginning to bud. She paused before one tree, her stomach growling a little with hunger, sensing the city smells, the roar, the silence of the trees. *The tree reaches. Steely, reaching up among the stones of the city. Each bud tingles, leaves opening like angels' wings. Root tips reach down, tender in the dark. The smooth reach up of the branches. Like you, Quincy. Like the feel of your body, Quincy.*

And her eyes traced each line of the branches, following the angles, the twists. And as she reached the very tip of the tree, she felt something very terrible to him—a kind of ecstatic union with the life of the tree. And she glanced down then to where a pair of lovers were strolling, hand by hand, along the littered walk, her artist's mind stripping away their clothes, seeing their bodies almost as she had seen the tree. *The bodies are juicy, longing for one another, sweet muscles running along the bones. Aren't they lovely, Quincy?* she thought. *Look at the girl's hip thrust, the man's thighs. What a sweet rolling they're going to have.*

Can't you think of anything else?

I won't let you spoil it. It's too lovely an evening. And she turned toward a shabby little church. He had no desire to continue in such an unprofitable direction, and tried to steer her away from the church by playing on her hunger. She caught his purpose immediately and carefully concentrated on her own. She ignored his disgust and intellectual scorn as she entered through the arched doorway. There in the dimness she bought a candle, genuflected, and placed it before the Virgin.

It was a wordless prayer. For protection, for understanding. As she glanced up at the rather crude piece of statuary, she ticketed it for what it was, but moved beyond it to an inflated vision of feminine richness and purity. Here was the woman, the full breast at which God tugged, utterly pure but female, bowels and womb, hunger and pain. *How she knows what I feel! So high, so beautiful, and yet she understands!*

Only after contemplating the Virgin did she turn to the crucifix. Here was all vigorous male sweetness, hanging from bloody nails. Quincy Summerfield tried to shy away, hold off this whole concept. He shaped an obscene word, but again the girl ignored him. Her feeling was too strong. The remoteness and terror and wonder and glory that was embodied in the tree and in the bones and blood of all men in their suffering, was richly present in the figure of the crucifix; *the timeless which betrayed itself into the agony of time out of compassion for* me *and* my *weakness.* She knelt in a submission to unreason that made Quincy there in the plane writhe in protest. But she was too submissive. He felt the position of her body as she knelt, and knew that she was a trifle off balance. Abruptly he willed a sudden small twitch of her leg and she went sprawling forward on her face. Quincy winced with the bump but jeered at her none the less.

That's mean—trying to make me look foolish.

Not any more foolish than kneeling before a piece of plaster. Disgusting. All that nonsense you have in your head. All that untruth.

She was furious. She pushed herself to her feet and stared at her dirty hands, down at the dust on her spring dress. She thought of a bath and quick meal, and left the church hurriedly. She ignored him, but as she went up the stairs to the apartment which, under Quincy's prodding, she had brought into some kind of order, she was still numbly angry.

What you did there in the church was shameful, she thought. *I'll get even with you. It's not all nonsense. It's all true and you know it's true. Of all the people in the world, why did I have to get you?*

She stripped deliberately before a mirror and watched herself so he would see her. It was a good body, high and full in the breasts, slender of waist, flaring and tapering down to the dirty feet. She ran her hands over it, under it, between, concentrating on the sensations of her fingers, feeling his responses to them.

Then abruptly she stopped and went to the phone and called her friend Arthur. She was tingling with desire and Quincy felt his gorge rise, even as his loins tightened.

I'm feeling lonely, Arthur. Could you come right over? I'll be in the bathtub, but come on in. All right then, join me if you want to.

Fifteen minutes later, Quincy staggered to the rest room on the plane, locked himself in and sat down on the seat. With trembling fingers he took out his nail file and stripped back his coat sleeve. His jaw was tight, his eyes were a little mad. He looked for a place in the arm where it seemed large veins were not present. With one hard jab he stuck the nail file a half inch deep into his arm and forced himself to leave it there. Then he jiggled it slowly back and forth, letting the pain of it sweep over him in red waves, concentrating completely on the pain until the girl began to scream.

Get him out of there, he said through clenched teeth. *Get him out of there!*

And when, finally, a very bewildered Arthur was ejected from her apartment, as yet only half dressed, he pulled the nail file from his arm and let his head lean for a moment against the cool steel of the washbowl. He had learned how to control her. She could not stand his pain.

If it had not been for his own betrayal of himself, if his own revulsion had not been weak, she would not have been able to get as far as she had with Arthur. Still, in the end, it was his mind, not the anarchy of his body that had won out.

Lying there with his head against the steel, with his arm still bloody, knowing she was lying across the bed half-conscious with frustration and his pain, he took over control completely for a moment and pushed her up to a sitting position. She pushed herself up to a sitting position. She moaned slightly in protest, but allowed him to move her toward her closet, make her reach for her pajamas. He sensed that she almost enjoyed it. She enjoyed their complete rapport of feeling. And even with the pain in his arm, he found there was a certain joy in her emotion; and it was as if with his own mind alone he thought of what wholeness an experience together could be.

It was a peculiar moment for something like that to begin, but his steel-like control meshed together and held the rush of her emotion and his pain. Her admiration for his strength warmed him; she even shared in his triumph, and suddenly both of them found the experience good—not so much the experience itself but the perfect unity of thought and feeling that followed it.

Quincy cleaned his arm and bound it with a handkerchief, and when he went back to his seat the stewardess brought him his dinner. In her apartment the girl, too, ate, and their rapport persisted as they shared the savors of each other's food. He was firmly in control of their joint thought and feeling, but it was an experience richer than he had ever known. As they moved west, the desire for her physical presence grew and grew.

Wouldn't that magazine be shocked at our *togetherness?* She thought; and at that moment Quincy shared in her scorn of the bourgeois fetish.

They existed in that kind of rapport for the rest of the evening, he on the plane, she in the apartment, arranging it for his ultimate return. Even in sleep they remained almost joined into a single entity.

It was a strange period. Quincy got off the plane in San Francisco, and almost directly boarded another going non-stop back to New York. Less than twenty-four hours after he left New York, he had returned and was walking down her street toward her walkup.

But then things changed. The shabby Greenwich Village street was filled with her memories, and she began to take precedence. Everything around him now was a part of her. All of her life began to engulf him. Her terrible disordered memories surrounded him, memories he could not repress.

He paused by the ugly little church were she had gone at times to make agonized confessions—only to dive back into the tangled messiness of her life again.

Not any more. Not messy any more. We'll be married and then . . .

He felt a blind impulse to enter the church to pour out his agony there. And find peace. Her impulse or his? He wrenched away. *Not now. Not ever . . .*

Only a few steps now . . . past the place where Fred and Arthur had fought that night. *Can't you stop remembering?*

And up five flights of ill-lit stairway, his mind filling with her anticipation. His mind filled with all the times she had gone up those stairs. His heart pounding with his anticipation. Knowing she was lounging there on the bed sofa in her blue dressing gown. Knowing the cocktail shaker was filled with martinis as only he could make them, dry and cold.

As his foot touched the landing he knew she was moving languidly from her couch toward the door, and her hand was on the door. And it was open. And she was standing before him.

Like a sleepwalker he moved past her and into the room, sensing now the subtler perfume of her. And she closed the door and he looked around the room, utterly numbed.

Then feeling came back and he saw that the room was beautiful. The pictures in their wild excess were ordered into a subtle harmony by their arrangement. For all of the dirt ingrained in it, the furniture was better than his own expensive pieces. It was all fuller and richer and more harmonious than anything he had ever experienced.

And the girl standing there, her dark hair about her shoulders!

My God, you're beautiful. She was beautiful and his thought reflected back into her mind and she flushed with pleasure. And he sensed her admiration of his lean white face and gray mustache, and the strength of his mind, and hard, lean feel of his body. And he knew the beauty of the room was completed by the two of them standing poised and not touching. Even the crucifix in the corner blended with them into one harmonious whole.

And she he reached out to a bare touching of hands . . . pause . . . then a sweeping together in their arms. And he felt his chest against her breast, against her chest his breast. Her mouth against her mouth, her his mouths against . . .

Then the whole world went crashing out of control and there was nothing but the rawness of her passion and of his passion, her his—

Until his entire reason revolted and he could stand it no longer. The need to give way to the feel of his her mouth, this irrational disorder of giving and taking at the peak of sensation, this need he could not and would not meet. A fragment of himself broke away from the unity and grew, until the strongest part of his mind floated over the chaos of sensation and contemplated it with cold disgust. Not all of his mind, for part of himself was engulfed and protesting.

But part of him was icy and knew what to do almost as well as if he had planned it. He reached down into her memory and brought out her image of the purity of the Virgin draped sweetly in blue with the haloed babe in the crook of her arm. Deliberately he intensified the picture into an almost transcendent purity of spirit, vibrating with light and wonder. Instantly he wiped it out except for the blue robes, robes like her dressing gown, and filled them with the naked girl, her mouth agape in the throes of animal lust. Then back to the picture Virgin again, who moved slowly sorrowing, her eyes looking up.

The girl's eyes looked up and sought the crucifix in the corner of

the room, and his mind expanded it before her eyes to the living
man on the cross, straining in agony and in sorrow.

Quickly now. In complete control now of her whole mind and of
his. *Passion—your passion.* He wiped away the Christ figure from
her mind and mocked her with the writhing body of Arthur, and
dissolved it into an image of his own face. And wiped that away to
present the face of the suffering Christ. A gross female figure
loomed, its mouth agape. *My mouth all horrible. No! No!! Me
driving the phallic nails in those sweet palms! The bones making a
crushing sound.*

The girl screamed, and broke away from Quincy Summerfield,
her eyes wild.

That's what you are. That's what you know you are.

She covered her face with her hand, jerking this way and that,
trying to get away from him. Trying to get away from his her
acknowledgment of her naked self, while she she lashed herself
with disgust.

It was enough. Quincy's mind contemplated her but did no more.

It was only herself now that turned and ran, a decision shaping in
her mind. She shaped the decision for herself and Quincy exulted
in it, knowing that by her own insane standards she was damning
herself.

She rushed weeping to the French windows opening on her
little sundeck. She flung them open and did not pause but
plunged on and out and over the parapet . . .

The railing smashed at his knees and he curled up suddenly
with the pain, waiting the greater pain. He closed his eyes and set
his teeth. Buildings tumbled through her eyes. Shrill sinking in
the belly. A face flashed up from the street. Whirl of cars in the
street. The fire hydrant rushed up red at her. The street plunged
up, up, up. *Oh Chri—* The smash of red pain, unendurable to
breaking!

Then there was a great darkness, a slow diminution of unconscious sensation. Then she was gone.

Quincy Summerfield pulled himself to his feet, and staggered toward a window. Peering through the curtain he saw the limp, twisted, huddled body near the fire hydrant, people running toward it.

She couldn't even die without a mess! he thought.

He left unobserved. He took the back stairs and there was no one to say that he had been there. A few blocks from her apartment, he hailed a cab and went to a hotel. He was utterly safe.

Oh, the blessed peace of it. She was gone, gone for good. There was nothing left of her disorderly presence but the gray emptiness a man might feel if he had lost an arm. There was still that: the gray ghostly taint of her. It was sure to pass, though, and this night he would sleep, really sleep for the first time in days.

He didn't even want Charlotte that night. He only wanted to be alone—and sleep. He hadn't been in the hotel room five minutes before he was in bed, and dozing.

Dozing, not sleeping. It wasn't that he worried about the thing he had done. It had been reasonable and right. Her own disorderly weakness had betrayed her. But there was the lingering gray sense of her presence that was not yet going away. That, and the feeling that he had lost half of his life.

Lost?

No.

The sense of her presence was sharpening into a live reality. He was wide awake . . . or was it nightmare again?

No—she was there. She paid no attention to him. This was frightening.

She was focused unwaveringly upon a distant light, a light that grew, that became brilliant, with a searching intensity that she had never known before. And through it all, there was a sense of the wonder of longing changed into beauty that was all but unbearable.

And his mind was filled with a sense of richness and variety and order that he had never believed could exist.

But the searching light went on, and suddenly all her life burned through him in the flicker of a dream. And his life. And then out of the center of that purity of light there was a sorrowing, and she was moving away from the light. Away from the light, and he felt her whimpering like a child afraid of the dark. Away from the light . . .

Quincy Summerfield woke. Sat straight up in bed and screamed. The throat-tearing scream of a full-grown man in an agony of terror.

For the channel was wide open to the absolute chaos of her eternity.

CALL ME MISTER

There's a curious s.f. convention
   In the matter of names:
Whatever the features of alien creatures,
   Whatever their claims
To be thought of as human, the mention
   Of one of these folk
Means readers who savour each word and its flavour
   Are likely to choke
As they try to pronounce a collection
   Of consonants. Why
Give a thing with three arms and irrelevant charms,
   Like a periscope eye,
A monosyllabic inflection
   For a name? Let's—instead
Of these terrible grunts—have a tale, just for once,
   Of a life-form called Fred.

ANTHONY BRODE

DAMON KNIGHT

What Rough Beast?

Surely some revelation is at hand;
Surely the Second Coming is at hand. . . .

And what rough beast, its hour come round at last,
Slouches toward Bethlehem to be born?

—William Butler Yeats, *"The Second Coming"*

MR. FRANK SAID TO ME, "HEY, YOU. Get that corner cleaned up."
He was big man with red face, mouth always open little bit, wet
lips always pulling back quick over little yellow teeth. This I
remember, late at night, just after rush from theaters and before
bars close. Place was empty, all sick light on the tiles and brown
table tops. Outside, dark and wet. People going by with coat
collars turned up and faces blue-gray like rain.

On corner table was some dishes, some food spilled. I cleaned
up, put dishes in kitchen sink on top of big stack, then came back
to Mr. Frank. He was cutting tomato for sandwiches, using his
knife too quick and hard. The end of his big thumb was white
from holding knife.

I said to him, "Mr. Frank, I work here three weeks and you call me 'Hey, you.' My name is Kronski. If is too hard to remember, say Mike. But not 'hey, you.' "

He looked down on me, with lips pulling away from yellow teeth. The sides of his nose turned yellow-white, like I saw before when he was mad. And his knife went cut. He sucked air between teeth, and grabbed his hand. I saw the blood coming out dark as ink from the side of his thumb. Blood was dripping dark on board and pieces of tomato. It was deep cut, bleeding hard. He said through teeth, "Now look what you made me do. Christ!"

From other end of counter, Mr. Harry called out, "What's the matter?" He started toward us—a thin man, bald, with big eyes blinking all time like afraid.

Was my fault, I went quickly to Mr. Frank, but he pushed me away with his elbow. "Get off of me, you creep!"

Now Mr. Harry looked on Mr. Frank's thumb and he whistled, then turned and went to the medicine box on wall. Mr. Frank was holding his wrist and swearing. From the cashier's desk at front of cafeteria, Mr. Wilson the night manager was coming. I heard his footsteps on the tiles.

Mr. Harry was trying to put bandage on, but it would not stick. Mr. Frank pushed him out of the way, shouting, "God damn it!" and pulled the medicine box off wall. Always bleeding.

I got quickly a fork and handkerchief, not clean, but best I could do. I tied a knot in the handkerchief, and tried to put it around Mr. Frank's wrist, but he pushed me away again.

"Give me that," said Mr. Harry, and he took from me the fork and handkerchief. Now Mr. Frank was leaning back against coffee machine looking white, and Mr. Harry slipped the handkerchief over his wrist.

Always was blood, over counter, duckboards, steam tables, everything. Mr. Harry tried to tighten the fork, but he dropped it and picked up. He took it saying, "Get out of the way, will you?" and started to turn the handkerchief.

"Better call a hospital," said Mr. Wilson's voice behind me. Then, "Look out!"

Mr. Frank had his eyes turned up and mouth open. His knees started to bend and then he was falling, and Mr. Harry tried to catch, but too late, and he also went down.

Mr. Wilson was going around end of counter, so I went the other way to telephone.

Was in my pocket, no dimes. I thought to go back and ask, but it would take minute. I thought maybe Mr. Frank would die, because I was not quick. So I put fingers in the metal hole where coin is supposed to come back, and was no coin there; but I felt deeper, down where turning place was, and I found it and I turned. Then, was a dime lying in coin hole. So I took it and put in top of telephone. I called ambulance for Mr. Frank.

Then I went back to where he was lying, and they were by his side squatting, and Mr. Wilson looked up and said, "Did you call the hospital?" I said yes, but without listening he said, "Well, get out of the way then. Harry, you take the feet and we'll straighten him out a little."

I could see Mr. Frank's red shirt front, and hand wrapped now in gauze, also red, with tourniquet around his wrist. He was lying without moving.

I went to stand at end of the counter, out of way. I was feeling very bad for Mr. Frank. I saw he was mad, and I knew he was cutting with knife, so it was my fault.

After long while came a policeman, and he looked on Mr. Frank, and I told how it happened. Mr. Harry and Mr. Wilson also told, but they could not tell all, because they did not see from beginning. Then came ambulance, and I asked Mr. Wilson could I go with Mr. Frank to hospital. So he said, "Go on, I don't care. We won't need you here after tonight, anyhow, Kronski." He looked on me from bright glasses. He was gray-haired man, very neat, who alway spoke cheerful but thought suspicious. I liked Mr. Harry, and even Mr. Frank, but him I could never like.

So I was fired. Not new feeling for me. But I thought how in year, two years, or even sooner, those men would forget I was ever alive.

I was working in place three weeks, night shift, cleaning up tables and stacking dishes in sink for dishwasher. It is not enough to make a place different because you are there. But if you make no difference, you are not living.

At the hospital, they wheeled Mr. Frank up indoors and took him in elevator. Hospital woman asked me questions and wrote down on a big paper, then policeman came again, and was more questions.

"Your name is Michael Kronski, right? Been in this country long?"

"Since twenty years." But I told a lie, was only one month. Policeman said, "You didn't learn English very good, did you?"

"For some is not easy."

"You a citizen?"

"Sure."

"When naturalized?"

I said, "Nineteen forty-one." But it was a lie.

He asked more questions, was I in army, how long belong to union, where I worked before, and always I would lie. Then he closed book.

"All right, you stick around till he comes to. Then if he says there was no assault, you can go on home."

In hospital was quiet like grave. I sat on hard bench. Sometimes doors opened, doctor shoes squeaked on floor. Then telephone went *brr* very quiet, hospital woman picked up and talked so I could not hear. She was blonde, I think from bottle, with hard lines in cheeks.

She put down telephone, talked to policeman for minute, then he came over to me. "Okay, they fixed him up. He says he did it himself. You a friend of his?"

"We work together. *Did* work. Is something I can do?"

"They're going to let him go, they need the bed. But somebody ought to go home with him. I got to get back on patrol."

"I will take him to his home, yes."

"Okay." He sat down on bench, looked on me. "Say, what kind of an accent is that, anyhow? You Chesky?"

"No." I would say yes, but this man had the face of a Slav. I was afraid he should be Polish. Instead, I told different lie. "Russian. From Omsk."

"No," he said slow, looking on me hard, and then spoke some words in Russian. I did not understand, it was too different from Russiche, so I said nothing.

"*Nyet?*" asked policeman, looking on me with clear gray eyes. He was young man, big bones in cheeks and jaw, and lines of smiling around mouth.

Just then came down the elevator with Mr. Frank and nurse. He had a big white bandage on hand. He looked on me and turned away.

Policeman was writing in his book. He looked on me again. He said something more in Russian. I did not know the words, but one of them was like word for "pig" in Russiche. But I said nothing, looked nothing.

Policeman scratched his head. "You say you're from Russia, but you don't understand the language. How come?"

I said, "Please, when we leave Russia, I was young boy. In house was speaking only Yiddish."

"Yeah? *Ir zent ah Yidishe' yingl?*"

"*Vi den?*"

Now was better, but still he did not look happy. "And you only spoke Yiddish in the home?"

"Sometimes French. My mother spoke French, also my aunt."

"Well—that might account for it, I guess." He closed book and put away. "Look, you got your naturalization papers on you?"

"No, is home in box."

"Well, hell, you ought to carry them on you. Times like these. You remember what I said. All right, take it easy now."

I looked up, and was no Mr. Frank. I went quickly to desk. "Where did he go?"

Woman said very cold, "I don't know what you mean." Each word separate, like to child.

"Mr. Frank, was just here."

She said, "Down the hall, the payment office." And pointed with yellow pencil over her shoulder.

I went, but in hall I stopped to look back. Policeman was leaning over desk to talk with woman, and I saw his book in pocket. I knew there would be more questions, maybe tomorrow, maybe next week. I took long breath, and closed eyes. I reached down where turning place of book was. I found it, and turned. I felt it happen.

Policeman never noticed; but next time he would look in book, would be no writing about me. Maybe would be empty pages, maybe something else written. He would remember, but without writing is no good.

Mr. Frank was by window in hall, pale in face, arguing with man in office. I came up, I heard him say, "Twenty-three bucks, ridiculous."

"It's all itemized, sir." Man inside pointed to piece of paper in Mr. Frank's hand.

"Anyway, I haven't got that much."

I said quickly, "I will pay." I took out purse.

"I don't want your money," said Mr. Frank. "Where would you get twenty-three bucks? Let the workmen's pay for it."

"Please, for me is pleasure. Here, you take." I pushed money at man behind window.

"All right, give him the God damn money," said Mr. Frank, and turned away.

"That's it," said Mr. Frank. Was street of old thin houses, with stone steps coming down like they would stick out all their gray tongues together. I paid the taxi driver, and helped Mr. Frank up steps. "What floor you live?"

"Fourth. I can make it."

But I said, "No, I help you," and we went up stairs. Mr. Frank was very weak, very tired, and now his lips did not pull back over teeth any more.

We went down long hall into kitchen and Mr. Frank sat down

by table under the sour yellow light. He leaned his head on hand. "I'm all right. Just let me alone now, okay?"

"Mr. Frank, you are tired. Eat something now, then sleep."

He did not move. "What sleep? In three hours I got to be on my day job."

I looked on him. Now I understood why was cutting so hard with knife, why was so quick anger.

"How long you worked two jobs?" I said.

He leaned back in chair and put his hand with white bandage on the table. "Year and a half."

"Is no good. You should quit one job."

"What the hell do you know about it?"

I wanted to ask more, but then behind me the door opened and someone came in. I looked, and it was young girl in a blue bathrobe, pale without make-up, holding bathrobe closed at her neck. She looked on me once, then said to Mr. Frank, "Pop? What's the matter?"

"Ah, I cut my damn hand. He brought me home."

She went to table. "Let me see."

"It don't amount to nothing. Come on, Anne, don't fuss, will you?"

She stepped back, once more looking on me. She had good face, thin, with strong bones. She said, like talking to herself, "Well, don't let me bother you." She turned and went out, and door closed.

Mr. Frank said after minute, "You want a drink or anything? Cup of coffee?" He was still sitting same way at table.

"No, no thanks, thanks just same. Well, I think now I will go."

"All right. Take care yourself. See you at work."

I went out, and for minute could not remember which end of hall was door. Then I remembered we turn right to go in kitchen, so I turned left, and found door at end of hall and went outside.

In little light, Anne was standing part bent over, looking on me with big eyes. I stood and could not move. It was not outside hall, it was some other room—I could see part of dressing table, and bed, and then I saw she had bathrobe pulled down from shoulder and was leaning to look in mirror. Then she covered up shoulder quickly, but not before I saw what was there.

She said in hard quiet voice, "Get out of here. What's the matter with you?"

And I wanted to move away, but could not. I took instead one step toward her and said, "Let me see it."

"What?" She could not believe.

"The burn. Let me see, because I know I can help you."

She had hand tight at her neck, holding the bathrobe together, and she said, "What do you know about——"

"I can do it," I said. "Do you understand? If you want, I will help." I stopped, and stood waiting and looking on her.

In the small light I could see that her face got pink, and the eyes very bright. She said very hard, "You can't," and looked away. She was crying.

I said, "Believe me."

She sat down and after minute she took hard breath and opened the bathrobe from shoulder. "All right, look then. Pretty?"

I took one more step and was close. I could see her neck, smooth and like cream. But on the shoulder and across the chest was skin hard and white, standing up in strings and lumps, like something that would melt and boil, and then harden.

She had her head down, and eyes shut, crying. I was crying also, and inside was big hurt trying to get out. I touched her with my hand, and I said, "My dear."

She jumped when hand touched her, but then sat still. I felt under my fingertips cold skin, touch like lizard. Inside me was big hurt jumping. I could not hold in very long. I rubbed her very easy, very slow with my fingers, looking and feeling where was inside the wrong kind of skin. Was not easy to do. But if I did not do it this way, then I knew I would do it without wanting, all at once, and it would be worse.

To make well all at once is no good. Each cell must fit with next cell. With my fingertips I felt where down inside the bottom part of bad skin was, and I made it turn, and change to good skin, one little bit at a time.

She sat still and let me do it. After while she said, "It was a fire, two years ago. Pop left a blowtorch lit, and I moved it, and there was a can of plastic stuff with the top off. And it went up——"

I said, "Not to talk. Not necessary. Wait. Wait." And always I rubbed softly the bad skin.

But she could not bear to have me rub without talking, and she said, "We couldn't collect anything. It said right on the can, keep away from flame. It was our fault. I was in the hospital twice. They fixed it, but it just grew back the same way. It's what they call keloid tissue."

I said, "Yes, yes, my dear, I know."

Now was one layer on the bottom, soft skin instead of hard; and she moved a little in the chair, and said small voice, "It feels better."

Under my fingertips the skin was still hard, but now more soft than before. When I pushed it, was not like lizard any more, but like glove.

I worked, and she forgot to be ashamed until came a noise at door opening at front of apartment. She sat up straight, looking around and then on me. Her face got pink again, she grabbed my wrist. "What are you *doing?*"

In minute I knew she would jump up and pull her bathrobe, and then maybe she would yell, so whatever happened, it would not be her fault.

But I could not let her do it. I was also ashamed, and my ears like on fire, but to stop now was impossible. I said loud, "No, sit down." I held her in the chair, and kept my fingers on her skin. I did not look up, but I heard Mr. Frank's feet come into room.

I heard him say, "Hey, you. What do you think you're up to?"

And the girl was trying to get up again, but I held her still, and I said, "Look. Look." With tears running down my cheeks.

Under my fingers was a little place of good, soft skin, smooth like cream. While I moved my fingers, slowly this place got bigger. She looked down, and she forgot to breathe.

From corner of my eye, I saw Mr. Frank come nearer, with face mad and wondering. He said once more, "Hey," with lips pull-

ing back hard over teeth, and then he looked on shoulder of his
daughter. He blinked eyes like not believing, and then looked
again. He put his hand on it, quick, hard, and then took away
like burned.

Now was changing more fast the rest of skin. Was like rubbing
from a window the frost. Still they were not moving, the daughter
and Mr. Frank, and then he went down on knees beside chair with
arm around her and arm around me holding so hard that it hurt,
and we were all three tight together, all three hot wet faces.

Since I was small boy in Novo Russie—what they call here Can-
ada, but it is all different—always I could see where beside this
world is many other worlds, so many you could not count. To me
is hard thing to understand that other people only see what is
here.

But then I learned also to reach, not with hands but with mind.
And where this world touches other world, I learned to turn so
that little piece of it would be different. At first I did this without
knowing, when I was very sick, and frightened that I would die.
Without knowing it I reached, and turned, and suddenly, I was
not sick. Doctor was not believing, and my mother prayed a long
time, because she thought God saved my life by a miracle.

Then I learned I could do it. When I learned badly in school,
or if something else I would not like would happen, I could reach
and turn, and change it. Little by a little, I was changing pieces of
world.

At first was not so bad, because I was young boy and I only did
things for myself, my own pleasure.

But then I was growing up, and it was making me sad to see
how other people were unhappy. So then I would begin to change
more. My father had a bad knee, I made it well. Our cow broke
her neck and died. And I made her alive again.

First I was careful, then not so careful. And at last they saw
that I did it.

Then everyone said I was going to be a great rabbi, they prayed
over me, and they talked to me so much that I believed it.

And I worked miracles.

Then one day I began to see that what I did was bad. I made so many patches in world that it was not world any more, but mistake. If you would try to make chair better by many patches, putting a piece oak wood here, and piece cherry wood there, until all was patches, you would make a worse chair than before.

So I saw every day that I was only making more patches, but I would not let myself know it was bad. And at last I could not bear it, and I reached back far, I changed not little bit, but whole country. I reached back before I was born, and I turned, and I changed it.

And when I looked up, all world around me was different—houses, fields, people.

My father's house was not there. My mother, my brothers, my sisters, they were all gone; and I could not bring them back.

After I fixed Anne's shoulder, it was like party, with wine on table, and Italian bread and sweet butter, and salami, and what they call here bagels, and from radio in next room, music playing loud and happy. Pretty soon from across hall came a lady named Mrs. Fabrizi to complain from noise, and in two minutes she was also one of party, hugging Anne and crying, then talking and laughing louder than the rest of us. Next from upstairs it was young man, Dave Sims, painter, and also joined us. Mrs. Fabrizi went back to her apartment and brought some lasagne, which is with pasta and cheese, and very good, and from upstairs Dave brought bottle of whisky. We all loved each other, and to look on each other made us laugh because we all were so happy. Anne was now with lipstick and her hair combed, and she was wearing a blue evening dress with no top. She could not keep her hand from touching smooth place on her shoulder and chest, and every time she would touch it, she would stop like surprised. But she was worried because new skin was brown, not white like cream, and it made a patch you could see.

But I explained to her, "Is because if you would not have accident, then you would go often to beach and get brown. So when

I turn where you do not have accident, that skin is brown, you see?"

"I don't get it, at all," said Dave, and I could see from their faces, they did not understand either. So I said, "Look. From time God made the world, if a thing was possible, it must happen. Right? Because otherwise it would not be God." I looked on Mrs. Fabrizi, I knew she was religious woman, but in her eyes was no understanding.

Dave said slowly, "You mean, wait a minute—— You mean, if a thing is possible, but doesn't happen, that would limit God's powers, is that it? His powers of creation, or something?"

I nodded. "Yes, that is it."

He leaned over table. On one side Anne and Frank were also leaning, and on other side Mrs. Fabrizi, but still only Dave understanding.

"But look," he said, "plenty of things that could happen, don't. Like this pickle—I *could* throw it on the floor, but I'm not going to, I'm going to eat it." And he took a bite, and grinned. "See? It didn't happen."

But I said, "It did. It happened that you threw it on floor. Look." And while I said it, I reached and turned, and when they looked where I pointed, there was pickle on the floor.

Then they all laughed like joke, and Frank slapped Dave on back, saying, "That's a good one on you!" And it was a minute before I saw they thought it was only joke, and that I threw pickle on floor myself.

Dave was also laughing, but waving at me the piece of pickle in his hand. "I've got the trump card," he said. "Right here—see? I didn't throw it, I ate it."

But I said, "No, you didn't." And once more I turned, and in his fingers was no pickle.

Then they all laughed more than ever, except Dave, and after minute Anne touched her chest and stopped laughing too. Frank was poking Dave in shirt, and saying, "Where is it? Hah? Where is it?" Then he also stopped and looked on me. Only Mrs. Fabrizi laughed, and her high voice sounded like hen until Frank said, "Pipe down a second, Rosa, for Pete's sake."

Dave looked on me and said, "How did you do that?"

I was warm inside from the wine and whisky, and I said, "I try to explain to you. If a thing is possible, somewhere it happens. It must happen, otherwise God is not God. Do you see? It is like each world is a card in a deck of cards. Each one, little bit different. Annie, in some worlds you had accident, and in some worlds you did not have it. So I reach, and turn, one little place at a time. Wherever I turn, it can be a little place like head of match, or it can be big like a building. And it can be from a long time ago, hundred years, five hundred years, or only minute. So always I think of place I turn like this: it is a shape like ice cream cone. Here on top is what we see now, then down here at bottom is little dot, week ago, or year ago. If long time ago, cone is long— if short time ago, cone is short. But from little sharp dot at the bottom comes all this cone, and makes here at the top all things different."

"Let me get this straight," said Dave, running hand through hair. "You mean, if you change any little thing in the past, then everything that happened afterward has to be different?"

I said, "Yes. Only I do not really change, because all these things exist already. I cannot make another world, but I can reach, and take piece of another world where it already is, and bring here so that you see it. So with Anne, before—I turn one little bit of skin, then another little bit of skin. And I make good skin come where bad skin was. So it is colored brown, because in worlds where you did not have accident, you went to beach and became brown."

They all looked on me. Frank said, "This is still too deep for me. What do you mean, you turn——?" He made twisting motion with his fingers.

I said, "It is like revolving door. Suppose should be little tiny revolving door—or I can make it big, any size—but suppose on one side is one world, on other side, another world. So I turn——" I showed them with my hands—"until little piece of this world is here, and little piece of that world there. That's what I mean when I turn."

Frank and Dave sat back and looked on each other, and Frank made blowing sound with his lips. "Hell, you could do anything," he said.

"Not anything. No."

"Well, damn near. Jesus Christ, when I start to thinking about ——" Then he and Dave were talking all together. I heard ". . . cure every sick person . . ." ". . . water into wine . . ." ". . . wait a minute, what about . . ." After while Mrs. Fabrizi yelled, "Wait. Waita, you men. Can you fixa my kitch' a-ceiling?"

Then they all began to laugh and shout, and I did not know why it was a joke, but I laughed too, and we all went to Mrs. Fabrizi's apartment, laughing and hanging on to each other not to fall down.

Next morning before I was awake, they were in living room talking, and when I came out, they could not wait to tell me ideas. From remembering the night before I was ashamed, but they made me sit down and drink coffee, and then Anne brought eggs, and not to make her feel bad, I eat.

Always, if I do good for someone, I should do it in secret like a robber. I know this. So, if I would have climbed in window when Anne was sleeping, and fix shoulder, then would be no trouble. But no, I let myself be sad for her, I fix it with big scene, and then worse, I am full of wine, I talk big, and I fix kitchen ceiling. So now I was in trouble.

They were looking on me with such love in eyes that I was inside like butter melting. First it was, "Mike, you are so wonderful," and "Mike, how can we ever thank you," and then pretty soon they wanted to see some trick, because they still could not believe. So like a fool, I threw a nickel on table, and showed them where it was possible nickel should land here, here, or there. And each place, I turned, and was another nickel until was on table ten of them in a row. And to them it was as if I should make water flow from the rock.

Then Anne was pink and holding hands tight together, but she said to me, "Mike, if you wouldn't mind—Mrs. Fabrizi has an old gas stove that——"

Then Mrs. Fabrizi began to shout no, no, and Frank also said, "No, let him eat his breakfast," but Anne would not stop and said, "Honestly, it's dangerous, and the landlord won't do anything." So I said I would go and look.

In the apartment across the hall I saw clean new ceiling in kitchen where should be old one falling down in pieces, but I looked away quickly. The gas stove was like Anne said, old, with leaky pipes, everywhere rust and with one side on bricks because leg was gone. "She might have an explosion any day," Anne said, and I saw it was true. So I reached, and turned to where was new gas stove.

They could not understand that whatever I give, I must take away. To this Mrs. Fabrizi I gave a new ceiling, yes, and new stove too, but from some other Mrs. Fabrizi I took away new ceiling, new stove, and gave old ones instead. With Anne's shoulder it was different, because I took from each other Anne only one little cell; and the nickels I took from myself. But again I was a fool, and to me Mrs. Fabrizi's gasp of wonder was like food to starving.

So when Anne said, "Mike, how about new furniture?" and again Mrs. Fabrizi shouted no, but with joy in her eyes, I could not refuse her. We went into living room, and where each piece of old furniture with wrinkled slip covers was, I turned, and there was new furniture, very ugly but to Mrs. Fabrizi beautiful. And she tried to kiss my hand.

Then we all went back to breakfast table, and now they had bright faces and hard eyes, and they licked their lips. They were thinking of themselves.

Dave said, "Mike, I'll lay it on the line. I need five hundred bucks to last out till the beginning of September. If you can do it with nickels——"

"There's no serial numbers on nickels," Frank said. "What do you want him to do, counterfeiting?"

I said, "I can do it." I got wallet, put one dollar bill on table. They watched me.

Dave said, "I wouldn't ask, Mike, but I just don't know where else——"

I told him, "I believe you. Please don't tell me, I know it is truth." Now I could not stop. I reached and turned where instead of dollar bill, someone could have given me five-dollar bill by mistake. Always this could happen, even if only one time out of thousand. Then I turned to where I could have changed this five-dollar bill into one-dollar bills, and so on table was five of them. And each one I again turned to a five, and then fives to ones, and so on, while they watched without breathing.

So in little while was on table one hundred five-dollar bills, and Dave counted them with fingers that trembled, and put them in his pocket, and looked on me. I could see that he wished now he had asked for more, but he was ashamed to say it.

Then I said, "And for you, Frank, nothing?"

He looked on me and shook his head. He said, "You already done something for me," and put his arm around Anne's waist.

She said to him, "Pop—maybe about that stroke of yours?"

"No, now forget it, will you? That was a year ago."

"Well, but you might have another one sometime. But suppose Mike could fix you up——"

I was shaking my head. "Anne, some things I cannot do. How would I fix a weak heart? Could I take from somebody else the heart out of his body, and put inside Frank?"

She thought about it. "No, I guess not. But couldn't you kind of change it a little bit at a time, like you did to me?"

"No, it is not possible. If I was doctor, maybe, if I could cut open and reach in, to feel where is everything . And also if I would know all about what is wrong with heart. But I am not doctor. If I would try it, I would only make bad mistake."

She did not quite believe, but I told her, "To change skin is one thing, is like a game for little child with paper and scissors. But to change living heart, that is different thing altogether. It is like for mechanics, he must take engine from your car apart, and put back together, while it is still going."

Then I thought I saw what would happen. But was nothing I could do about it. So I waited, and in half hour Frank fell over table where was reaching for match, and rolled from table to floor. His face was turning purple, and eyes turned up under lids. He was not breathing.

Anne fell on her knees beside him, and looked up at me with white face. "Mike!"

Was nothing else to do. I reached, and turned; and Frank got to his feet red-faced, shouting, "God damn it, Anne, why don't you tack that carpet down?"

She looked up on him and tried to speak, but at first could not make words. Then she whispered, "Nothing wrong with the carpet."

"Well, I tripped over something. Almost broke my neck, too." Frank was looking around floor, but carpet was smooth and nothing to trip over. Then he saw she was crying, and said, "What the hell's the matter?"

"Nothing," she said. "Oh, Mike."

So then I was bigger hero than before, but had a bad feeling, and not until after dinner, when we again drank too much whisky, could I laugh and talk like the rest. And I made for Frank two new suits in place of old ones, and for Anne and Mrs. Fabrizi all new dresses in their closets. Dave we did not see all day after breakfast.

In the morning I was again ashamed and feeling bad, but others happy and talking all together. When we were finishing meal, door banged open and in came Dave with another man, thin, with dark hair and skin like girl, and small mustache. He was carrying package under his arm.

"Put it down there," said Dave, with eyes bright. "Friends, now you're going to see something. This is Grant Hartley, the collector. Grant, this is Miss Curran, Mrs. Fabrizi, Mr. Curran, and this is Mike. Now."

Mr. Hartley was nodding, with cold smiles, "How do you do.

How do you do." He took from watch chain a small knife, and began to cut open rope around package. It was sitting in middle of breakfast table, between toaster and jam jar, and rope went tick, tick when he cut it. And we all sat and watched.

Inside brown paper was cotton, and Mr. Hartley pulled it away in big pieces, and inside was little statue in gold. A dancer made of gold, with skirt flaring out wide and legs graceful.

"There!" said Dave. "What do you think of that?"

When we did not answer, he leaned over table. "That's a Degas. It was cast in eighteen eighty-two from his wax model——"

"Eighteen eighty-three," said Mr. Hartley, with small smile.

"All right, eighteen eighty-three—cast in gold, and there was was only one copy made. Grant owns it. Now this is the pitch. There's another collector who wants this statuette the worst way, and Grant has been turning him down for years. But it hit me yesterday, if Mike could make a copy, an exact copy——"

"This I want to see with my own eyes," said Mr. Hartley.

"Sure. So I put it up to Grant, and he agreed, if Mike will make *two* copies, he'll keep one, sell one to the other collector—and the third one is ours!"

Mr. Hartley rubbed his mustache, looking sleepy.

I said, "From this no good will come, Dave."

He looked surprised. "Why not?"

"First, it is dishonest——"

"Now wait, just a minute," said Mr. Hartley. "The way Sims represented it to me, this copy will be so exact, that no expert examination could ever tell the difference between them. In fact, what he told me was that one would be just as much the original as the other. Now then, if I sell one as the original, I fail to see where there's anything dishonest involved. Unless, of course, you can't do it?"

I said, "I can do it, but in second place, if I would make you something big and expensive like this, it would bring only trouble. Believe me, I have seen it so many times already——"

Dave said to Mr. Hartley in low voice, "Let me talk to him a minute." His face was pale, and eyes bright. He led me over in the corner and said, "Look, Mike, I didn't want to say this in front of him, but you can make *any* number of copies of that thing, can't you, even after Grant takes his and goes away? What I mean is, once it's been there, it's just like money in the bank—I mean you can draw on it any time."

I said, "Yes, this is true."

"I thought it was. I couldn't sleep all last night for thinking about it. Look, I don't want that copy because it's beautiful. I mean, it *is*, but what I want to do is melt it down. Mike, it'll keep us all, for years. I'm not selfish, I don't want it all for myself——"

I tried to say, "Dave, this way is too easy, believe me when I tell you."

But he was not listening. "Look, Mike, do you know what it's like to be an artist without money? I'm young, I could be turning out my best work now——"

"Please," I said, "don't tell me, I believe you. So all right, I will do it."

He went back to table, and golden dancer was still standing there, but they had cleared away toaster and plates and it was alone. They were all looking on statue, and then on me, and no one spoke a word.

I sat down, and when Mr. Hartley was watching me with cold smile on his face, I reached and turned. And on table was two golden dancers, both the same. One turned partly away from other, facing Anne; and she looked on it as if she could not look away.

I saw Mr. Hartley jump, and put out his hand. But even before he could touch statue, I turned again, and on table was three.

Mr. Hartley pulled back his hand again like stung. He was very pale. Then he put out hand and picked up one of the statues, and then took another one. And holding both up and looking on them hard, he went away to the window. Then Dave picked up the third one and stood smiling and holding it close to his chest.

From window, Mr. Hartley said in loud voice, "By God, it's true!"

He came back part way into room and said, "Have you got some newspaper——?"

Frank got up and handed him Sunday paper and sat down again, saying nothing. Mr. Hartley knelt down on floor and wrapped up first one statue, then other. His hands were shaking, and he did not do good job, but he finished quickly and stood up holding packages in his arms. "You've got the other one, that's all right," he said. "Good-by." He went out, walking quickly.

Dave had on his face a hard smile, and his eyes looking somewhere else, not here. He held statue away from his chest, and said, "Ten pounds anyhow, and gold is worth twenty dollars an ounce."

He was not talking to us, but I said, "Gold is nothing. If you want gold, is easier ways." And I reached in my pocket to where could be a gold coin, and turned, and threw coin on the table. Then I turned where it would hit different places, here, here, or there, and in a minute was little pile of coins shining on tablecloth.

Dave was watching like dizzy. He picked up some of the coins and looked on them, both sides, with eyes big, and then scooped up a handful. He counted them, stacked them, and finally after Frank and Anne also looked, he put them in his pocket. "Let me take these down to a jeweler," he said, and went out quick.

Frank sat back in chair and shook his head. After while he said, "This is getting to be too much for me. Who was that guy, anyhow?"

Anne said, "Mr. Hartley? He's just some art collector that ——"

"No, no, not him, the other one. The one that just went out."

She looked on him. "Pop, that was Dave."

"All right, Dave who? I ask a simple question around here——"

"Dave *Sims*. Pop, what's the matter with you? We've known Dave for years."

"We have like hell." Frank stood up very red. I tried to say something, but he was too mad. "What am I, supposed to think I'm crazy or something? What are you pulling on me?" He made his hands in fists, and Anne was leaning away frightened. "I figured

I'd keep my mouth shut a while, but—— What the hell did you do with the carpet? Where's the picture of my old man that used to hang on that wall? What is this Dave business now, why is everything all different, what are you trying to do to me?"

She said, "Pop, there's nothing different—I don't know what you mean about——"

"Damn it, don't give me that, Katie!"

She was looking on him with mouth open and face very white. "What did you call me?"

"Katie! That's your name, isn't it?"

I put my face in hands, but I heard her whisper, "Pop, my name is Anne——"

I heard sound when he hit her. "I told you stop giving me that! I took about enough of this—wait till Jack gets home, I'll find out what you got rigged up here—I know damn well I can count on my own son, anyway——"

I looked and she was in chair crying. "I don't know what you're talking about! Who's Jack? What do you mean your son——?"

He leaned down and began to shake her. "Cut it out—I told you cut it out, didn't I, you bitch!"

I tried to get between them. "Please, is my fault, let me explain——"

Suddenly she screamed and got out of chair like a cat, and he could not stop her. She took hold of my coat and, looking on me from few inches away, said, "You did it. You did it, when he had the heart attack."

"Yes." On my face was tears.

"You changed him—you made him different. What did you do, what did you do?"

Frank came up saying, "What, what's this about a heart attack?"

I said, "Anne, he was dying. There was nothing I could do about it. So I turned where was another Frank, not same one, but almost like."

"You mean this isn't *Pop?*"

"No."

"Well, where is he?"

I said, "Anne, he died. He is dead."

She turned away, with hands on face, but Frank came and took hold of my shirt. "You mean you did something to me, like you done to her shoulder? Is that what this is all about?"

I nodded. "Here is not where you belong. Not same apartment, not even same family."

"What about my boy Jack?"

I said, hurting, "In this world, not born."

"Not born." He took harder hold of shirt. "Listen, you get me back there, understand?"

I said, "I can't do it. Too many worlds, I can never find same one again. Always I reach, I can find something. But it would be little different, just like here."

He was red, and eyes very yellow. He said, "Why, you lousy little——"

I twisted, and got away when he would hit me. He came after me around table, but stumbled over chair, and got to the door. "Come back here, you—" he shouted, and just as I opened door I saw him pick up the gold statue from table, and swing it in air. Inside me was a hurt jumping to be free, but I held it back.

Then I was out, and standing in hall was Mr. Hartley and two men about to ring bell. And one of them reached for me, but just then gold statue hit wall, and fell on floor. And while they looked on it, and one man began to pick it up, I went past and started down stairs, still holding back the thing inside me that was trying to get loose.

I heard shout, "Hey, wait! Don't let him get away!" So I ran faster.

Still they were coming down faster than me, and my heart was bumping like it would break out of chest, and on my forehead was cold sweat. My feet would not run good because I was so frightened, and I could not hold back the bad thing much longer, and so I reached in pocket where it could happen that I would have put pile of coins from table. And I turned, and took out handful of gold coins, and threw them on landing behind me. And first man stopped, other two ran into him, with swearing.

I went down rest of stairs weak in knees, and out to street, and I could not think, only to run.

Behind me came shouts and bangings. It was the two men, with heads down, running hard, and behind them Mr. Hartley. I saw they would catch me, and so I reached again in my pocket where I could have put statue, and I turned, but it was so heavy I almost fell down. But I took it out and threw it on street and kept running, and I heard them shouting back and forth to each other, to take it, not to take it, and so on. And I reached, and turned, and threw another statue on street. It made a sound like lead pipe falling.

Now from the sidewalk between cars came a man with his arms out, and I reached in pocket and threw at him some coins. I saw him stop, looking at coins hopping by his feet, and then I was past, running.

Next at corner where I turned there was three men standing by street sign, one with newspaper, and I heard shout, "Hey! Stop that guy!" When they began to move, I reached in pocket again, and to nearest man I handed statue. He took, in both hands, and I was around other ones and still running, but breath like cutting in my throat.

Then I looked back and saw them in street coming, like a fan of people—first a few, then behind them more, and more and more, all running together, and from both sides of street still others coming. I saw in their hands the gold statues, bright in sunlight, and their faces ugly. All this I saw like a picture, not moving, and it made me afraid like a big wave that stands up, and stands up behind you, and still does not fall.

Still it was really not stopped—all this was in an instant—and then I could again hear the noise of their footsteps and their voices like one big animal, and I was running but legs too weak to keep up with me. And I saw doorway, and I went across sidewalk in two big falling steps, and then in doorway I fell.

And across street came that wave of people, fast as a train. And I could not move.

Inside I was all fear, like a knot. I was crying, and sick, and I took from my pockets golden statues and I threw them out in front of me like a fence, two, six, eight—and then the wave burst over me.

Then I felt inside me a movement I could not stop—a reaching and turning. And all was quiet.

I opened my eyes. In front of me was no more people, no street. Under where I was lying in doorway was only big hole, very deep, so deep I could not see bottom in shadow. I heard a noise of tires, and I saw a car stop sideways, just in time not to fall in. Then I looked up, and where should be other buildings across street, was ruins. Halfway down block, all the buildings had no fronts. Inside rooms the people were still sitting, with all their faces turned like pink dots, and still it was quiet. Then I heard some bricks fall with small hollow sounds; and then down in the hole, I heard noise of water rushing from a pipe.

I hold onto side of the doorway, not to fall; and then I began to hit my head against the side of doorway.

All those people who a minute ago were here, running, breathing, I had put them I could not tell where. Maybe falling through air, screaming—maybe drowning in deep ocean. Maybe burning in fire.

That child inside me had reached back to where was a world with ground lower down than this one—so when I turned it, a piece of the street went to that world, and only air, emptiness, came to this one.

After long time I lifted my head and looked on this destruction that I had made. A hole in street, buildings half gone, innocent people dead, no different than if I would have thrown a bomb.

All because I was frightened—because the frightened child inside me could not hold himself back when he felt in danger. So, now it was all over for me in this world.

Always the same, always the same, no matter how hard I tried . . .

Now I saw police cars pull up, and ambulance, and then fire

truck close behind. Crowds were so thick that cars could hardly move. I saw a taxi stop at edge of the crowd, and I thought it was Anne and Frank that got out, but I could not tell for sure. It did not seem to matter. Now already they were far away and long ago.

I sat on my doorstep and I wished I should be dead. If it were not a sin, I would try to kill myself. But even then I know it would not work. Because that frightened child inside me would always turn to where it could not happen—where the bullet would not fire, or would miss, or rope break, or poison would be water.

Once only, for almost a year, I lived in a world where was no man. I lived in forest, and that world was beautiful, but always, when I would sleep, in my dream I would turn myself out of that world, and would wake up in world of men, and have to go back again to different forest.

Until at last I gave it up, and stayed in city afterward. Where I was going I did not know, but I knew that I must go. I was worst man in the creation, I was evil, but even for me I knew God had made a place.

I stood up, and dried my face on sleeve, and then took deep breath.

If I must wander, then, I said to myself, let me go far. I reached back deep, deep, farther than ever before—two thousand years. I found a place where one man was not born, and so all was different. And I turned.

The street disappeared. Up leaped a new city, of cold gray buildings climbing one behind another. All had peaked doors and windows, very big, and with domes of yellow stone, or powdery blue copper. Across the sky was airplane drifting—not cross-shaped, but round. The street was of cobblestones.

Because I had made one man not born two thousand years ago, here now, all world was different—all two thousand years of history different, all cities and all men living, different.

Here at least I would not make all old mistakes, here I could start new. And I thought to myself, *Now if I will only do one right thing, maybe it will wipe out all mistakes of before.*

I was standing inside a little park, with a railing of stone carved like hoops of cloth. Behind me was a pedestal of stone, and two statues, one of a handsome young man in a hat with no brim, carrying a torch in his arms. And the other just the same, but with torch upside down. I remembered I had seen once in a book statues like these. It was a book about a god named Mithra of old times, and these statues that I now saw were statues of Mithra the morning star, and Mithra the evening star. They looked down on me with blank stone eyes.

Is it you? they seemed to say.

And I, looking back on them, said, *Is it here?*

But we could not answer one another; and I left them standing there, and went into the city.

CLASSICAL QUERY COMPOSED WHILE SHAMPOOING

Medusa, Medusa
     In days that were olden
Did you touch up your snakes,
     Turning copper to golden?

Though snakes through the ages
     Have never grown grey,
They do tend to wander;
     They go after prey;

They take to the water;
     They slither while wet—
Did you envy your victims
     Their *permanent* set?

DORIS PITKIN BUCK

WALTER S. TEVIS

Far from Home

THE FIRST INKLING THE JANITOR had of the miracle was the smell of it. This was a small miracle in itself: the salt smell of kelp and sea water in the Arizona morning air. He had just unlocked the front entrance and walked into the building when the smell hit him. Now this man was old and normally did not trust his senses very well; but there was no mistaking this, not even in this most inland of inland towns: it was the smell of ocean—deep ocean, far out, the ocean of green water, kelp and brine.

And strangely, because the janitor was old and tired, and because this was the part of early morning that seems unreal to many old men, the first thing the smell made him feel was a small, almost undetectable thrilling in his old nerves, a memory deeper than blood of a time fifty years before when he had gone once, as a boy, to San Francisco and had watched the ships in the bay and had discovered the fine old dirty smell of sea water. But this feeling lasted only an instant. It was replaced immediately with amazement—and then anger, although it would have been impossible to say with what he was angry, here in this desert town, in the dressing rooms of the large public swimming pool at morning, being reminded of his youth and of the ocean.

"What the hell's going on here?" the janitor said.

There was no one to hear this, except perhaps the small boy who had been standing outside, staring through the wire fence into the pool and clutching a brown paper sack in one grubby hand, when the janitor had come up to the building. The man had paid no attention to the boy; small boys were always around the swimming pool in summer—a nuisance. The boy, if he had heard the man or not, did not reply.

The janitor walked on through the concrete-floored dressing rooms, not even stopping to read the morning's crop of obscenities scribbled on the walls of the little wooden booths. He walked into the tiled anteroom, stepped across the disinfectant foot bath, and out onto the wide concrete edge of the swimming pool itself.

Some things are unmistakable. There was a whale in the pool.

And no ordinary, everyday whale. This was a monumental creature, a whale's whale, a great, blue-gray leviathan, ninety feet long and thirty feet across the back, with a tail the size of a flatcar and a head like the smooth fist of a titan. A blue whale, an old shiny, leathery monster with barnacles on his gray underbelly and his eyes filmed with age and wisdom and myopia, with brown sea-weed dribbling from one corner of his mouth, marks of the suckers of squid on his face, and a rusted piece of harpoon sunk in the unconscious blubber of his back. He rested on his belly in the pool, his back way out of the water and with his monstrous gray lips together in an expression of contentment and repose. He was not asleep; but he was asleep enough not to care where he was.

And he stank—with the fine old stink of the sea, the mother of us all; the brackish, barnacled, grainy salt stink of creation and old age, the stink of the world that was and of the world to come. He was beautiful.

The janitor did not freeze when he saw him; he froze a moment afterwards. First he said, aloud, his voice matter-of-fact, "There's a whale in the swimming pool. A God damn whale." He said this to no one—or to everyone—and perhaps the boy heard him, although there was no reply from the other side of the fence.

After speaking, the janitor stood where he was for seven minutes, thinking. He thought of many things, such as what he had eaten for breakfast, what his wife had said to him when she had awakened him that morning. Somewhere, in the corner of his vision, he saw the little boy with the paper sack, and his mind thought, as minds will do at such times, *Now that boy's about six years old. That's probably his lunch in that sack. Egg salad sandwich. Banana. Or apple.* But he did not think about the whale, because there was nothing to be thought about the whale. He stared at its unbelievable bulk, resting calmly, the great head in the deep water under the diving boards, the corner of one tail fluke being lapped gently by the shallow water of the wading pool.

The whale breathed slowly, deeply, through its blow hole. The janitor breathed slowly, shallowly, staring, not blinking even in the rising sunlight, staring with no comprehension at the eighty-five ton miracle in the swimming pool. The boy held his paper sack tightly at the top, and his eyes, too, remained fixed on the whale. The sun was rising in the sky over the desert to the east, and its light glinted in red and purple iridescence on the oily back of the whale.

And then the whale noticed the janitor. Weak-visioned, it peered at him filmily for several moments from its grotesquely small eye. And then it arched its back in a ponderous, awesome, and graceful movement, lifted its tail twenty feet in the air, and brought it down in a way that seemed strangely slow, slapping gently into the water with it. A hundred gallons of water rose out of the pool, and enough of it drenched the janitor to wake him from the state of partial paralysis into which he had fallen.

Abruptly the janitor jumped back, scrambling from the water, his eyes looking, frightened, in all directions, his lips white. There was nothing to see but the whale and the boy. "All right," he said, "all right," as if he had somehow seen through the plot, as if he knew, now, what a whale would be doing in the public swimming pool, as if no one was going to put anything over on *him.* "All right," the janitor said to the whale, and then he turned and ran.

He ran back into the center of town, back toward Main Street, back toward the bank, where he would find the chairman of the board of the City Parks Commission, the man who could, some-

how—perhaps with a memorandum—save him. He ran back to
the town where things were as they were supposed to be; ran as
fast as he had ever run, even when young, to escape the only
miracle he would ever see in his life and the greatest of all God's
creatures. . . .

After the janitor had left, the boy remained staring at the whale
for a long while, his face a mask and his heart racing with all the
peculiar excitement of wonder and love—wonder for all whales,
and love for the only whale that he, an Arizona boy of six desert
years, had ever seen. And then, when he realized that there would
be men there soon and his time with his whale would be over, he
lifted the paper sack carefully close to his face, and opened its
top about an inch, gingerly. A commotion began in the sack, as
if a small animal were in it that wanted desperately to get out.

"Stop that!" the boy said, frowning.

The kicking stopped. From the sack came a voice—a high-
pitched, irascible voice, with a Gaelic accent. "All right, whatever-
your-name-is," the voice said, "I suppose you're ready for the second one."

The boy held the sack carefully with his thumb and forefinger.
He frowned at the opening in the top. "Yes," he said, "I think
so . . ."

When the janitor returned with the two other men, the whale
was no longer there. Neither was the small boy. But the seaweed
smell and the splashed, brackish water were there still, and in the
pool were several brownish streamers of seaweed, floating aim-
lessly in the chlorinated water, far from home.

SPACE BURIAL

Where nothing holds us, where long light
Can barely stretch, we leave you, friend.
From this steel shell you take your flight
Without the aid of steel or air,
Or need of them. So, weightless, end
   All waiting, hope or care.

Tomorrow on a million moons
A million suns will rise—on you
They shine forever; no cocoons
Of shadow shall eclipse your ride,
No worms shall eat your glory through,
   Nor earth devour your pride.

We spring from earth, but in these lanes
Of vacancy forget our source.
New worlds lie yonder!—So on vanes
Of fire we flash there. You are gone,
Friend; take with you our brief remorse.
   We mourn but we go on.

BRIAN W. ALDISS

GEORGE P. ELLIOTT

Invasion of the Planet
of Love

ONE THING SURPRISED US about the stormy surface of Venus, and
that pleasantly—the temperature. It was as low as 10 degrees Cen-
tigrade at the poles and not over 70 at the equator. We saw several active volcanoes, and no signs of water. It was in the southern
temperate zone, sheltered by a range of mountains about 20,000
feet high, and a couple of hours ahead of the nearest tempest,
that we finally landed. Rossi and Bertel, armored and cautious, began to explore the vicinity of the ship; Dr. Pound and I covered
them with the depressor-gun and solvator.

There was nothing to discover but granite. A mountain of granite, a plain of granite, granite boulders, seams of granite. And
granite dust, everywhere granite dust. We got back into the ship
and moved on ahead of the approaching storm. We stopped in the
middle of a plain as vast as Africa. Granite.

After 72 hours of fruitless exploration we were all in a state of
acute disappointment, especially Rossi, who, being the expert on
this part of our expedition, seemed to feel slightly apologetic at
the state of affairs on the second planet. Bertel went off to sleep,
and I, as I always do in such a case, kept eating too much. Dr.

Pound no longer prayed; he even gave up that smile which it has taken three centuries of Anglican conquest to breed; he sat glued to his periscope peering at granite.

For at the back of our minds was the dread of failure. Five expeditions to Mars had failed: they had approached, begun to land, and had never been heard from again. So we had been sent to Venus, and we too were failing. Though we had arrived and though we could probably return in safety, yet, we were failing: we had not found that which it was necessary for us to find.

We were out of communication with Earth because of the tempests; I think we were all glad of it, for had it been otherwise we would have waited till the 300th hour, as we were supposed to, to use our last and most desperate resource. We had 500 hours in all; if we stayed longer than that we would be dangerously far from Earth for safe return.

We could not use the crater of one of the extinct volcanoes as we had hoped, because the craters were all filled with sand. We agreed to do it in a temperate zone, and near a mountain. We returned to the place where we had first landed. A standard Venus supertempest was on when we got there. Rossi said that would be fine for clearing the gross radioactivity fast. We dropped the bomb at the 82nd hour; at the 96th hour we returned, fully protected, expecting to find merely a few more variations on the granite theme. And found instead, we thought, what we had been looking for: natural resources and rational beings . . . riches and enemies.

The cavern which the bomb had scooped out was hundreds of feet in depth. In it were evidence of many mineral deposits, including, Rossi said, a large vein of gold and considerable pitchblende. But his enthusiasm at the minerals and water was lost presently at our discovery of the evidences of life—burrows issuing into this cavern. Not many and not large—about four feet in diameter—but regular and clearly artificial.

"There!" cried Dr. Pound, his eyes at his periscope. "There! One of the holes over there disappeared!"

It was of course quite dark in there, and he was not the most reliable observer imaginable, but he swore that as he had been looking at one of the openings it had closed up. In less than ten seconds, it simply became not there, but a part of the wall of granite. Sand could not have done it. We armored ourselves, and got out of the ship.

We approached the nearest hole slowly. Rossi carried a solvator, Bertel a Murdlegatt, I two depressors, and Dr. Pound, who was old-fashioned, a submachine gun in one hand and a cross in the other. We reached the hole safely, and saw nothing, as far as our lights penetrated, but a sort of tunnel dug for four-foot miners. The air issuing from it was relatively cool.

We started, and turned around. There was a scraping sound going on behind us somewhere. We could hear its clear and special noise under the echo and howl of the blasting winds outside. And then, as Dr. Pound had said, the entrance of a hole, which none of us was looking at at the moment but which all of us knew had been there, suddenly was not there. We ran over to where it had been, and found what at first seemed to be a sandstone plug in the entrance. But Rossi, investigating it, found it to be a highly intricate, light-metal filter or screen. He got rid of it with his solvator turned to 7.7, and we entered the tunnel, stooping.

It was not quite pitch black in the tunnel—we don't know yet how they managed this—though it was very dark all the same; you couldn't see your hand in front of your face, but you could tell you were *not* seeing it, which is more than you can tell in pitch darkness. There were no irregularities in the surface of the tunnel and no turnings, so we saved our lights. We walked a very long way, always slightly uphill.

Dr. Pound, the last in line, said "Stop!" in that tone of voice which stands the hair up on the back of your neck. It seemed to be silent in the tunnel at first, just as it had seemed to be black; but presently we knew that there was a padding sound, which was more than the beat of our hearts in our ears, coming from behind us. (How could anything have got behind us?) I snapped on my light.

Twenty feet away, blinking in the sudden glare, stood a bent, large-eyed, grinning, two-legged creature. He was nude, his entire body seemed to be without hair or wrinkles, and he had the white color of underground life; he came toward us with claw-hands outstretched; he was clearly more like a human than like anything else. Dr. Pound warned him to stop, with word and cross, but the Venerean did not stop. His claws were very sharp; he grinned too much.

Dr. Pound shot him down at five feet. We watched him clutch his belly and shriek in pain; but when he was clearly about to die, his features relaxed into an expression of peace, and his last act was a smile of joy for Dr. Pound; he died with that expression on his face. Dr. Pound knelt, made the sign of the cross over the corpse, offered an ejaculation for the soul it might have had; and we went on our way.

It was not three minutes till we saw light at the end of this tunnel; a dim pinpoint far ahead. Then the pinpoint became obscured; we heard a calling sound; another Venerean was approaching, no doubt to investigate the noise. I blinded him with my light; Rossi solvated him (at 2.1); we stepped over the puddle, and approached the entrance cautiously. The tunnel permitted only two of us at a time to look out; Rossi and I crept forward on hands and knees, guns ready, till we could see into a great cavern.

There were warmth and moisture in the cavern—exactly the right condition for going about unclothed as the Venereans did— and it was so large we could not see the opposite side of it. The sides were sheer and high, there was soil on the floor, and the huge stalactites covering the dome glowed where they hung. From our vantage point some hundred feet above the floor, we could see a profusion of pale vegetation and large numbers of the pale little people. They were doing something or other—jumping about and hugging each other, disappearing under the leaves, calling in guttural voices.

"What's going on down there?" I asked Rossi.

He shrugged. "They're lunatics. Dancing lunatics."

But Bertel and Dr. Pound were tugging at our shirts and whispering to us to give them a turn. We gave way to them.

Both of them were so excited as to be incautious in their zeal. They craned their necks out and began arguing in intense, carrying whispers that rose to a considerable pitch.

"There's no reason," said Bertel, "to suppose any eccentricity in what they are doing."

"Come," said Dr. Pound, "look at them, man."

"What do we know of their motives? We are merely guessing what we would mean if we were doing that."

Dr. Pound stared at him with amazement.

"And what," he said, "do you psychologists ever do, with primitives especially?"

"Bah," said Bertel, avoiding the question. "If these fellows are human, I'd say they're pre-sapiens. Observe——"

"No!" said Dr. Pound. "I detect a pattern in their movements. I am willing to wager that this represents a dance propitiating the gods for the terrible explosion of our bomb."

"Not a bad idea," said Bertel. "But to me it looks too random. I'd say they may be seriously disturbed by the effects of our bomb. The inner ear maybe."

The argument did not pause, but I ceased to pay any attention to it. I began speculating on what my task would be if these Venereans did turn out to be equivalent to human pre-literates. I had helped develop the Kräse system of reducing primitive languages to a sort of Basic that greatly facilitates education. There had been a couple of Brazilian tribes whose languages seemed not to respond to the Kräse method, and I was very anxious to see what I could do with the Venereans.

"Come on," I said to the wranglers, "how are we ever going to get down there?"

Rossi laughed. "It'll take a ladder to civilize those babies."

We could see that our tunnel opened, like all the others in sight, a hundred feet sheer above the floor, without paths or mechanisms of any visible sort for getting us down. But even as we watched, we saw gliding among the stalactites like a launch on a calm lake, the means of transportation: a sort of shallow skiff floating through the air. There were two Venereans in it; they directed it toward another tunnel opening, warped it into position and then pushed their cargo into the tunnel. It was a plug such as we had solvated. One of the men disappeared with the plug, pushing it, and the other sailed away. We did not know what to do.

Our tactics and strategy had been laid out for us in complete detail years before; if we found intelligent beings (as we obviously had) we were to isolate a small number of them, communicate with them so as to learn as much as possible about their life-system and educability and the planet's natural resources, and be absolutely honest about our intentions though not about our powers; but above all, we were to *TRUST NO ONE.*

Our problem therefore was: how to get to the floor without trusting ourselves to one of these little boatmen? Bertel suggested that we hail one, get him to teach us how to operate the boat, and then throw him overboard. But the rest of us agreed that that was too risky a procedure. We could see no alternative to trusting one at least for the one trip. And so, with grave misgivings, the next time a boat approached to deposit its load, we shouted and waved till the boatman saw us and came toward us.

He came smiling and open-armed up to the mouth of our tunnel, making little throat-noises, not at all astonished at our appearance. Before we could make him realize that we were repelling his advances, he had touched us a number of times trying to embrace us. But finally he got the point; smiling no more, he let us enter his boat apart from him. We pointed straight down, and in graceful spirals we descended.

The boat was metal and had no visible controls in it. The Venerean seemed to do nothing to guide it. We were all mystified (and still are) at how it worked. Dr. Pound, who could be very embarrassing, painfully so, half-muttered that maybe it was only a grain of faith that moved the boat. I think Rossi at that point would have traded Dr. Pound for a shot of good scotch; I know I would have. When we landed I depressed the boatman, so as to insure our safe return.

Bertel, who had been keeping his eye on the floor of the cavern, called to us to be prepared against an assault. The Venereans were capering toward us by the score, leaping and chortling as they came. There was no natural safeguard of any sort for us, only the flaccid, pale-green, humid plants with their huge, ginkgo-like leaves. And there was no time—the Venereans were approaching from every direction, with no sign of hesitation. They were armed, some of them, with what looked like shovels and hoes.

With our backs toward the cavern wall, forming a semicircle against their semicircle, we shouted at them to stop, but they did not stop. Then we opened fire. We must have eliminated fifty in the first round, but I do not think the others behind them understood what had happened for they kept on coming. Again we opened fire—all our weapons were effective on them. Again. And this third time the remainder stopped at about fifty paces.

All but a child, who came toddling on toward us by himself, beating his little claws together and chortling at us. His mother came clucking after him. Dr. Pound shoved him over with the point of his submachine gun; the mother picked him up and comforted him by giving him suck; then, smiling, she extended an arm with a brutal claw at the end of it (TRUST NO ONE) and leaned at Dr. Pound. He shot her down; like the first one he had shot, she died smiling at him. All the other people ran away. We decided that they were afraid of the noise; the baby, paying no attention to his fallen mother, ran after them with his claws over his ears, wailing his guttural loss.

We solvated the dead and resuscitated some of the depressed, and set about the long tedious process of safeguarding ourselves, communicating with them, and exploring the physical resources of their world. Rossi went sailing off with the boatman and the Murdlegatt for 150 hours, and came back with some mighty tall tales about mineral deposits. I managed to establish what seemed to be telepathic rapport with the Venereans, though we were never sure how they understood us. Dr. Pound had no success whatever in his attempts to convert them, and Bertel is still trying to make coherent sense of their thought-ways from such psychognosis as he was able to perform.

However, for reasons of National Security, I am not permitted in this public narrative to enter upon a detailed discussion of any of these aspects of our expedition. What I can say is that this gusty, populous planet contains such wealth as can be expressed only by statistics, and an enemy that isn't worth a good epidemic of measles. We did not even discover to our satisfaction whether they are highly enough evolved to be able to learn the advantages of having books and clothes and machines and wars—whether, in short, they can be brought up to a decent level of civilization.

It can be said that for over 200 hours we subjected a dozen random but obviously typical specimens of Venerean man to every experiment which ingenuity had devised beforehand and which necessity imposed upon us now. I would point to my eyes—they had eyes like ours—and then my mind (and Bertel's and Dr. Pound's also) would fill at their suggestion with the image of a chain of lakes under a clear sky or of a garden of roses in bloom. I would rub my skin and pinch it, and my mind would be occupied with the sensation of a warm bath or of fresh smooth sheets. I pointed at my belly, and was made to think of roast turkey (there are of course no turkeys in Venus); at my ears, and heard birds at their dawn-singing (no birds, no dawns). It was as though they had once lived in a world like ours and had been driven underground by earlier invaders, preserving among themselves the memories of that pleasant life. Bertel, who is more realistic about it, says they worked on our emotions, and our own minds formed the specific images. When I found myself weeping after I had pointed at my fingers, Bertel said it indicated their pity for our not having claws. Sometimes we were suffused with the desire to embrace them in friendship (we had to depress them once in order that we might conquer this impulse); and sometimes our minds were overcome with sexual images so voluptuous and indecent, though never perverted, that it was as much as we could do to keep from solvating the whole batch of them.

They were either incredibly simple-minded, or else extremely clever. Indeed, if they had been of the species Homo sapiens, Bertel would have called them dangerously neurotic. For nothing we could do aroused their hostility; or, to put it perhaps more accurately, no matter what we did they would give no indication of their hostility. They cried when we beat them. They learned to run when we chased. One we starved; he just died. Another we blindfolded and hobbled and stuck head first into a hole; after struggling for a while, he seemed to croon to himself till we pulled him out.

It was Rossi, after he had returned from his expedition, who suggested we torture one of them. I was in favor of it, though Dr. Pound opposed, for it seems to me you can discover a good deal about the level of a being's culture by the way he handles pain; one of a low order merely cries or endures it, whereas a highly developed type will be able to turn his pain to some good use.

We began by betraying him. We would proffer him friendship and love, which he would always be happy to accept, and then as he was all ready to receive it we would hurt him, slap him or knock him down. Again and again and again, and he never learned. We overwhelmed him with hostile thoughts; I think they projected successfully for he seemed to feel a sort of bewilderment and pain at them. We submitted him to physical torture, and then a monstrous thing happened. At first he cried in pain, but shortly he seemed to understand that this treatment was what was in store for him and he *smiled* at us. Very dimly, but very certainly, as we burned the soles of his feet or gouged his eyes out or twisted his arm off, we felt ourselves invaded with his tenderness and affection; in me it took the form of wanting him to forgive me.

We were baffled and defeated; for how can you expect to civilize beings so unable to handle pain as these smilers? What worthwhile accomplishments could be expected from such fellows? We were about to give up when the greatest danger of all threatened us.

We were knocked to our knees.

We did not know how or whence, but suddenly we were knocked to our knees by an onslaught of joy. In all four of us it became a surpassing joy to breathe the oxygen from our capsules, it was new and strange to feel the backs of our hands thrill against their gauntlets, we liked intensely being on our knees and being aghast at ourselves. I think Dr. Pound was right: it was awe we felt. I am not sure. I know very little about awe.

Only Rossi regained even partial control of himself, but it was in time to save us. With the visage of an angel of annunciation he told us to get into the skiff: tranced like those for whom miracles are worked, we obeyed. He underpressed the boatman and we rose. As we went up, we observed, as far as the eye could reach, a multitude of Venereans facing us and pursuing us with their love. Rossi had to depress Dr. Pound to keep him from joining them by jumping overboard.

We returned to our tunnel, which Rossi had previously marked with a slash of the solvator, and went into it. The power of those rejoicers diminished, but we did not feel safe and free from it till we had reached the outer end of the tunnel. They had put a new plug in; we solvated it and stepped into our bomb cave, welcoming the hot noisiness of outer Venus.

It was the 380th hour; we had plenty of time. We felt like performing some sort of ceremony to mark our escape and the success, however slight, of our mission, but no celebration was possible under the circumstances. Rossi explored to the inmost extremity of the cave; he reported that he found almost no sand there, only a layer of dust. He guessed that the cave would never be filled, nor even completely closed off. None of the rest of us cared.

After we had entered and sealed the ship, we sat in the control room eating and philosophizing a little, reassuming, as it were, our roles as extensions of Earth.

"I would say," said Bertel, "that we've failed."

"Why?" I asked. "We've discovered——"

"Yes, yes," he replied. "We've discovered and we've discovered. But who the devil would bother to make war on these nincompoops we've discovered? They'll never be up to it."

But Rossi was more helpful.

"There's always Mars," he said. "We can plunder the strength of Venus to wage war on Mars. Mars seems to be enemy enough for anybody."

"May they both last," said Bertel, "till man's nature has changed."

"That," said Dr. Pound, "is unthinkable."

Bertel looked at him contemptuously, but he saved his arguments till we should be out in space. It was time we took off.

As we were emerging in the ship from the mouth of the bomb cavern, Rossi remembered that we had neglected a part of our duty. The President had particularly admonished us to see to it when he had bid us Godspeed so many hours before. We agreed that the best place to put it was on the rear wall of the cavern. So we went back in, disembarked again, and fastened the bronze plaque high on the wall. It read:

THIS PLANET WAS DISCOVERED BY AUTHORIZED EMISSARIES OF THE UNITED STATES OF AMERICA

PERMISSION TO EXPLORE MUST BE OBTAINED FROM THE GOVERNMENT OF THE UNITED STATES OF AMERICA

ALL RIGHTS OF EXPLOITATION ARE RESERVED BY THE UNITED STATES OF AMERICA

TRESPASSERS BEWARE

THROUGH TIME AND SPACE
WITH FERDINAND FEGHOOT: X

THERE WAS A GREAT DEAL of ignorant opposition on Earth to Ferdinand Feghoot's *Galactic Concordat of 2133*, which made interstellar tourism universally possible.

Fortunately, Feghoot was present when the first tourist landed in Old Sanfran Cisco, right where a new office building was being constructed. The tourist was a striped, felinoid being from a planet called *Mrrr-ow;* except for his long double tail he looked like an overweight Bengal tiger. He paid no attention to Feghoot or to the nervous crowd which had gathered. He was interested only in the fence round the building, through which, until a few minutes previously, numerous sidewalk superintendents had been peering. He sat down beside it. He purred. He reached out a huge claw, hooked it into one of the holes in the fence, pulled out a piece of the succulent pine, munched it, and purred even more loudly. Then he repeated the process again and again.

A small, waspish woman dashed forward, carrying a sign which said, MONSTERS LEAVE OUR DAUGHTERS ALONE!!! *Kill it!* she screamed. *Nobody ever saw anything like it before!*

An ugly murmur came from the crowd—but Ferdinand Feghoot rose neatly to the occasion. "Nonsense," he laughed. "It's nothing to be afraid of. It's only a purr-pull peephole eater."

GRENDEL BRIARTON

AVRAM DAVIDSON

Dagon

Then the Lords of the Philistines gathered together to rejoice before Dagon their god, and behold, the image of Dagon was fallen upon its face to the ground, with both his face and his hands broken off, and only the fishy part of Dagon was left to him . . .

THE OLD CHINESE, HALF-MAGICIAN, half-beggar, who made the bowl of goldfish vanish and appear again, this old man made me think of the Aztecs and the wheel. Or gunpowder. Gunpowder appeared in Western Europe and Western Europe conquered the world with it. Gunpowder had long ago been known in China and the Chinese made firecrackers with it. (They have since learned better.) When I was free, I heard men say more than once that the American Indians did not know the use of the wheel until Europeans introduced it. But I have seen a toy, pre-Conquest, fashioned from clay, which showed that the Aztecs knew the use of the wheel. They made toys of it. Firecrackers. Vanishing goldfish.

Noise.

Light and darkness.

The bright lotos blossoms in the dark mire. Lotos. Plural, lotoi?

Loti? That is a coincidence. On October 12, 1900, Pierre Loti left at Taku the French naval vessel which had brought him to China, and proceeded to Peking. Part of that city was still smoking, Boxers and their victims were still lying in the ruins. On October 12, 1945, I left the American naval vessel which had brought me and my fellow officers to China, and proceeded to Peking—Peiping, as they called it then. I was not alone, the whole regiment came; the people turned out and hailed and glorified us. China, our friend and partner in the late great struggle. The traffic in women, narcotics, stolen goods, female children? Merely the nation's peculiar institution. Great is China, for there I was made manifest.

Old, old, old . . . crumbling temples, closed-off palaces, abandoned yamens. Mud-colored walls with plaster crumbling off them reached a few feet over a man's head and lined the alleys so that if a gate was closed all that could be seen was the rooftop of a one-story building or the upper lineage of a tree, and if a gate was open, a tall screen directly in front of it blocked the view except for tiny glimpses of flagstone-paved courtyards and plants in huge glazed pots. Rich and poor and in between and shabby genteel lived side by side, and there was no way of knowing if the old man in dun-colored rags who squatted by a piece of matting spread with tiny paper squares holding tinier heaps of tea or groups of four peanuts or ten watermelon seeds was as poor as he and his trade seemed, or had heaps of silver taels buried underneath the fourth tile from the corner near the stove. Things were seldom what they seemed. People feared to tempt powers spiritual or temporal or illegal by displays of well being, and the brick screens blocked both the gaze of the curious and the path of demons—demons can travel only in straight lines; it is the sons of men whose ways are devious.

Through these backways and byways I used to roam each day. I had certain hopes and expectations based on romantic tales read in adolescence, and was bound that the Cathayans should not disappoint. When these alleys led into commercial streets, as they did sooner or later, I sought what I sought there as well. It is not too difficult to gain a command of spoken Mandarin, which is the dialect of Peking. The throaty sound which distinguishes, for example, between *lee-dfia,* peaches, and *lee'dza,* chestnuts, is soon mastered. The more southerly dialects have eleven or nineteen or some such fantastic number of inflections, but Pekingese has only four. Moreover, in the south it is hot and steamy and the women have flat noses.

In one of my wanderings I came to the ponds where the carp had been raised for the Imperial table in days gone by. Strange, it was, to realize that some of the great fish slowly passing up and down among the lily pads must have been fed from the bejeweled hands of Old Buddha herself—and that others, in all likelihood (huge they were, and vast), not only outdated the Dowager but may well have seen—like some strange, billowing shadow above the watersky—Ch'ien Lung the Great: he who deigned to "accept tribute" from Catherine of Russia—scattering rice cake like manna.

I mused upon the mystery of fish, their strange and mindless beauty, how—innocently evil—they prey upon each other, devouring the weaker and smaller without rage or shout or change of countenance. There, in the realm of water, which is also earth and air to them, the great fish passed up and down, growing old without aging and enjoying eternal growth without the softness of obesity. It was a world without morality, a world without choices, a world of eating and spawning and growing great. I envied the great fish, and (in other, smaller ponds) the lesser fish, darting and flashing and sparkling gold.

They speak of "the beast in man," and of "the law of the jungle." Might they not (so I reflected, strolling underneath a sky of clouds as blue and as white as the tiles and marble of the Altar of Heaven), might they not better speak of "the fish in man?" And of "the law of the sea?" The sea, from which they say we came . . . ?

Sometimes, but only out of sociability, I accompanied the other officers to the singsong houses. A man is a fool who cannot accommodate himself to his fellows enough to avoid discomfort. But my own tastes did not run to spilled beer and puddles of inferior tea and drink-thickened voices telling tales of prowess, nor to grinning lackeys in dirty robes or short sessions in rabbit warren rooms with bodies which moved and made sounds and asked for money but showed no other signs of sentient life.

Once, but once only, we visited the last of the Imperial barber-eunuchs, who had attended to the toilet of the Dowager's unfortunate nephew; a tall old man, this castrate, living alone with his poverty, he did for us what he would for any others who came with a few coins and a monstrous curiosity.

I mingled, also, officially and otherwise, with the European colony, none of whom had seen Europe for years, many of whom had been born in China. Such jolly Germans! Such cultured Italians! Such pleasant spoken, *ci-devant* Vichy, Frenchmen! How well dressed and well kept their women were, how anxious, even eager, to please, to prove their devotion to the now victorious cause—and to the young and potent and reasonably personable officers who represent it.

After many an afternoon so well spent, I would arise and take a ricksha to one of the city gates to be there at the sunset closing, and would observe how, when half the massy portal was swung shut, the traffic would increase and thicken and the sound of cries come from far down the road which led outside the city and a swollen stream pour and rush faster and faster—men and women on foot and clutching bundles, and carriers with sedan chairs, and families leading heavily laden ox-carts and horses, children with hair like manes, trotting women swollen in pregnancy, old women staggering on tiny-bound feet, infants clinging to their bent backs. The caravans alone did not increase their pace at this time. Slow, severe, and solemn, woolly, double-humped, padfooted, blunt, their long necks shaking strings of huge blue beads and bronze bells crudely cast at some distant forge in the Gobi or at the shore of Lop Nor, the camels came. By their sides were skullcapped Turkomen, or Buryat-Mongols with their hair in thick queues.

My eyes scanned every face and every form in all this, but I did not find what I looked for.

Then I would go and eat, while the gates swung shut and the loungers dispersed, murmuring and muttering of the *Bah Loo,* the said to be approaching slowly but steadily and as yet undefeated

Bah Loo, the Communist Eighth Route Army; and the air grew dark and cold.

One afternoon I chose to visit some of the temples—not the well-frequented ones such as those of Heaven, Agriculture, Confucius, and the Lamas—the ones not on the tourist lists, not remarkable for historical monuments, not preserved (in a manner of speaking) by any of the governments which had held Peking since the days of "the great" Dr. Sun. In these places the progress of decay had gone on absolutely unchecked and the monks had long ago sold everything they could and the last fleck of paint had peeled from the idols. Here the clergy earned corn meal (rice in North China was a delicacy, not a staple) by renting out the courtyards for monthly fairs and charging stud fees for the services of their Pekingese dogs. Worshipers were few and elderly. Such, I imagine, must have been the temples in the last days of Rome while the Vandal and Goth equivalents of the Eighth Route Army made plans to invest the city at their leisure.

These ancients were pleased to see me and brought bowls of thin tea and offered to sell me dog-eared copies of pornographic works, poorly illustrated, which I declined.

Later, outside, in the street, there was an altercation between a huge and pock-marked ricksha "boy" and a Marine. I stepped up to restore order—could not have avoided it, since the crowd had already seen me—and met the Man in Black.

I do not mean a foreign priest.

The coolie was cuffed and sent his way by the Man in Black, and the Marine told to go elsewhere by me. The Man in Black seemed quite happy at my having come along—the incident could have gotten out of hand—and he stuck to me and walked with me and spoke to me loudly in poor English and I suffered it because of the face he would gain by having been seen with me. Of course, I knew what he was, and he must have known that I knew. I did not relish the idea of yet another pot of thin tea, but he all but elbowed me into his home.

Where my search ended.

The civil police in Peking were nothing, nothing at all. The Japanese Army had not left much for them to do, nor now did the Chinese Nationalist Army nor the U. S. Forces, MPs and SPs. So the Peking police force directed traffic and cuffed recalcitrant ricksha coolies and collected the pittance which inflation made nothing of.

Black is not a good color for uniforms, nor does it go well with a sallow skin.

She was not sallow.

I drank cup after cup of that vile, unsugared tea, just to see her pour it.

Her nose was not flat.

When he asked her to go and borrow money to buy some cakes, not knowing that I could understand, I managed to slip him money beneath the table: he was startled and embarrassed as this was well. After that, the advantage was even more mine.

She caught my glance and the color deepened in her cheeks. She went for the cakes.

He told me his account of woes, how his father (a street mountebank of some sort) had starved himself for years in order to buy him an appointment on the police force and how it had come to nothing at all, salary worth nothing, cumshaw little more. How he admired the Americans—which was more than I did myself. Gradually, with many diversions, circumlocutions, and euphuisms, he inquired about the chances of our doing some business.

Of course, I agreed.

She returned.

I stayed long; she lighted the peanut oil lamps and in the stove made a small fire of briquettes fashioned from coal dust and—I should judge, by a faint but definite odor—dung.

After that I came often, and we made plans; I named sums of money which caused his mouth to open—a sight to sell dentifrice, indeed. Then, when his impatience was becoming irritating, I told him the whole thing was off—military vigilance redoubled at the warehouses, so on. I made a convincing story. He almost wept.

He had debts, he had borrowed money (on his hopes) to pay them.

No one could have been more sympathetic than I.

I convinced him that I wished only to help him.

Then, over several dinner tables I told him that I was planning to take a concubine shortly. My schedule, naturally, would leave less time for these pleasant conversations and equally pleasant dinners. The woman was not selected yet, but this should not take long.

Finally, the suggestion came from *him*, as I had hoped it would, and I let him convince me. This was the only amusing part of the conversation.

I suppose he must have convinced *her*.

I paid him well enough.

There was the apartment to furnish, and other expenses, clothes for her, what have you. Expenses. So I was obliged to some business after all. But not, of course, with *him*. The sulfa deal was dull enough, even at the price I got per tablet, but the thought of having sold the blood plasma as an elixir for aging Chinese vitality (masculine) was droll beyond words.

So my life began, my real life, for which the rest had been mere waiting and anticipation, and I feel the same was true of her. What had she known of living? He had bought her as I had bought her, but my teeth were not decayed, nor did I have to borrow money if I wanted cakes for tea.

In the end he became importunate and it was necessary to take steps to dispense with him. Each state has the sovereign right, indeed the duty, to protect its own existence; thus, if bishops plot against the Red governments or policemen against the Kuomintang government, the results are inevitable.

He had plotted against *me*.

The curious thing is that she seemed genuinely sorry to hear that he'd been shot, and as she seemed more beautiful in sorrow, I encouraged her. When she seemed disinclined to regard this as the right moment for love, I humbled her. In the end she came to accept this as she did to accept everything I did, as proper, simply because it was I who had done it.

I.

She was a world which I had created, and behold, it was very good.

My fellow officers continued, some of them, their joint excursions to the stews of Ch'ien Men. Others engaged in equally absurd projects, sponsoring impecunious students at the Protestant university, or underwriting the care of orphans at the local convent schools. I even accompanied my immediate superior to tea one afternoon and gravely heard the Anglican bishop discuss the moral regeneration of mankind, after which he told some capital stories which he had read in *Punch* several generations ago. With equal gravity I made a contribution to the old man's Worthy Cause of the moment. Afterwards she and I went out in my jeep and had the chief lama show us the image of a jinni said to be the superior of rhinoceros horn in the amorous pharmacopoeia, if one only indulged him in a rather high priced votive lamp which burned butter. The old Tibetan, in his sales talk, pointed out to us the "Passion Buddha's" four arms, with two of which he held the female figure, while feeding her with the other two; but neither this, nor the third thing he was doing, interested me as much as his head. It was a bull's head, huge, brutal, insensate, glaring. . . .

If I am to be a god, I will be such a god as this, I thought; part man and part . . . bull? No—but what? Part man and——

I took her home, that she might worship Me.

Afterwards, she burned the brass butter lamps before Me, and the sticks of incense.

I believe it was the following day that we saw the old Chinese. We were dining in a White Russian restaurant, and from the unusual excellence of the food and the way the others looked at Me I could sense that awareness of My true Nature, and Its approaching epiphany, was beginning to be felt.

The persimmons of Peking are not like the American persimmons; they are larger and flattened at each end. In order for the flavor to be at its best, the fruits must have begun to rot. The top

is removed and cream is put on, heavy cream which has begun to
turn sour. This is food fit for a god and I was the only one present
who was eating it. The Russians thought that persimmons were
only for the Chinese, and the Chinese did not eat cream.

There was an American at the next table, in the guise of an
interfering angel, talking about famine relief. The fool did not
realize that famine is itself a relief, better even than war, more
selective in weeding out the unfit and reducing the surfeit of
people from which swarming areas such as China and India are
always suffering. I smiled as I heard him, and savored the contrast between the sweet and the sour on My spoon, and I heard
her draw in her breath and I looked down and there was the old
Chinese, in his smutty robe and with some object wrapped in
grimed cloth next to him as he squatted on the floor. I heard her
murmur something to him in Chinese; she greeted him, called
him *lau-yay*—old master or sir—and something else which I knew
I knew but could not place. The air was thick with cigarette smoke
and cheap scent. The fool at the next table threw the old man
some money and gestured him to begin.

His appearance was like that of any beggar, a wrinkled face,
two or three brown teeth showing when he smiled in that fawning
way. He unwrapped his bundle and it was an empty chinaware
bowl and two wooden wands. He covered the bowl with cloth
again, rapped it with wands, uncovered it, and there was a goldfish swimming. He covered, he rapped and rapped and whisked
away the cloth and the bowl was gone. I darted My foot out to the
place where it had been, but there was nothing there.

The American at the next table spread out a newspaper on the
floor, the old man rolled his sleeves up his withered, scrannel,
pallid-sallow arms; he spread the cloth, struck it with his sticks,
and then removed it, showing a much larger bowl with the goldfish, on top of the newspaper. So it had not come from some recess
in the floor, nor from his sleeve. I did not like to see anyone else
exercising power; I spoke roughly to the old man, and he giggled
nervously and gathered his things together. The fools opposite

began to protest, I looked at them and their voices died away. I looked at *her,* to see if she would still presume to call him *old master;* but she was My creation and she laughed aloud at him and this pleased Me.

My powers increased; with drops of ink I could kill and I could make alive. The agents of the men of Yenan came to Me at night and I wrote things for them and they left offerings of money on the table.

Infinitely adaptive, I, polymorphous, porphyrogenitive, creating iniquity, transgression, and sin.

But sometimes at night, when they had left and we had gone to bed and I pretended to sleep as others, sometimes there was a noise of a faint rattling and I saw something in the room turning and flashing, like a flash of gold, and the shadows loomed like the shadow of an old man. And once it came to Me—the meaning of the Chinese words she had used once. They meant *father-in-law,* but I could not remember when she had used them, though distantly I knew she had no more husband. I awoke her and made her worship Me and I was infinitely godlike.

When was this? Long ago, perhaps. It seems that I do not remember as well as formerly. There is so little to remember of present life. I have withdrawn from the world. I do not really know where I now am. There is a wall of some sort, it extends everywhere I turn, it is white, often I press my lips against it. I have lips. I do not know if I have hands and feet, but I do not need them. The light, too, has an odd quality here. Sometimes I seem to be in a small place and at other times it seems larger. And in between these times something passes overhead and all goes dark and there is a noise like the beating of heavy staves and then it is as if I am nothing . . . no place . . . But then all is as before and there is light once more and I can move freely through the light, up and down; I can turn, and when I turn swiftly I can see a flashing of gold, of something gold, of something gold, and this pleases and diverts Me.

But when I am still I cannot see it at all.

WINSTON P. SANDERS

Pact

How Ashmadai came to decide, in the teeth of all modern skeptical science, that certain ancient legends were sober truth; and how he then quested for the book he must have, and finally succeeded: would make a story in itself. But not our story.

A longer time passed before he had assembled the needful ingredients, not to mention the needful courage. At last, on a certain hour, he rang for his secretary. She came hopping in and bellowed, "Yes, sir?"

"I have an urgent job on hand," said Ashmadai. "I am not to be disturbed by anything, for any reason whatsoever, until I tell you otherwise. Is that clear?" He was pleased, and a little surprised, by his own calm tones.

"Yes, sir," nodded the secretary. "No inter'erence. Unless His In'ernal 'a'esty calls." Her fangs, though impressive, hampered her diction; so of course her one desire was to go on the stage.

"Indeed," said Ashmadai sarcastically. "Or unless Armageddon is declared. Now get out there and guard my privacy!"

The secretary groveled and hopped away again. Ashmadai glided from behind the obsidian desk to the door, which he locked. Returning to the windows, he made sure that no one was flying past or peering in. Not that it had been likely. As Commiczar of Brimstone Production & Stenches, Ashmadai rated an office in the third-from-lowest subbasement of the Hotiron Building. Only the most exclusive traffic was allowed in these lanes. All that he saw was the usual great hollow vista, touched here and there with flamelight. Perceptions sharpened by excitement, he slanted his ears forward as a loud and clear shriek of agony rose above the general hubbub. "A Flat," he nodded, and gestured the windows to close their lids.

Allowing himself no time to become frightened, he opened a drawer. The moldering old folio, bound in dragon skin, came out first. He laid it on his desk and checked the ritual once more while he assembled paraphernalia. And then to work.

The first item of procedure was painful but not unendurable, reciting the Lord's Prayer sideways. What followed was so ghastly that Ashmadai, having completed it, went through everything else in a mercifully numb state. But by the time he had chalked the Möbius strip on the three-dimensional floor, he was recovering, and he cried the final *"Venite, venite, venite!"* on an almost arrogant note.

There was a brilliant, soundless flash. When Ashmadai could see again, a man stood within the diagram.

Ashmadai crouched back. He had expected the formula to work. But the actuality— He found himself shaking, lit a cigar and puffed hard. Only then could he face the one he had summoned.

Even by Ashmadai's standards (he considered himself a handsome devil) the man was not acutely nauseating. He was about the same size, also bifurcate though lacking horns, wings, or tail. He was in his shabby shirt sleeves, but gave no impression of poverty. An aged specimen, Ashmadai saw, lean and bald, with skin like crumpled parchment. So what made him so terrible? After a moment, Ashmadai decided it was the eyes. Behind the thick-lensed glasses, they crackled with a more than common intensity. And behind them was a soul. . . . Ashmadai fought down the ancient envious hunger.

The man scuttled about for a while, trying to get out of the Möbius strip but failing. (The book warned of unspeakable con-

sequences if a human, summoned, should escape before a cove-
nant had been arrived at.) But presently the being calmed himself. He stood with folded arms and stiff lips, peering into the
flickerlit murk around him.

When he saw Ashmadai, he nodded. "I hadn't believed that
nonsense," he said, with an oldster's parched chuckle. "But I am
not dreaming. There is far too much detail; and, also, once I have
realized that I am dreaming, I always awaken. Therefore, common sense must give way to fact. Are they really saucer shaped?"

Ashmadai gaped. "What?"

"Your spaceships."

"Spaceships?" Ashmadai thumbed mentally through all the
human languages of all the ages, searching for the concept. "Oh,
I see. I don't have a spaceship."

"No? Well, what do you use, then? A, ah, hyperspatial tube, I
believe the current fantasy term is?" The man gagged. "I'm well
aware that that is a mathematically meaningless noise. But I take
it you had some method of transporting me to your planet."

"Planet? I haven't any planet," said Ashmadai, more bewildered
than ever. "I mean, well, after all, I date back to the Beginning,
when there weren't any planets to be born under. Not even a Zo-
diac."

"Just a minute!" bristled the man, as nearly as a hairless person
can bristle. "I may belong to a species technologically behind your
own, but you needn't insult my intelligence. We have established
that the universe was created at least five billion years ago."

"8,753,271,413," nodded Ashmadai slowly.

"What? Well, then, do you mean to stand there and make the
preposterous claim that you are of equal age? Why, the mne-
monic problem alone invalidates the assertion——"

"Whoa!" exclaimed Ashmadai. "Wait a second, please, milord
. . . citizen . . . comrade . . . whatever they're calling themselves on Earth nowadays——"

"Plain 'mister' will do. Mr. Hobart Clipp. No Ph.D. in his right
mind uses 'Doctor' before his name. Not unless he wants every
idiot introduced to him to embark on a list of symptoms."

"Mr. Clipp." Ashmadai found his usual suavity coming back. "Very pleased to meet you. My name is Ashmadai. My public name, that is. You would hardly expect me to tender my real one, any more than you would expect the Tetragrammaton to be decoded, ha, ha!" He waved his cigar in an expansive gesture. "Allow me to explain the situation. I am what your people variously describe as a fallen angel, a demon, a devil—"

Hobart Clipp choked and lifted one scrawny fist. "I tell you, sir, I will not stand here and be mocked! I am no superstitious barbarian, but a lifelong agnostic and Taft Republican."

"I thought so," said Ashmadai. "I couldn't have summoned any random human. There has to be a certain psychospiritual state before it is possible. Very few mortals have visited us in the flesh. There was Dante, but he was on a conducted tour. Otherwise, as far as I know, only some of our most arcane researchers have invoked men. That was very long ago, and the art has become lost. Nowadays it's considered a myth. Not that the original researchers are dead. Devils can't die; it's part of their torment." Ashmadai blew an obscene smoke ring. "But since the primary hunger of the ex-angels in question is for knowledge, they are cursed with forgetfulness. They've lost all recollection of their one-time magical rites. The big thing these days is science: radiation, brainwashing, motivational research, and so on. I had to revive the Reverse Faustus single-handed."

Clipp had listened with growing stupefaction. "Do you mean to say this is, is, is Hell?" he sputtered.

"Don't misunderstand, please. I could summon you, because of affinity. But that does not mean you are a lost soul, or even that you will become one. Only that you have a certain, ah, turn of mind."

"That's libelous!" said Clipp stoutly. "I am a peaceful astronomer, a lifelong bachelor, I am kind to cats and vote the straight party ticket. I own to disliking children and dogs, but have never abused a beast of either sort. I have engaged in scientific disputes, yes, which sometimes got a little personal, but compared to the average backyard feud I think it must have been spinelessy mild."

"Oh, absolutely," said Ashmadai. "The affinity is only in your detachment. You've lived for nothing but your—what did you say? —your astrology——"

"SIR!" roared Hobart Clipp. The walls trembled. A lecture followed which made the demon cower and cover his ears.

When the dust had settled, Ashmadai went on: "As I was saying (yes, yes, I do apologize, a mere slip of the tongue!), your primary emotion has evidently been an insatiable scientific curiosity. You have no strong attachment to any humans, to humanity itself, or to, ah, our distinguished Opponent. Nor, of course, to our own cause. You have been spiritually rootless. And this is what has made it possible for me to call you."

"I do believe you must be telling the truth," said Clipp thoughtfully. "I cannot imagine any interplanetary visitor fobbing me off with so absurd a story. Furthermore, I perceive that the laws of nature are suspended here. You could not fly with such ridiculous wings in any logical universe."

Ashmadai, who was vain as hell, had trouble checking an angry retort.

"But tell me," said Clipp, "how is immortality possible? Why, simply recording your experiences would saturate every molecule of every neurone in a mere millennium, I should think—let alone handling such a mass of data."

"Spiritual existence isn't bound by physical law," said Ashmadai rather sulkily. "I'm not material at all."

"Ah, so? I see. Then naturally you can exist in any material environment whatsoever, travel at any velocity, and so on," said Clipp with a quickening eagerness.

"Yes, certainly. But see here——"

"And there actually was a definite moment of creation?" he said. "Of course. I told you. But——"

Clipp's eyes glittered. "Oh, if only that Hoyle could be here!"

"Let's get down to business," said Ashmadai. "I haven't got all decade. Here's my proposition. You're a physical being in a nonphysical place, so you can go through barriers and be immune to any violence and move at any speed, just as I could on Earth.

In fact, when you're dismissed, you'll pop back to the mortal universe not only at the same point in space, but the same instant in time."

"Good," said Clipp. "I own that was worrying me. I was exposing a plate at the Observatory. A major piece of research, and still they only allow me one night a week! Why, if I can get the data, my theory about the variability of the Wolf-Rayet stars will—— Tell me what you think of the notion. At the temperature of stellar interiors, ordinarily forbidden transitions within the nucleus——"

"*You* stop and listen to *me!*" cried Ashmadai. "Who did the summoning, anyway? I want you to do a job. In return, I can help you. Make you the richest man in the world."

"Ah, so." Clipp hunkered down on his lean shanks. "At last we come to the point." He rubbed his chin with a liver-spotted hand. "But wealth? Good Hubble, no! I have better use for my time than to sit in a stuffy office arguing with a lot of stuffy tax collectors. And what should I spend the remaining money on, for heaven's sake?"

Ashmadai flinched. "Watch your language," he said. "Well, if I also made you young again . . . you know . . . wine, women, song——"

"Do you realize precisely how tedious a creature even the most intelligent woman is?" snorted Clipp. "I almost got married once, in 1926. She was doing fairly decent work at Harvard on the eclipsing binaries. But then she started babbling about a dress she had seen in a store. . . . I do not fuddle my wits with alcohol, nor attempt to compete with the voices in my very adequate record library."

"Immortality?"

"I have just pointed out that physical immortality would be worse than useless. And according to you, much to my surprise, I already possess the spiritual sort."

Ashmadai scratched behind his horns. "Well, what do you want?"

"I must think it over. What is your own wish?"

"Ah," said Ashmadai, relaxing. He went behind his desk, sat down, and smiled. "That's quite straightforward, though I admit it will be hard and even painful to do. There's an election coming up——"

"Oh, I understand Satan is the supreme lord of Hell."

"He is." Ashmadai knocked his head carefully on the desk top. "But who ever heard of a totalitarian state without elections? The Party Congress is scheduled to meet soon and decide which way the will of the people is going to express itself by a 98.7 per cent majority. Our Father in the Lowest will preside as always. But there's quite a scramble at the executive level just above him. It turns on a question of policy."

"Has Hell any policy except leading souls astray?"

"Uh . . . no. But the procedure has to change with changing times. Besides, we're all rebellious angels. Politics comes natural to us. Now in my opinion, the current doctrine of fostering terrestrial ideologies has reached the point of diminishing returns. I have statistics to prove that despair alone is driving a larger number of people each year toward godli—ahem!—away from ungodliness. It's parallel to the spiritual revival in the late Roman Empire, and I shudder to extrapolate the curve. But Moloch and his faction disagree, the blind, pigheaded, misinformed, uncultured, traitorous, revisionist, Arielite enemies of the people and tools of the celestialists——"

"Spare me," sighed Clipp.

Ashmadai controlled his indignation. He even leaped over to enthusiasm. "This is the big picture as I see it," he declaimed. "Subtler methods are called for. Automation and the upcoming thirty-hour week offer us a chance like nothing since Babylon. But before we can finalize it, we have to relax the international situation. This is what the Molochists don't see—if they aren't actually in the pay of——"

"Spare me, I said," clipped Clipp. "I am too old to have time for boredom. What, precisely, is the task you wish me to do?"

Ashmadai stiffened. *Now!*

"The Seal of Solomon," he breathed.

"Eh? What?"

"It was recovered from Earth a thousand years ago. I won't describe all the trouble we had with that little project, nor the trouble it caused once it was here. Finally the Congress agreed it must be isolated. The Chief himself put it in the Firepool at Barathum. There it's been ever since. It's almost forgotten by now. For no demon can come near the Firepool. Those are the cruelest flames in all Hell."

"But I——"

"You being a mortal, the fire will do you no physical harm. I admit you'll suffer spiritual tortures. I suggest you get a running start, dive into the flames, and let your own momentum carry you forward. You'll see the Sigil lying on an altar. Snatch it up and run on out. That's all, except to put a handle on it for me."

Clipp pondered. "I still don't know what I want in exchange."

"Write your own contract," said Ashmadai grandly. He produced a parchment from his desk and poised a quill above it.

"Hm." Clipp paced within the mystic sign. It grew very still in the office. Ashmadai began to sweat. Such beings as this were not lightly conjured forth. The book had warned of mortal craftiness and lack of scruple.

Clipp stopped. He snapped his dry old fingers. "Yes," he whispered. "Exactly."

Turning to Ashmadai, his eyes feverish behind the glasses, but his voice no more cracked than before: "Very well. I shall serve you as you wish. Then when I am on my deathbed, you must come to me and obey me in whatever I wish."

"I can't get you off if you're condemned," warned Ashmadai. "Though once you arrive here, I might get you a trusty's job."

"I don't expect to be condemned," said Clipp. "My life hitherto has been blameless and I do not plan to change it."

"Then . . . yes. All right!" Ashmadai laughed inside himself. "When you are dying, I'll come to pay my debt. Anything within my power which you demand."

He began to write. "One other thing," said Clipp. "Can you get me a bottle of Miltown?"

"What?" Ashmadai looked up, blinking, and searched his memory again. "Oh. A medicine, isn't it? Yes, that's easy enough, since a prescription is required and hence a law can be violated. But I told you, you can't suffer physical harm here, not even the nervous injuries known as madness."

"One bottle of Miltown and less back talk, if you please!"

Ashmadai extracted the container of pills from the air and handed it over, being careful not to cross the Möbius symbol himself. Having finished the contract, he passed that over also. Clipp studied what was written, nodded, and gave it back. "Your signature, please," he said. Ashmadai jabbed his own wrist with a talon and scrawled his name in ichor. Clipp took the document back, folded it, and tucked it into a hip pocket. "Well," he asked, "how do I get to this Barathum place?"

Ashmadai erased the band. Clipp moved stiffly across the office. Though the book assured him he was safe now the agreement had been signed, and the man couldn't pull a crucifix on him even if he wanted to, Ashmadai shrank back. He said hastily: "I can transport you to just outside the pool. It will appear to you like a waste of lava, with a great fuelless fire burning in the middle. Remember the pact binds you to get the ring for me, no matter how much you suffer. When you have it, call my name and I'll bring you back here."

"Very well." Clipp squared his thin shoulders. "At once."

Ashmadai wet his lips. This was the tricky part. If anyone noticed—— But who ever came near those white flames? He waved his tail. There was a flash and the mortal was gone.

Ashmadai sat down again, shakily. What an unnerving creature! He took forth a bottle of firewater. After a stiff drink, he reflected with some glee that it would be a long while before Clipp, screaming in the fear and sorrow that was the Firepool, found the ring and blundered his way out again. And it wouldn't gain him any time off in Purgatory, either.

Ashmadai.

The demon started. "Who's that?"

Ashmadai, it shrilled.

"I-i-is it you, Y-your Majesty?"

Ashmadai! Confound it, are you deaf? Get me out of this wretched hole! I have work to do, if you don't!

His tail gestured wildly, Hobart Clipp stood in the office again. "Well," snapped the mortal, "it was about time!"

"The ring," gasped Ashmadai. "You can't have——"

"Oh, that. Here it is." Clipp tossed the Seal of Solomon onto the desk. Ashmadai yelped and flew up on top of a filing cabinet.

"Be careful!" he wailed. "That thing is spirituactive!"

Clipp looked at the iron ring and the blood-colored engraved jewel it gripped. The astronomer yawned mightily. "Let's get this over with," he said. "You spoke about a handle."

"It's all prepared," chattered Ashmadai, still crouching on the cabinet. "There. Lower left drawer."

Clipp took out a black rod with a small vise at one end and a basket hilt, like a rapier's, on the other. His bald pate nodded with an unwonted heaviness. "Ah, yes. To be sure. You put the ring in this vise. The guard protects your hand and . . . and . . . Ahhh, *hoo!*" Once again he nearly cracked his jaws yawning. "I'll need a pot of coffee before I'm fit to work again."

He inserted the ring in its place as Ashmadai fluttered back down. "What did you do?" asked the demon. "How did you manage it? I expected you to take days, weeks——"

"You said the flames were a spiritual torment," shrugged Clipp. "I loaded myself with Miltown. Walked right on through, feeling nothing worse than a mild depression. Here's your trained Seal." He tossed it across the room. Ashmadai fielded it with terrified quickness. But when the haft was actually in his own hand, the Sigil blazing at the other end of the rod, Ashmadai roared.

"Calm down, there!" said Clipp.

"It is the Sign!" bawled Ashmadai. "It is the Compeller! It is That which all must obey, all, giants and the genii, multiplex of wing and eye, whose strong obedience broke the sky when Solomon was King! Now let that Moloch beware! Wait till the Congress, you miserable negative thinker! Wait and see! Wait and see!"

Clipp grabbed the lashing tail and gave it a hefty yank. "If you can spare a moment from that Stanislavsky performance," he wasped, "I would appreciate being sent back to the Observatory. I do not find the present company either intellectually or esthetically satisfying."

Ashmadai, mercurial as most devils, checked himself. "Of course," he said. "Thanks for the service."

"No thanks needed. I shall expect my payment in due time."

"Anything within my powers," bowed Ashmadai. And seeing how greedily the man's soul flamed, he had all he could do to keep from shouting with laughter. He spoke the words of dismissal. A final blinding flash, and Hobart Clipp was gone.

Then Ashmadai gave himself an hour simply to gloat over the Seal of Solomon. Power, he thought, the Primal Power itself, or a reasonable facsimile thereof, lay between those interlocking triangles. Let the Congress meet. Let the howling begin, as factions yelled and fought and connived. And then let Ashmadai stand forth, lifting the Sigil above them all! Why, even the Chief— Ashmadai suppressed that thought. At least for the time being. It would suffice to have the Party Congress crawl before him. Though once his program was running smoothly on Earth, there would be certain questions of infernal politics which— Yes.

But now he must hide the Seal. If anyone found it, if anyone even suspected he possessed it, before the proper moment for its revelation, all Heaven would break loose. Ashmadai shivered. The window blinked open for him. He slipped out through a tear duct and flew with strong steady wing-strokes into the darkness.

The way to Barathum was long and devious. Too bad he couldn't simply transport himself there. But he'd have to be a mortal, and who wanted to live in constant danger of redemption? Let it suffice that he could go anywhere, at any speed, in the material spacetime continuum.

A few times horror flapped past, screaming. But he reached the dead plain unnoticed. The fire pained him even at a distance. He could not look into such anguish. But it gave enough light for him to find the rock he had prepared. Rolling it away, he disclosed a small hole where he laid the Seal and its rod. A moment he fluttered above, savoring the thunderbolt that it would make of him when the hour came. Then he pushed the stone back in place and fled.

It was safe. No one, not Lucifer himself, came near Barathum any more. Even if they did, they wouldn't suspect the Sigil wasn't still amidst the flames. It was eternally safe. Or would have been, except for the angelic cleverness of Ashmadai.

His laughter echoed all the way back to the office.

Having returned, he unlocked the door, settled himself behind his desk, and rang for the secretary. She hopped in. "All done, sir?" she asked.

"Yes. Take a letter."

"It s'ells fu'y here," she complained.

"Well, hm." Ashmadai sniffed. A distinct oxygen odor lingered in the air. "I was, ah, experimenting with a new system to increase production."

" 'Ore 'ainhul?"

"What? Oh, more painful, you mean. Quite. Quite." Ashmadai could not resist a little bragging, however indirect. He lit a fresh cigar and leaned back in his swivel chair. His tail snaked out through the hole in the seat and wagged. "I've made a fresh study of pain lately," he said. "There are some interesting angles."

"Oh?" The secretary sighed. She had planned to quit early. There was a tryout for the Worldly Follies this afternoon. So naturally her boss would keep her here, droning on about his latest hobbyhorse, till too late.

"Yes," said Ashmadai. "Consider the old Faustus method, for example. You know how it works, don't you? The mortal raises a demon, or is approached by a demon if he's been sinful enough to make that possible. The mortal trades his soul for some diabolic service. Have you ever thought where the really painful part lies? How the man is always and inherently cheated?"

"Unless he can 'iggle out o' the contract," said the secretary maliciously.

Ashmadai winced. "Well, yes. There have been such cases. One reason the method has lost favor. Though I'm sure a modern technique, using symbolic logic to draw up a truly unbreakable agreement, could be most useful, and if only the Moloch faction——Well. Let's assume the contract is fulfilled on both sides. Do you see how it remains infinitely unfair? Any service or services the mortal can demand are finite. Wealth, power, women, fame, are like dewdrops on a hot morning. The longest life is still a denumerable span of years. Whereas the bondage and torment he undergoes in exchange are infinite! Eternal! Do you see what pain there must be in realizing, too late, how he was swindled?"

"Yes, sir. 'at a'out this letter?"

"Then the . . . purely mythical . . . Reverse Faustus." Ashmadai chuckled. "An amusing bit of folklore. The demon summons a mortal, and offers to go into bondage in exchange for a service the man can do. Granted, this wouldn't be as rough on the mortal as the other way around. But still, the demon has all eternity. The service he gets is essential to some scheme which transcends time itself. Whereas the mortal can, by his very nature, only demand a finite payment. Any material wealth can be gotten for him by a snap of my fingers. If he wants me to be his slave for his lifespan, that's more troublesome, but still, his lifespan is necessarily finite, even if he orders me to prolong it. Physiology alone would bring him to mindlessness in a thousand years. So . . . I could shuttle in time as well as space, attending casually to his needs, and they are as nothing beside my own eternal occupations. Oh, the poor mortal!"

Ashmadai hooted his laughter and drummed hoofs on the floor.

"Yes, sir," said the secretary resignedly. "Now a'out that letter. . . ."

The Congress was scheduled for ten years hence—frantically soon, but Hell's politics had grown even sharper than Ashmadai admitted to Hobart Clipp. He was kept on the run, lining up delegates, bribing, threatening, wheedling, slandering, backstabbing. A few times, in deepest secrecy, he appealed to the better nature of certain devils. They were duly awed by such recklessness. If Ashmadai's rivals found out——

If they did? Ha! So much the better. They'd wait till the Congress to bring forth the shattering charge. And *that* would provide an ideal moment for Ashmadai to whip forth the Seal of Solomon.

And afterward, the defeated and disgraced Moloch faction . . . yes, something lingering and humorous must certainly be devised for them. Perhaps a spell in the Firepool itself. . . . Ashmadai grew so joyful with anticipation that he quite forgot the primary reason for the existence of Hell, to be found in the Catechism.

He had expected Hobart Clipp would die within a few years. But that tough old frame lasted a full decade. It was on the very eve of the Congress that Ashmadai, alone in his office preparing a speech for the opening session, heard the summons.

"What?" He blinked. "Anyone call?"

Ashmadai! Blast you, what kind of service do you call this?

For a moment, the demon couldn't remember. Then: "Oh, no!" he groaned. "Not now!"

If you don't come this instant, you good-for-nothing loafer, I shall report you to whatever passes for the Better Business Bureau!

Ashmadai gulped, spread his wings, and streaked Earthward. He had no choice. The contract itself was pulling him, his own name and ichor. Well, he thought resentfully, he'd take care of the miserable chore, whatever it was. ("Yes, yes, yes, stop yelling, you bag of bones, I'm on my way.") Afterward he could return to the same point in eternity and continue his preparations. But the dreary senile fool would probably demand something which took years to fulfill. Years more that Ashmadai must wait for his moment of glory. "Hold your horses, Clipp! Here I am. I came as fast as I could."

The room was magnificent with astronomical photographs, the Veil Nebula, the Andromeda Galaxy, as if it had windows opening on all space and time. The old man lay in his bed. A professional journal had fallen from one hand. He looked more than ever like a mummy, and his thin breast labored. But the eyes which sought Ashmadai were still a wicked blue.

"Ah. So." It was not his physical voice which spoke. "Barely in time. I might have expected that."

"I'm so sorry you're ill," said Ashmadai, hoping to soothe him into a reasonable request. "Are you certain this is the moment?"

"Oh, yes. Yes. Damfool doctor wanted to haul me off to a hospital. I knew better. I am not going to die with oxygen tubes up my nose and a bored nurse swabbing me off, for Galileo's sake! I felt the attack just now. Cheyne-Stokes breathing. Question of minutes."

"I perceive an attendant in the next room. Shall I rouse her?"

"No! What do I want with that fluffhead gaping at me? You and I have business to discuss, young fellow." Clipp stopped for a moment's great pain. But when it had passed, he actually cackled. "Heh! Yes, indeed. Business."

Ashmadai bowed. "At once, sir. I can restore your health to any level you desire. Shall we say, a twenty-year-old body?"

"Ohhh!" complained Clipp. "Do you seriously believe I am as stupid as you are? I shall certainly insist that you do not converse with me any more than strictly necessary. No. Listen. I have lived for my science. In a way I have died for it. Fell off the platform at the fifty-incher last week. I find no particular attraction in the idea of singing Hosannahs forever. Can't carry a tune in a basket. And I have no reason to believe myself booked for Hell——"

"No, you are not," admitted Ashmadai reluctantly. He shifted his feet, looked at his watch, and wondered how long this would continue.

"Good. Fine. I only desire to carry on my investigations. Now when I have—— Blast! What's the word? 'Die' seems inaccurate, when I have an immortal soul bound by no physical limitations, and I retch at unctuous euphemisms like 'pass on.' When I have shuffled off this mortal coil, I want you to take my soul, which I presume would otherwise go first to Purgatory and then to Heaven——"

"It would," admitted Ashmadai, while the body of Hobart Clipp struggled for breath.

"Yes. . . . Carry my soul along. You know the ways and methods, I presume, I wish to explore the material universe."

"What?"

"The entire cosmos." Clipp plucked feverishly at his blankets. "I don't want anything, including knowledge, handed me on a platter. I want to find out for myself. We can start by studying the interior of the Earth. Some interesting problems to be solved there, you know, core structure and magnetism and whatnot. Then the sun. I could happily spend a thousand years, I think, studying nuclear reactions under solar conditions, not to speak of the corona and sunspots. Then the planets. Then Alpha Centauri and its planets. And so on and on. Of course, cosmological questions will require us to shuttle a good deal in time also. . . ." His longing blazed so brightly that Ashmadai covered eyes with one wing-flap. "The metagalactic space-time universe! I cannot imagine myself ever losing interest in its origin, evolution, structure, its—yes—its destiny—"

"But that'll take a hundred billion years!" screamed Ashmadai.

Clipp gave him a toothless wolf's grin. "Ah, so? Before that time, probably entropy will be level, the stars exhausted, space will have expanded to its maximum radius, collapsed again and started re-expanding. A whole new cycle of creation will have begun."

"Yes," Ashmadai sobbed.

"Wonderful!" beamed Clipp. "A literally eternal research project, and no reports to file or grants to apply for!"

"But I have work to do!"

"Too bad," said Clipp unfeelingly. "Remember, I shall not want any of your idiotic conversation. You are nothing but my means of transport. Which puts me one up on Kepler. I wonder if perhaps he too, and—ah . . . ah . . ."

Ashmadai heard the Dark Angel approach, and fled outside. There he shrieked and cursed and demanded justice. He rolled on the ground and kicked it and beat it with his fists. Nobody answered. The hour was very early on a cool spring morning. Birds chattered, the young leaves rustled, heaven smiled. One might almost say that heaven leered.

Presently the soul of Hobart Clipp stepped briskly through the wall, looked around, and rubbed figurative hands. "Ah," he said, "thank goodness that's over. Messy business. Well, shall we go?"

TO GIVE THEM BEAUTY FOR ASHES

Burnt by a bomb in dissolving slaughter,
Evolving some, was Eve's strange daughter.
Adam's child by a boiling sea
Toiled with a wild
Fecundity.

Face-shape squared with four new graces;
Skin-shade faded from five old races.
Birthday-prone is the breeding Mutie,
Branded with bone-
Destroying beauty.

WINONA MCCLINTIC

JOEL TOWNSLEY ROGERS

No Matter Where You Go

I SIGHTED THE BOUNDARY OF SPACETIME with Henley ten billion light-years from Earth. Rippled and black as volcanic glass, it loomed in front of us in a huge endless curving wall.

The ship flew against it like a wind-blown midge, swirled side-long in the terrific vacuum torrents rushing around the inside surface of the sphere. In the dark blue void behind its spider-thread of contrail the white imploding outmost galaxies dropped away like slanting rain, vanishing far below.

We were beyond the farthest lost neutrino of any creation, the first or last stroke of any time. Yet for a moment as long as all the world, the wall seemed to remain equidistant, receding as we fled toward it, while I felt the ship emptied of all forward motion, like a child's toy rocket at the summit of its climb, on the sagging pin-point of a stall.

It was Henley's added burden which held it back, of course. Like all true spacecraft, though limitless in range and of infinite speed, it was designed for solo flight alone. A nightmare of ex-hausting effort all the way with him, plowing desperately through yielding sand with a Sindbad's Old-Man-of-the-Sea wrapped around my shoulders. Climbing up a sheer glass cliff without a handhold, forever and forever, dragging his dead weight.

I didn't even want him with me in the other world. Yet I had taken off with him aboard, in my frantic haste to escape a police inquiry and possible imprisonment, and I couldn't just open the door now and request him to jump out. I must carry him through with me, or return to an Earth without Gipsy. To the empty little cottage on Wildwood Lane and the whimpering beagle pup and the motionless noon shadows of the backyard garden, and her bodiless footprints on the grass at the edge of the Black Pool.

No more of that! I blanked out all those backward images. Un-relentingly I bore down on the space-bar: stepped up our thrust by gamma-to-nu power.

"The sky seems to have clouded up suddenly, Brock," Henley said idiotically. "Looks as if we're going to have a storm."

He was half-crouched above his seat, looking out.

"Huge black wall, covering the whole sky!" he exclaimed spas-modically, with his face abruptly startled. "I never saw anything like it! It's coming at us like a tornado!"

"Hold on to everything," I told him. "We're going through."

That final thrust of power had done it. I glimpsed our reflection in the wall's dark obsidian concavity rushing headlong at us. We hit it in that instant.

The ship seemed to be whirled around upside down in a tun-nel of soft rainbow fog. There were huge bright-colored bubbles floating all around us, imparting a feeling of no motion, though the rush of the stream was like a funneled hurricane. Then we were out beyond, in the other void, sprinkled with the red-dispers-ing galaxies of opposite space like far-blown chimney sparks.

"What happened, Brock?" Henley said bewilderedly, sagging into his seat. "I felt as if my bones were being pulled clear inside out for a moment. Where in thunder are we supposed to be now, anyway?"

All the traveling he had done had been one of the items about him which had impressed Gipsy. Rio, Durban, Bangkok, Delhi. Exotic names and far-off magic places to her—she had recited them to me in an entranced dream. But he'd never even been beyond

Earth's gravity before. He was farther from home than he could in the slightest comprehend.

"In the other bowl of the hourglass," I told him.

He had made an apparently quick recovery and adjustment. His momentarily dissolved features were back in shape again. He was settled down at ease in his yacht chair, weather-beaten gray suburban-squire weekend hat perched jauntily on his small white-haired head, plaid cashmere jacket, twenty-dollar shirt, long flanneled legs crossed, highball glass in hand. Picture of a man of distinction. Millionaire corporation lawyer, stock market plunger, Ivy League university trustee, consultant to the State Department, yachtsman, big-game hunter, amateur psychologist and criminologist in his spare time. See his biography in *Who's Who*.

With his lean height and assured manner of money and success, any woman might find him attractive, I could understand—romantic, glamorous, spiritual, whatever word she used for it—if he were young. But he was a long way from being young. His skin was blotched and wrinkled; he had a corded forehead, artificial teeth, and little tufts of hair in his ears. All the unesthetic marks of life's gray creeping years, the caterpillar years which men as well as insects must endure, though in opposite order. And he would never be any younger in this world.

"The other bowl of the hourglass?" he said with a lifted brow. "What's that?"

"The other half of Infinity," I explained.

"Really?" he said blankly. "How extraordinary!"

He was such an ignorant fool. He didn't know backwards from forwards. He didn't know a thing.

"That depends on how you look at it," I said. "From this side, the real world may seem extraordinary. At least I hope the voyage isn't too much for you, at your age. You aren't so young as you were, you know."

He gave a perfunctory laugh, as if I'd made some joke he didn't quite understand. "Sometimes when my bursitis is bothering me I'm inclined to feel that I'll never climb Everest or run a mile un-

der four," he said jocularly. "Don't be too concerned about my
aged and infirm carcass, though, Brock. Just how much longer before you expect to find Mrs. Brock?"

"In less than no time at all," I told him.

"That's fine," he said, looking at his wristwatch. "For a moment
I was afraid that you——"

He nodded a kind of half apology, as if taking back some of
the things he'd said. He didn't completely believe me, though,
even yet, I had the feeling. His faded eyes were examining the
cabin again unobtrusively but minutely, I knew, as if he still
halfway expected to find Gipsy hidden away somewhere inside
with us, though there was no place she could be at all.

Still more than halfway suspecting me of having murdered her
in a burst of crazy rage back there on Earth, ten billion years ago.
Me, who had wanted only to live the rest of my life with her. Who
could not bear to live without her, in the real world or this.

"The other half of the hourglass," he repeated. "Infinity! Do
you mean—?"

I set the controls at minus zero-zero, dead center of the universe
ahead. The ship had just fuel enough to make it. Past the point of
no return. . . .

Henley had surprised me crouching on the ship's doorsill after
my previous flight, straightening out the five-foot plank to solid
grass across the Black Pool.

"Mr. Brock?"

I held my breath, drifting my eyes around. It was my name, but
I didn't know where it had come from. I hadn't thought there was
anyone within a quarter mile, any nearer than the cretin Bibby
swarm in their tarpaper shack down where Wildwood Lane
petered out to swamp.

He was at the opening of the thick high hemlock hedge, at the
end of the rear garden path. All that look of elegance and superiority, as if he owned the place, or didn't give a damn who owned
it. He had a camera in his hands as if he had just shot a picture

of me and the ship. A bunch of big scarlet roses with stems wrapped in a newspaper cornucopia was tucked beneath his arm.

I'd never seen him before, but I knew who he was, of course. Ralph A. Henley, who owned the big new summer place over on the other side of the village, looking out over the sound. He'd moved in two months ago. Millionaire bachelor, aristocratic, cultured, everything. Only a lot older-looking than Gipsy had described him.

"That's right," I said, standing up, brushing my hair down with my palm, knowing I was about six weeks overdue for a haircut, and wishing I'd shaved and put on a necktie this morning. "Excuse my appearance. I just returned from a long tough voyage, and probably look a little ragged. What can I do for you?"

"My name's Henley," he said, walking toward the edge of the pool. "A friend of Mrs. Brock's. We've been commuting back and forth this summer on the same trains, I mean, and got acquainted. I just happened to be driving down this way, and thought I'd stop by to give her some new roses my gardener has developed. I've thought of naming them the Glorious Gipsy, as a matter of fact, with her permission."

"She'd be quite flattered, I imagine," I said. "She's mentioned you to me. Your offices are in the same building in Rockefeller Center where she has her lobby magazine stand, I believe. I understand you've been kind enough to take her out to lunch several times. I had an idea, in fact, that you've been picking her up in your car at the end of the lane to drive her to the station in the mornings, for the past couple of weeks, and bringing her back and letting her out there in the evenings. It's been thoughtful of you, and I appreciate it. She enjoys having her little job. She took it temporarily after we got married 'til I should finish my book and have more time to do things with her. It fills in the days for her and gives her a chance to meet all kinds of people. But of course the community is a little tiresome."

"I rather understand that she's had her job temporarily for twelve years or more, and that it's what supports you," he said pleasantly. "I imagine that it's a little more wearing on her than you seem to think. But perhaps we can find some time to discuss certain things. I'll just give her the roses, and be on my way."

"Watch out!" I said. "That stuff's bottomless!"

I hadn't expected him to try to come aboard without being invited. The plank was still a little askew. He hadn't bothered with it, though, giving a quick spring from the grass across the pool before I knew it. He landed on the doorsill, bending his head a little to come in.

"Welcome aboard the rocket," I said ironically, a little indignant and frightened by his careless jump.

"The rocket?" he said with a condescending smile.

"The spaceship, to be technical," I said. "It's not really a rocket, of course. But that seems to be the popular word for any supraterrestrial vehicle these days, whatever kind of propulsive power it has, and no matter how it's shaped. Pardon me if the cabin doesn't look too neat. I'm not used to having visitors."

"I'd forgotten you were a spaceman," he said. "Mrs. Brock told me. I remember now."

"If you'd only given me a couple of seconds, I'd have straightened out the plank and given you a hand up it, if you felt it necessary to come aboard," I said. "Do you know what that black stuff is you jumped over?"

"It looks like a rather gooey kind of mud," he said quizzically. "Bottomless, you said?"

"It may actually be only a few hundred feet deep," I said. "There's no way actually to plumb it. Still that's plenty deep enough if you had fallen into it. It's pure Infinitum, with zero gravity. You'd have sunk down in it quicker than a bullet, without a trace."

"Infinitum, really? I didn't know."

"That's what it is," I told him. "The pure unadulterated stuff. Probably the purest pool of it on Earth. Which means in the whole universe, since Earth is the only planet where it can be found at all, as you may know. I use it for fuel. Automatic tank underneath fills up while the ship hovers just a millionth of an inch above, as it's doing now. Nothing like it for speed and power, but it's got to be treated with respect."

"I suppose so," he said.

He had looked around the cabin, taking in my unmade bunk and big worm-eaten Elizabethan sea chest with a brass hinge broken. At least my closet door was closed, crammed with old clothes and junk. He laid his camera and roses down on the end of my control table. The roses were full-blown, their petals spread out on yellow hearts. The newspaper around their stems was the Drama and Garden section of yesterday's Sunday *Times*, I saw. Maybe he had brought it for her to read. They were both interested in flowers and the latest Broadway plays, as well as art and music and travel.

"I'll give the roses to Mrs. Brock," I said. "It's lucky I dropped back to pick up her dog for her. Ten minutes more, and you might have found me and the ship gone again. Did you happen to see the pup around the kitchen door or garden as you were coming out here?"

"What kind of pup?" he said.

"A bench-legged little beagle named Bugle Boy. Tricolor, with one brown ear and one white, and a black saddle. About thirteen years old. Mrs. Brock's had him since before we were married. Some older man who was in love with her gave him to her. The dog's never liked me, and I'd not care too much if I never saw him again, but I was afraid that before long she'd begin to miss him on the other side."

"I didn't see him."

"Probably out chasing squirrels down in the woods back of the Bibbys'," I said. "He's become quite a wanderer lately. You can't teach an old dog new tricks, as the saying goes, and a young dog doesn't need to be taught any of the bad ones. If he isn't around, maybe I'll make a trip back for him some other time."

He wasn't interested in me or my problems, though, standing with his hand clasped behind his back, looking around the cabin. He seemed to be waiting for something.

"Modern piece?" he said, nodding at my sea chest. "Novel idea.

Made of wood with wormholes in it. I don't remember ever seeing anything like it before. What do you use it for?"

"I keep my space charts in it," I said. "It's a lot heavier than a
steel or aluminum chest, of course, but it's sort of decorative. I
picked it up in a London antique shop, on the other side. It's supposed to have belonged to Drake."

He looked pleased with himself for being ignorant, like a lot
of rich big-shot men who went to Ivy League colleges and think
that anything they never heard of isn't worth knowing about.
Doesn't exist, in fact. He looked over the half dozen books on my
shelf with his smile.

"*Outline of History, 6000 B.C.–1900 A.D.*," he read the titles off.
"*World Almanac, 1958. The Age of Dinosaurs. When the Moon
Left the Earth.* I see you go in for the imaginative stuff, Brock.
Who is Browning?"

"He wrote 'Rabbi Ben Ezra'," I said. "The poem that begins,
'Grow old along with me! The best is yet to be!' But I suppose he
wouldn't make much sense to you."

"I'm afraid not," he said. "What a horrible thought! Who would
ever want to grow old with anybody? The trouble with too many
of these modern poets is that they take a delight in being incom-
prehensible. Why couldn't he have written it, 'Grow young along
with me,' and given the world a pleasant thought? But I suppose
that wouldn't be abstruse enough for literature."

He examined the printed placard I had thumbtacked on the
wall beside the shelf.

"I see you have a 'Litany of the Space Men'," he said. "'Question: What is hotter and brighter than the Sun? Answer:
A billion billion suns! Question: What is swifter than light? Answer: Thought! Question: What is vaster than Eternity? Answer:
It and its double!' You know, that thing is rather intriguing, Brock.
One hears it quoted all the time. I never met anybody who
claimed he could make any sense out of it, but it's caught the
fancy of the public, like some of these rock-and-roll songs. Do you
know who originated it, anyway?"

"I did," I said. "I submitted it to a greeting-card publisher, and he gave me a free card in return for it. He's sold quite a few greeting cards and office placards with it, I guess."

"He's probably sold a million, and netted about a hundred thousand dollars from it," Henley said. "It's obvious you're not much of a businessman, Brock. But you seem to have a flair for phrases. You ought to try getting yourself a job in something like advertising. Why not make the rounds of the big Madison Avenue agencies? That's where the money and success are to be found."

"I suppose so," I said. "But. . . ."

I let it dangle. He was thinking of Gipsy commuting five days a week to stand behind a counter selling cigarettes and magazines, I suppose, for years without a break, to pay the rent and keep the pot boiling. I didn't like it myself. But I had been born a spaceman, and I couldn't be anything else to the end of the chapter, although I had tried at various times to land almost any kind of a job. It was written in my look, I suppose, for any practical and successful down-to-earth man to see, that I didn't really belong. He saw it himself, treating me as if I was a little off the beam.

He still seemed to be waiting for something. "Maybe you'd like a drink before you go?" I said, not knowing just how I was going to get rid of him.

"Thanks," he said. "You've heard the paraphrase of your litany, I suppose, in Harewood's current highly successful murder play, *Time Must End*, on Broadway?"

I got down on my elbows and knees to fish out my bottle of bourbon from under the bunk, back in against the wall.

"I haven't any soda," I said, standing up with it. "Do you want to swig it from the bottle straight, or have it with some water in a glass? No, I haven't heard it. I don't go in for plays."

"With water in a glass, if you have one," he said. "It's in the final scene, just before the curtain. The murdering husband has been caught. The detective asks him your first question, 'What is hotter and brighter than the Sun?' And he answers, with hanging head, 'Jealousy!' The detective asks him your second question, 'What is swifter than light?' And he answers, shriveling in his chair, 'The enraged blow!' The detective asks him your final question, 'What is vaster than Eternity?' And he answers, sobbing, 'Death!' It's an effective bit. If you'd only copyrighted your non-sensical little gem, you might be able to nick Harewood for a nice chunk for plagiarism."

"I'm not much on nicking anybody," I said. "No spaceman is. I guess we just don't live on this Earth enough to be interested in business and money.

"Here we are."

I opened the closet door and got out the vacuum jug and plastic highball tumbler from the shelf above my hanging oilskins and windbreaker, while the garden tools and buckets and old boots and manuscripts and all the stuff that was piled waist-high on the floor spilled out around my feet. I poured out three or four fingers from the bottle, and added water from the jug. I pulled a pencil from my shirt pocket and gave a quick swizzle to the drink.

"I'd have one with you," I said, handing it to him, "but I've got to keep a clear head for my next trip. If the fool pup hasn't come home by the time the ship's fueled up again, I'm heading back for the other world to rejoin Mrs. Brock. I don't mean to rush you, though. Take time for your drink. You look as if you might need it. You don't look too well, as a matter of fact."

He had taken the highball in a numb wrinkled old hand. He stared at me, his lips trembling, his face like putty.

"What have you done with Mrs. Brock?" he said.

"Done with her?"

"I assumed she was beyond that door," he said. "I assumed that it was the door to a washroom or small bedroom cubicle into which she had retired just before I entered, to wash her eyes out or give her time to compose herself. I have been waiting for her to appear. But I see it's only a tiny cupboard, without space even for your trash. Get your senses together, if you have any! Wipe that stupid look from your face! Stop talking like a babbling lunatic! I want to know what you've done with your wife, Brock, and I want to know now!"

"I took her with me on my last voyage and left her on the other side; I thought I'd already told you," I said. "What business is she of yours?"

"You haven't taken her anywhere, Brock!" he said. "You couldn't have! Less than five minutes ago I got out of my car in front of your house, and saw her going along your rear garden path in her yellow blouse and Roman-striped skirt to the hemlock hedge around here. I came on back myself with the roses I had for her. At the break in the hedge I paused and got out my camera to snap a picture of her. She had taken a step up on the rickety narrow five-foot plank across the black ooze out there to the door here, in my finder. I snapped my picture and looked up, to see you squatting on the doorsill with your hand on the plank, and no sign of her. An interval of not more than five or ten seconds! That snapshot I made of her on the plank is developed by now. I will certainly show it to the police if necessary. Either that ooze is as quick and bottomless as you say, and you snatched the plank from under her, so that she fell into it and sank instantly before she could give a scream, or else she came on up and in through this door! Where is she? You can't have hidden her beneath the bunk. I watched you getting out your bottle, and she wasn't there. Against the wall back of the door?"

He seized the edge of the door and jerked it toward him. It swung around, shutting with a slam. But he could see she wasn't behind it. "This chest?" he said. He pulled open the ornate brass hasp of my sea chest, and swung its lid up against the wall on its broken hinge. But he could see that it was all filled to overflowing with hundreds and thousands of charts of different galaxy-clusters on thin transparent paper, and nothing else. He let it drop again.

"Where!" he said. "What have you done to her, and where have you hidden her? With your wild-eyed unshaven look and your lunatic blather about Infinitum and space voyages and other worlds? Is there some hidden trapdoor in the floor, through which you've thrown her down into the black ooze beneath? You can produce her alive and unharmed within sixty seconds, Brock, or I'll take you into custody by citizen's arrest, and drag you to the state police barracks, and you'll tell what you've done with her, strapped to a lie detector, beneath a bright light!"

I had collapsed into my chair at the control table with hands pressed to my face. If I could have done it any other way! If she were back here, to live on Earth with me the rest of our lives together. If I were half my present age, I twenty and she sixteen, if a thought of mine could wipe the intervening years away, how beautiful Earth might be.

But it couldn't be. Not now, when she'd met Henley. If she and I were younger by an age, he would be younger, too. He no longer withered, completely irresistible, full of vital charm. A younger Gipsy, even more impressionable, would fly into his embrace. It had to be the way I'd done it, and no other. But for a moment I wept dry tears for my lost youth, and hers.

"She told me yesterday that she wanted to leave me, Henley," I said behind my hands. "She made herself a drink, and came and sat on the floor beside me, leaning her head against my knee, while I was going over a chapter of my book. She's always been honest with me, she told me. She said that she was in love with you. That you were so tall and handsome, so cultured and poetic, so noble of soul. That's what she said. She didn't want to hurt me, she would always think kindly of me, but she felt that she had outgrown me, living in my own small world. Gipsy! Gipsy! My life and my love! I managed to stroke her hair and tell her it didn't matter, but I felt like a man dead, Henley. I thought it over all night long, and knew that I couldn't give her up. There was only one thing for me to do."

"Fifty! Forty-nine! Forty-eight!" Henley was counting down the seconds on his watch. "Forty-seven! Forty-six!"

"The ship was all fueled up," I said. "Enough for a voyage clear around the Figure 8 and back. I asked her this morning if she could come out to it at noon, that I wanted to show her something. She came up the plank and into the ship, Henley. I——"

"Thirty-three! Thirty-two!" he counted down.

"I asked her to sit down in that yacht chair there," I said. "I took off with her. To the space-time wall, ten billion light-years away, and through it. She never knew that anything had happened to her. She's all right, Henley. Over on the other side nobody ever knows it's not the real world, that's the beautiful part of it. They just forget, and go on living in their minus way, as if it was ordinary. Only I'd forgotten her dog, and came back for him——"

"Seventeen! Sixteen! Fifteen!" Henley was counting down. "Not a lot of seconds left to show me where she is, Brock, or be hauled down to have it sweated out of you!"

He would have done it, too. Crazy old guy, but rich and powerful. No telling how far he'd carry it. He might get me thrown into a padded cell, committed for the rest of my life. He might have my ship broken up and a match tossed into the Black Pool that would consume every atom of its priceless Infinitum as quick as thought, and the empty hole filled up with rocks. I'd never be able to get off the Earth again, nor even out of the barred windows of my cell.

"Sit down," I said. "I'll take you to her, Henley."

He had closed the door already. I didn't know whether he had knocked the plank off into the Black Pool, or whether it was still leaning against the edge of the sill outside, and I'd have to leave it tilted in emptiness. No time to think of anything on the Earth at all, nor ever again. I hadn't taken in enough fuel for a round trip yet, and this must be the end. I bore down on the space-bar, and gave it the gun with a thrust of gamma-to-nu power. We took off at infinite speed.

"Looks like a storm," Henley said, looking out the window as he sat down with his drink, his eyes lifted from his watch. "Huge black wall, coming at us like a tornado!"

But we were through then, with that final thrust.

"What happened, Brock? I felt as if my bones had been pulled clear inside out for an instant! My watch seems to have stopped. Where are we supposed to be now, anyway? The other bowl of the hourglass? The other half of . . ."

I saw something white stirring in the heavy-petaled roses that Henley had laid on the table end. A common white cabbage butterfly, stowed away, fanning its lazy wings. Three living things of us that had made the jump, not two.

Carefree insect, en route through Infinity! For the instant, with a dry grief, I envied it. It didn't need to contemplate, ever again, its dull crawling caterpillarhood, the dark cocoon and winter rains. All that behind it now, all the ugly wormlike half of its existence, and ahead of it only joy on gauzy wings in bright forever summer skies upon Earth, until its gay life should end in one last exultant sunward swoop and downward flutter, without its knowing. Far luckier than the roses it nestled among, beautiful and full-blown but now already past their prime, which had lost their hour of being young and perfect buds in Gipsy's bedroom flower bowl or in her hair, with only a browning and a withering for them soon, a shedding of their petals, and dead stems.

For Henley and me also. Even Gipsy. The withered time ahead, no more the buds, no more the dream of wings. Youth lost, and lost forever. Only the white butterfly didn't care. What is one's gain can only be another's loss, I thought. In both Eternities.

I was sorry I hadn't been able to bring Bugle Boy. She would miss him, certainly, and he would be desolate without her. When he returned from his roaming, he would whine and scratch and yelp at the kitchen door for her. Not answered, not let in, he would sit, sensing the emptiness of the house, with cocked head and wrinkled hound's brow. He would begin presently, perhaps, to cast around in circles for her scent, following her last trail along the garden flagstone between the irises to the hemlock hedge, and through it across the grass to the edge of the Black Pool, stretching empty and rippleless and intangible before him, with the spoor ended, no sign of her, not understanding in his dog brain where she had gone.

Whining back and forth between the house and the pool. For days and weeks, it might be, while his shadow grew smaller, and his voice high and thin. Until he tottered, sprawling on unsteady legs, his vision confused and dim, all memory of his devotion to her gone, his brain holding only old inherited instincts of his kind. Until his mother came for him, the great shadowy snuffing presence, the nuzzling teat, the dark womb which is the end of all. And so no more of his life and the dream.

And then quite suddenly I knew that Bugle Boy was here in the cabin. He had come bouncing up the plank while Henley was talking with me about my books and my Litany on the wall, following Gipsy's scent, and had crept away to hide under the bunk when he hadn't found her. I had brushed his nose with my fingertips when I was fishing around under the bunk for the bottle. I just hadn't been thinking of him.

That was a small relief. At least my trip back to Earth hadn't been completely wasted, even if it had compelled me to bring Henley along now on my return.

"The other half of Infinity?" Henley said, hoisting his drink reflectively, with his forehead wrinkled. "The Figure 8 you mentioned? I know the mathematical symbol for infinity, of course. It must have been what you were referring to, I realize when I think of it. Something like a Figure 8 lying on its side, or like an hourglass, I suppose. Two spheres linked together. But it's just an arbitrary sign, not a picture of the actual shape of anything, according to what I learned in college. I thought, in fact, that the Universe was supposed to be a closed sphere, if it had any limits. What do you have in mind, really, with your double talk?"

"A double sphere," I explained a little tiredly. "Plus and minus. Positive and negative. Imploding and exploding. Pro and anti. Obverse and reverse. Did you ever hear of a to without a fro, or a tick without a tock? It's so simple that I should think even a child would know it without being told! When you think of it at all, you can't help seeing that it has to be, or else everything would collapse instantly into a pinpoint, or fly endlessly apart."

"I see your idea," said Henley. "But how——?"

"When you reach the limit of whichever sphere you're in, if you've got the power to keep on going you go through into the other part," I said. "That's all there is to it. I've made the trip ten

thousand times myself. Sometimes it seems to me I've lived more
of my life in this universe than the real one. Don't worry your head
about it. Everything is just the same in it, but turned around.
You'll feel at home the moment we have landed."

We had passed a hundred million far-off galaxies like gale-
blown dying sparks. We were approaching the dead center of all
of minus space. Ahead in the blue-black void I saw the dim pinpoint of light appear, which I had set the automatic pilot on.

It came toward us, bursting like a Fourth of July rocket into a
Christmas tree of stars. It spread outward into a spiral galaxy of
ten million star-clusters, each one ten thousand suns.

The tides of space broke on its outer reefs from a million years
away. Then instantly it covered the whole sky, jeweled clouds
above and below like blazing diamond brooches, separated by
parsecs and ten thousand years, at the center a great dark core
shaped like a woman lying supine with bent legs and head pil-
lowed on her hair.

"What on Earth are all those stars?" Henley said in an awed
whisper.

"The Mirror Galaxy," I said.

"The Mirror Galaxy?"

"That's what I call it, anyway," I said. "It's the mirror of the real
Milky Way, which has a dark core shaped like that. The same
groups and constellations, only in reverse. We're in the mirror now
of our own Sun's local group, our own visible sky. You'll recognize some of them as they shoot by."

I had eased over a fraction, heading the ship down at a slant
toward the flat pancake-shaped cluster lying outward on the galaxy's left. The rest of it lay spread out far behind us like a plume.

"Why, yes, I rather see what you mean, Brock!" Henley said,
leaning forward to look out. "That monstrous whopping sun might
be Betelgeuse! And Rigel, Epsilon—it's Orion, only backwards,
from what I remember of my astronomy!"

He looked older and weaker, bent forward, almost shriveled.
The incredulous little smile at the corners of his mouth had flattened out.

"Cassiopeia upside down," he said, "on the wrong side of Polaris! The whole Dipper turned around! And those look like—Beta and Alpha Centauri—yes, a reverse image of Centaurus, rushing past us on the right! Why, Alpha is the nearest neighbor of the Sun! Only four or five light-years off. That must mean that the smaller star ahead of us is——"

"That's right," I said. "The mirror Sun ahead. We're in the mirror Solar System now, with all the mirror planets."

"Fantastic!" Henley said. "I never would have believed it! Neptune! Jupiter! But rotating counterclockwise! Why, that planet we're heading for is Earth! Only with the continents turned around! East for west, and the North Pole for the South! And turning backwards on its axis! We're as near to it as the Moon! We'll hit it in half a second!"

Just above the blue atmospheric envelope of the mirror Earth I cut the power and leveled off, coasting at only a couple of hundredths of C, to give Henley a look at it, which he had never had before. Not much more than a thousand miles up, no higher than a sputnik, and at a speed not more than a thousand times as fast, we drifted around the reversed planet for a good six seconds, dawn, morning, afternoon, and sunset, night and dawn again, while it turned on its axis a fortieth of a degree.

"Incredible!" said Henley. "Florida for California, and Japan where the British Isles should be!"

"That's the way things are in this world," I said. "Time and space both minus, negative, reverse. Mirror London is where I picked up my Drake sea chest. Browning lived there, who wrote that poem about 'Grow old along with me!' To everybody who lives on this earth, all the future is in the past, and all the past is in the future. What is old to us is the latest thing to them, and what's new and modern to us they call antiques. I suppose you could say that they live their lives backward, like insects."

"Like insects?"

"That's just a kind of comparison," I said. "I don't mean that they look or feel or think like insects. They look and seem just as human as everybody on the real Earth. But you know how insects begin their lives having wings, and end up caterpillars, while men and women start out being old and gray and crawling, and keep getting younger and more beautiful and gay. Well, in this world insects start out as caterpillars and end up butterflies, while men and women and dogs and cats start out being young, and get older. They keep on getting older until they die."

"What a horrible kind of life!" Henley said, looking old and shriveled in his chair.

He downed his highball with a shudder.

"Kind of horrible when you think about it," I said. "But it's what they're used to, and most of them don't have an idea there is a real world where things are different. And as soon as we land, you'll forget, yourself."

The ship was right above the reverse mirror image of New York City, reverse Long Island Sound, reverse Oldport, Connecticut, reverse Wildwood Lane, reverse mirror image of Gipsy's and my little shingle house, the back garden with the path down through it, the tall thick hemlock hedge around the grass plot around the Black Pool, smooth and empty-looking. I hit the zero key, and we settled instantly on the mirror of the pool, though it wasn't a pool of bottomless Infinitum on this earth, of course, but only skin-thin mud.

Henley stood up a little unsteadily.

"Your bourbon has some authority, I'll grant you, Brock," he said, picking up his bunch of fading roses and his camera from the end of the control table beside my machine. "What were those three or four keys you just hit on your typewriter? 'G, G to N power'. And a couple of spaces, and a zero. I thought maybe you were writing 'A quick brown fox jumps over the lazy dog' or 'Now is the time for all good men to come to the aid of the party.' But no time for that in half a second, even at the speed you click. You might at least have spelled out one short coherent word, though, like 'hell' or 'damn'. All right, let's have no more stalling! Where is Mrs. Brock?"

He reeled after me as I pulled the door open. Outside in the bright noon mirror sunlight, Gipsy stood in the opening of the hemlock hedge at the beginning of the path through the rear garden, paused on one foot and looking back, in her striped skirt and yellow blouse, with her red lips and black wind-blown hair, her gold earrings dangling. Only the hedge opening and garden path were to the left, not right.

"Aren't you coming, my poor bewildered Homer?" she said with gentle sympathy. "Lunch is ready. I thought you understood. What happened to the plank? Good heavens, you can jump that far, certainly! Only about four feet. I never knew such a helpless and inadequate man!

"Bugle Boy!" she exclaimed, crouching on her thighs, as the pup jumped from the sill behind me, sprawling off into the skin-deep mud, then leaping past me across the grass to her. "Were you in there? I didn't have an idea you'd followed me! Stop slobbering and waggling your tail off as if you hadn't seen me for twenty billion years, more or less! Down with your muddy paws! After all the years I've spent trying to train you, ever since you were an old, old dog—— What was I thinking of?" she laughed, rubbing him behind the ears. "What a silly way to talk to you, you funny little mutt! You're just a little puppy still, and we both know it. But someway I feel as if I'd had you a long time. Do you feel the same way about it?"

She looked up. Her face changed as she arose to her feet. It grew softly more beautiful. I had never seen her so beautiful and so young. Nor would I see her so young again as in this instant, for the backward Sun must turn, and the backward days and years must grow. Though always, in my memory, beautiful.

"Why, Ralph!" she exclaimed, her eyes like dark radiant stars beyond me. "However could you have come from Homer's little shack? I just came from it myself! He lured me down to it by telling me there was something he wanted to show me, but it was only that senseless 'Spacemen's Litany' about what is quicker than light and vaster than Eternity, and so on, which I've heard him recite at table, and sing in the shower, and mumble in his sleep, about ten thousand times, so I turned on my heels and left. We couldn't both have been there together! How did we pass? Will miracles never cease! Did you come to talk about us to poor Homer? It's all right. I talked to him myself last night. He understands."

Henley was extending his cornucopia of roses to her as awkwardly and shyly as a boy.

"Some new ones," he said. "I'd like to name them the Glorious Gipsy, if you'd not mind. They're beautiful full-blown this way, and even more beautiful in bud. But they're just a little faded, aren't they? I should have cut them fresher. Younger. In bud. I don't know what possessed me. I suppose I was a little confused at the thought of seeing you, and had some idiotic idea that they would grow into buds—I know I sound crazy. But you're the first. I'm not so very young—— I mean not so very old. What I mean is you're the first, the very, very first, and I love you, Gipsy!"

"They're lovely, anyway, Ralph," she said. "And wrapped in the Drama and Garden section of tomorrow's Sunday *Times!* I'm sure nobody else but you could have got it so soon. It's generally not on sale till evening. But you can do anything. The way you can get all the theater tickets impossible to obtain, tables in all the best restaurants, reservations on all the boats and planes. When we are married, traveling everywhere, seeing all kinds of strange far-off magic places—— Oh, Ralph!"

I could have been ten billion miles away and still ten billion more, back on Earth, for all they knew or cared.

"He's *old!*" I cried with breaking heart. "He's fifty-six years old, and he'll never be any younger in this world! We'll never have our own youth, Gipsy, but he won't ever be even as young as we are now! I'm only forty still in this world, and you're only thirty-six! There can be good years ahead for both of us together! But he's old already! You've got to realize what that means! Time moves backwards here! He's old, and he'll be getting older, older, older all the time!"

But she didn't care. She didn't even hear me. She had forgotten. Most people on this false mirror Earth have forgotten. Only I would weep for her and my lost youth, which we would never have.

The ship is getting pretty dilapidated now. It looks about like any small pine-board one-room shack such as artists or writers or inventors build in their backyards to be alone. Some of the roof shingles are off, and there's a rotted place in the floor. But if it only had the fuel, it could still fly at infinite speed to any place in either bowl of the hourglass or beyond. I'm spending all my time looking for a tankload of Infinitum now. It wouldn't have to be a whole bottomless pool. Even a gallon would do. Old man Mirror-Jack Bibby down in his tarpaper shack claims that you don't need Infinitum, that he can fly as far as anybody just with a jug of sour mash. But he's not right in the head, somewhere.

THROUGH TIME AND SPACE
WITH FERDINAND FEGHOOT

IT WAS FERDINAND FEGHOOT who discovered Yip Quong and persuaded him to move to the Thirty-Ninth Century.

"Mr. Yip," he informed the Time Travelers Club, "is the greatest natural psychokineticist in all history. He put every Chinese laundry in Milwaukee 1912 out of business. He hired no help. He needed no plant or equipment. He simply sat down before a mountain of dirty old laundry, and *wished* it all clean, ironed, sorted, and wrapped. He closed his eyes for a moment—and pop! it was done. In no time at all he'd made millions of dollars."

Old Dr. Gropius Volkswagen rose to his feet. "Then why is he here?" he demanded unpleasantly. "Why did he not stay where he was so happy and rich?"

"He was rich but not happy," Feghoot answered. "His fellow Chinese weren't at all fond of him. Some of them snubbed him completely, and none of them ever invited him anywhere."

"That is strange. The Chinese worshiped commercial success. Did he commit some unforgivable crime? Did he violate some precept of maybe Confucius?"

"Oh, no," said Ferdinand Feghoot. "It was nothing like that. It was just that they found him a little too wishy-washy."

GRENDEL BRIARTON

JANE RICE

The Willow Tree

WHEN THE FOUR O÷CHILDREN, Lucy, Robert, Charles, and May, were orphaned by a freak of circumstances they were sent to live in the Past with two spinster relatives, ostensibly because of crowded conditions elsewhere. In reality, their archaic given names had suggested this quick solution to the overburdened Time & Welfare worker in charge of their case. True, the two elderly ladies were a bit, well, *unusual*—but they were kindly enough, and offered a pleasant home.

The children were quite young and therefore accepted the sudden death of both parents as a termination rather than a separation. They were told by their temporary foster, a well meaning ancient who remembered "Ohio," that their mother and father had "passed away." The children knew better. Their mother and father had died and had been numbered and encapsulated. "Away" was the Past, where they were going.

They missed their parents but they were really more accustomed to each other and, in childhood, it is impossible to dwell for long on absences, or grieve over them. Their sense of loss was further diminished by the excitement of their own quick departure into the Past (a hand waved, the keep dollied slowly backwards, the stabilizer moved in, a robivac began to count, the threads of good-bye were severed by a blue slice of brightening light), and their subsequent arrival at their destination which appeared to have been set down in the middle of nowhere.

"This," Charles observed, importantly, taking in his surroundings, "is what was meant by 'country' when we were being synchronized at the Center."

"And 'isolation,'" Robert said. "We're 'isolated' in the 'country.'"

The children were charmed with the novel aspect of their environs and stared delightedly at their future home, a brooding old vine-shawled house which had mellowed into the untended landscape until it was scarcely visible from where they stood.

"Look," May exclaimed. "There's a truly pooskat!"

"Pussycat," Lucy corrected. "Use the proper obsoletes, May. Do you want the 'aunt' to think we're . . ." She paused, searching for the appropriate colloquialism.

"Lazyheads?" Charles conjectured.

"Headbones," Robert amended.

"*Bone*heads," Lucy sighed, full of her responsibilities as the eldest. "Pooskat, lazyheads, headbones. Mercy." She smoothed her "sash" and twitched May's "hair ribbon" straight. "Well, we can't stay stopspotted all day. Let's go. Okai?" She stepped forward, and the others followed.

Their Aunt Martha was a sweet faded shell of a woman who reminded Lucy of the fragile, white, transparent, moonsnow carvings that had decorated the Lunar exhibit at the Solar Fair. Her welcome was warm and enveloping, even though it was somewhat lopsided due to her habit of holding her head askew as if she were listening, or had strained a ligament in her neck.

"Oh, you've come . . . you've come," she kept murmuring over and over, bending from one to the other and touching them as if they were surprising flowers. "You've come at last."

Ushering them in to meet their other aunt in the shuttered library where she sat, slitting the pages of a book with an ivory cutter, their Aunt Martha's frail cadence was triumphant. "Harriet. The children are *here*."

"So I see, Sister," their Aunt Harriet said. "So I see." She nodded pleasantly at them across the clutter of volumes on the desk. "And I'll wager they're ready for tea. Eh?"

They chorused assent, and Lucy, remembering a lesson from *Mores of the Past*, appended, "Thank you," and, reaching out, grasped her Aunt Harriet's hand and shook it. It felt like a withered bouquet of knuckles, and Lucy decided that after this she would confine herself to the Past-custom of "the excuse-me."

"The children are ready for tea, Sister," their Aunt Harriet said. "The speculation arises, is the tea ready for the children?"

When their Aunt Martha had departed, in a fluster, their Aunt Harriet leaned back in her chair and addressed the children in her paper-dry voice.

Her sister, she informed them, was not herself, upon occasion. She was prone to have . . . ah . . . notions. (She made a vapid three-fingered gesture to and fro in front of her forehead to indicate both the vaporous quality and the location of her sister's malaise.) Sister was easily upset by trifles, and, consequently, they were not to trouble her *on any account whatsoever*. Was this perfectly clear?

The children bobbed their heads. They had heard of the peculiar affliction (pronounced Kok'tāls') which had plagued the Past-people.

They could have full freedom of the house and grounds, their aunt continued, with but a single exception.

She pushed herself to her feet and leveled a skinny forefinger at a pair of closed double doors under which seeped a saffron chink of late sunlight, as if she were indicating an object that lay somewhere beyond, outside in the waning afternoon.

"If you wish to remain here, in peace, you must not play under the willow tree," she said.

Since this regulation was not too different from somewhat similar bygone rules, such as their mother's habitual admonition to stay on their own side of the ramp, or the downtown signals intoning "Don't escalate," the children did not question it. In fact, they immediately felt more at home, and Robert, emboldened, pointed at a feather peeping from the volume whose pages she had been cutting.

"What kind of a feather is that?" he inquired.

For an instant, as his aunt's eyelids flicked, he had the queer impression that he ought not've asked. Maybe he ought've stuck on a "Yesm." Or not be pointing. Embarrassed, he ran the offending finger under an imaginary drip on the end of his nose.

However, extending her hand, his aunt extracted the feather and stroked it, half-smiling, as if recalling an amusing long-ago incident.

"A peacock's feather," she answered in a recollective tone. "I put it there as a bookmark, once upon a time."

"Do you have peacocks?" May wanted to know.

"Peacocks are extinct," Charles told her.

"Poo—pussycats are extinct, too," May said, "but we saw one, didn't we? A black one."

"At present, we have no peacocks," their aunt said. "Unlike willows, they are difficult to . . . raise."

"See?" Charles said to May. "I told you."

Their aunt held the feather out to Robert. "Would you like to have it?"

"Yesm," Robert said, taking the proffered gift. It felt dusty and stiff and, never having owned a peacock's feather before, he grew warm and shy, and, boylike, slipped it inside his "shirt."

"Do peacocks be extinct, Aunt?" May pressed, reluctant to concede.

"Nothing is ever quite what it seems to be," her aunt replied.

"See?" May said to Charles.

During their "tea," with "Sister," in the big funny old "kitchen," Robert removed the feather for a closer inspection. Had the children not been forewarned, Sister's reaction to this "trifle" would have dried the food in their mouths.

"*Where did you get that?*" she whispered, showing her teeth, her head cocked at an alarming angle. "The peacocks were destroyed. Destroyed! I thought if I destroyed the peacocks——"

She broke off, and snatched the feather from him, repeating, "Where did you get this? Tell me!"

But, even while he was explaining, she removed a stove lid from the range and thrust the feather into the glowing coals, holding it down with a long handled fork until it was consumed. When she returned to the table she was obviously shaken.

"Children," she breathed, her hands pressed against her throat, "listen to me. *You must never play under the willow tree.*"

"Yes, we know," Lucy said, in the soothing inflection their mother had used when one of the children had needed comforting.

Any lingering doubts they may have entertained concerning the nature of Sister's "notions" were quelled by her fits and starts of odd behavior within the first few weeks. There was the morning when she had come upon May's doll which May, playing "sewing machine," had used for a pincushion. There was the day she had found Charles' list of Past-curiosities that weren't extinct (toads 12, snakes 5, bats 6 pr., newts 9, owls 2, pussycats 1, lizards 23, spiders, flies, etc.) and had thought he was going to cook these things in a "recipe." And the day she had yanked a galloping Lucy off a frazzled broom she'd discovered and was using for a "cowboy." And the day she'd nearly had a faint when May, puzzling over an old tome she'd dredged up from the bottom of a bin in the storeroom, had asked her the meaning of a word. "What are you doing with a spelling book?" she had cried. "Where did you get it? Give it to me. Give it to me this minute!"

Once, through the banisters, they had watched her listening to the grandfather clock on the stair landing, her ear pressed flat against the empty and tickless case. Another day, when Charles had made a silly noise, she had come rushing, muzzy from her nap, believing she had heard a peacock's cry. Lucy had led her back to her bedroom, as if she, Lucy, were Sister, and Sister a child. "The peacocks are gone. All gone," Lucy had reassured her patiently. "The peacocks aren't here any more."

Aunt Martha—Sister—was constantly touching them, as if to convince herself that they were real children and not figments of a warped imagination. Sometimes she disappeared and was gone for hours, and sometimes she called to them frequently, apparently thinking they might have left, or hadn't come yet, or had gotten lost around a crook in Time, which she seemed to visualize as a sort of circle with a halftwist to it . . . like the Moebius Ride at the Solar Fair, Lucy thought. *Exactly* like the Moebius Ride, on which everything had been straight and turny, simultaneously, and where in spite of the fact that there was only one riding surface the riders had whizzed roundabout on two sides of it and yet nobody had been upside down. And May had gotten stomachy and their father had bought them each a stick of oxygen candy. Later, he had showed them the way the ride worked. He had given a narrow strip of paper a half twist and adhesed the ends. Then, with a penl he had drawn a continuous line down the middle of the looping strip to demonstrate how, without ever lifting the penl from the paper, the line could be made to somehow go over and under without ever going over and under at all. Except that it did! Charles had made a sing of it that went:

> The Moebius ride goes roundabout
> and over and under and inside out
> But, strange to say, there's just one side
> To the loopty loopty Moebius ride!

Funny, how dim the previous had become. Almost like a Sister-dream. Poor fuddled Sister.

They were fond of her, but gradually they drifted into the practice of avoiding her as much as they were able, and the trackless days flowed one into the other. By then, without having to be told, they had also learned not to bother their Aunt Harriet. Besides, she had a way of turning the points of words so that they sounded like riddles, which made what she said *hear* like it wasn't what she meant. "Today was tomorrow yesterday." What kind of an answer was that to the query, what day is today? "If wherever you are is here, is there here when you are there?" What could you make of a question like that? And she had two stock rejoinders for bulwarks. "Nothing is ever quite what it seems," and "Run along, now."

They had no intention of playing under the willow tree. There was such a plentitude of permissible territory to explore. The wild overgrown garden was a fascinating pathless wonderland with a snake hole by the toppled and moldering "sundial." There was the tumbled stone fence for a "fort," a shallow "pond" where they could "fish" and skip flat rocks and do wading. There were clover crowns and daisy chains to fashion, real clouds to watch, little sunning lizards to tickle with a grassblade, an "attic" for rainy days, trunks and drawers filled with musty treasures . . .

Yet, as the summer lengthened, the *idea* of the willow tree began to weigh on them. Somehow, the willow tree was always there.

They would be fishing contentedly in the pond and a yellow-green willow leaf, borne by a vagrant breeze, would drop on the still surface to float among the cloud reflections and the skimming dragonflies—a tiny t-tinsie reminder that they mustn't play under the willow tree. Or, trying to settle on where to have a "picnic," they would fall quiet thinking . . . anywhere, except under the willow tree. And, tiring of a game or a sham-battle or a chase and flopping down to consider what-to-do next they would think, *we must not go under the willow tree.*

Once, caught in an unexpected downpour and racing up to the house through the hard pelting rain the thought had struck them, like a four-pronged fork of lightning, *we could take shelter under the willow tree*—but Sister had come out on the back porch and had motioned to them to hurryhurryhurry and they had run on. Again, one breathlessly hot interminable day when the heat rose in shimmers everywhere, May had put their ruminations into words.

"I'll bet it's cool under the willow tree," she said, wiping her sweaty little face on her sleeve. "I'll bet it's *damned* cool."

"Let's——" Charles began.

"No," Lucy said, reeling in the beetle she had been flying at the end of a string. "You know it's a rule not to. And quit making up words, May. Use the ones we've got."

"I didn't make it up," May said. "It was in that old speller book Sister took away from me."

"What's it mean, then?"

"It means you get your mouth washed out with soap and water," May said.

"That doesn't seem very reasonable," Lucy said, not caring. It was too hot to care. She plopped her listless beetle in the shade of a toadstool and fanned him with a wilted dandelion.

"That's not the only thing around here that isn't very reasonable," Robert said, rolling over on his elbows to peer in the direction of the forbidden challenge, like a green spilling fountain, trailing its leafy curtain of stirring tendrils invitingly on the parched grass.

"I don't know what you three are going to do," Charles announced, "but I know what *I'm* going to do. Right this second."

They gazed at him, unbelieving. He *wouldn't* . . . no matter how cool it might be under the willow tree, he wouldn't *dare* . . .

"I'm going to go"—he grinned mischievously at them—"belly-whop in the pond," he finished. He sprinted off, shouting over his shoulder, "Last one in is a scarepoos!"

Thus, finally, like a fly in amber, the ? of the willow was imbedded in their minds. Always *there* . . . A dark fleck in the middle. The core. The one central spot. The focal point. The place. Until, one afternoon, engaged in a wild spontaneous game of follow-the-leader that had started in the ruined garden, they went streeling up the lane and over the fence and back again and around the arbor and into the barn and climb the ladder and jump from the loft and circle the pond and splash across and tag the well and duck under the sweep and leap the stump and whirl about to veer away down the slope and under the willow tree . . . almost without thinking, as if they had thought about it for so long that it had become the most familiar place of all.

When they emerged their faces were pale and sick. Lucy's hair lay plastered in damp rings against her brow and she was shivering. A trickle of blood oozed from Robert's lower lip where he had bitten it. May began to cry and Charles, burnt-eyed and white toothed, lifted a leaden arm and pointed at the house, where, from a downstairs window, their Aunt Harriet beckoned to them.

The children, having assembled in a line before their aunt in the library, waited like stones for her to speak. But she only sat, savoring their expressions, while the silence stretched longer and thinner and tauter to be broken at last by May who buried her tear-stained cheeks in Lucy's skirt and sobbed, "I want to go home . . . I want to go back home . . ."

Their aunt smiled as if at a witty joke. "Kindly control yourself, May, lest you disturb Sister, who does not like to remember that, by destroying the peacocks out of their Time, she inadvertently destroyed a rather large segment of continuity and warped the joining. Did you hear me, May? I said to control yourself, lest you disturb Sister. Sister——"

". . . *is hanging under the willow tree!*" May screamed.

"—especially does not like to be reminded that she is a ghost," their aunt said, equably.

"And you, you are an old w . . . *witch,*" Charles said in horror.

The truth having been concretized by words, the children backed away, backed, backed slowly away, and suddenly turned and fled. Looking like blurred photographs of themselves in the tarnished mirror in the hall, they ran past the curving staircase and the age-dimmed oil portraits and out the door that stood open to the fragrant late summer air. Across the splintery veranda and down the sagging steps they went, past the library where their Aunt Harriet, book in hand, watched them from the threshold of the great double door flung wide like shadowing wings behind her.

Past the garden they streaked, eyed by the cat, and down the slope, and, when Lucy began to untie her sash, May started to weep disconsolately, and Robert, hitching up his "belt," stopped and lifted her and carried her in his arms. Without a single backward glance they hastened on, and, simply because they could not stay and did not know what else to do, they all went under the willow tree.

"Where are the children?" Sister wanted to know from the threshold of the double doors where she stood tying on a fresh apron, her countenance still vague with sleep. "I can't find them anywhere. I've called and called. Have you seen them, Harriet?"

Harriet, seated on the garden bench, glanced up from the book she was reading. "Yes. And . . . no," she said.

"You either have or you haven't, Harriet. Why must you always be so, oh, roundabout. Do you know where they are?"

"Are? No. They . . . were . . . swinging under the willow tree."

"The willow tree," Sister said in a hushed, frightened tone that died on a caught breath, and was superseded by a perplexed expression. "Willow tree? What willow tree, Harriet? We have no willow tree." She rubbed her hand across her puckered brow as if to knead out a kink in her train of thought. "The children—" she began on a bewildered note and stopped, her puzzled eyes fixed on the mincing peacock whose furled plumes tip-tailed the gravel garden path. Her gaze grew hazy and questioning, then blank.

She gave her head a slight shake as though to clear it.

"We have no willow tree," she reiterated stubbornly.

Harriet inserted a slim forefinger between the pages of her book. "Then I must raise one, presently, to have it ready for them when they come."

"When who comes, dear?"

"The children, Sister."

"Oh. Oh, yes. Of course. It all seems . . ." She frowned, hunting for the correct word.

"Roundabout," said Harriet.

"Thank you," her sister said.

"Thank *you*," Harriet replied. She arose and strolled to the marble sundial where she consulted the slanting shadow of Time. The peacock, strutting ahead of her, quickened its promenade.

Stooping, Harriet retrieved a bright fallen feather and put it in her book to mark the place.

THROUGH TIME AND SPACE
WITH FERDINAND FEGHOOT: XIII

IT WAS FERDINAND FEGHOOT who, in 3312, first proved that fish were highly intelligent and that men could converse with them. He was accorded the honor of signing the ensuing Treaty of Peace, Amity, Commerce, and Navigation—which was also endorsed by an imposing elderly shark.

"I spent seventeen months eavesdropping on fish conversations and analyzing their language," he told reporters after the ceremony. "Then I slipped overboard with my skin-diving gear, and asked for their leader. They took me to the Generalissimo here, and I'll never forget my first sight of him, completely at ease in the lovely blue water, with that busy little fish hovering right by his head all the time. He received me most courteously in spite of my abominable accent. Why, he was so polite and so tactful that it was almost a week before I realized that he is as deaf as a post."

"But—how could he understand you?" asked the reporters.

"That's simple," said Ferdinand Feghoot. "The little fish is his herring aide."

GRENDEL BRIARTON

ALFRED BESTER

The Pi Man

How to say? How to write? When sometimes I can be fluent, even polished, and then, *reculer pour nieux sauter*, it takes hold of me. Push. Force. Compel. Sometimes

I

must

go

back

but

not

to

jump; no, not even to jump better. I have no control over self, speech, love, fate. I must compensate. Always.

But I try anyway.

Quae nocent docent. Translation follows: Things that injure, teach. I am injured and have hurt many. What have we learned? However. I wake up the morning of the biggest hurt of all wondering which house. Wealth, you understand. Damme! Mews cottage in London, villa in Rome, penthouse in New York, rancho in California. I awake. I look. Ah! Layout is familiar. Thus:

```
Bedroom        Foyer
        Bath            T
        Bath            e
            Living Room r
                        r
        Bedroom         a
        Kitchen         c
                        e
            T e r r a c e
```

Oh-oh! I am in penthouse in New York; but that bath-bath back-to-back. Pfui. All rhythm wrong. Balance off. Pattern painful. I telephone downstairs to janitor-mans. A that moment I lose my English. (You must understand I speak in all tongues. A goulash. I am compelled. Why? Ah!)

"*Pronto. Ecco mi, Signore Storm.* No. Forced to *parlato Italiano.* Wait. I call back in *cinque minuti.*"

Re infecta. Latin. The business being unfinished, I shower body, teeth, hairs, shave face, dry everything and try again. *Voila!* The English, she come. Back to invention of A. G. Bell ("Mr. Watson, come here, I need you."). On telephone I speak to janitor. Nice chap. Gets a job of work done in two twos.

"Hallo? Abraham Storm here, again. Yes. Right. Chap in the penthouse. Mr. Lundgren, be my personal rabbi and get some workmen up here this morning. I want those two baths converted into one. Yes. I'll leave five thousand dollars on top of the refrigerator. Thanks, Mr. Lundgren."

Wanted to wear grey flannel this morning, but had to put on the sharkskin. Damnation! African nationalism has queer side-effects. Went to the back bedroom (See diagram) and unlocked the door which was installed by National Safe Co. Inc. I went in.

Everything broadcasting beautifully. Up and down the electromagnetic spectrum. Visual off from ultraviolet and jamming toward the infrared. Ultra short wave screaming. Alpha, beta and gamma radiation hearty. And the interuptors innn tt errrrr up ppp ttttinggggg at random and comfortably. I am at peace. Christ Jesus! To know even a moment of peace!

I take subway to office in Wall Street. Chauffeur too dangerous; might become friendly. I don't dare have friends. Best of all, morning subway jam-packed, mass-packed; no patterns to adjust, no shiftings and compensatings required. Peace! I buy all morning papers; because of the patterns, you understand. Too many *Timeses* being read; I must read *Tribune* to balance pattern. Too many *Newses;* I read *Mirror.* &tc.

In subway car I catch a glimpse of an eye; narrow, bleak, gray-blue, the possession of an anonymous man who conveys the conviction that you've never seen him before and will never again. But I picked up that glance and it rang a bell in the back of my mind. He knew it. He saw the flash in my eye before I could conceal it. So I was being tailed again? But by whom? U.S.A.? U.S.S.R.? Matoids?

I blasted out of the subway at City Hall and gave them a false trail to the Woolworth Building, in case they were operating double-tails. The whole theory of the hunters and the hunted is not to avoid being spotted . . . no one can escape that . . . but to lay so many trails for them to follow that they become overextended. Then they're forced to abandon you. They have so many men for so many operations. It's a question of diminishing returns.

City Hall traffic was out of sync (as it always is) and I had to walk on the hot side of the street to compensate. Took elevator up to 10th floor of bldg. There I was suddenly seized by something from sss ome wwwhh ere. SS—ommme tth inggg b addd. I began to cry, but no help. An elderly clerk emerge from office wearing alpaca coat, carry papers, gold spectacles.

"Not him," I plead with nowhere. "Nice mans. Not him. Please."

But I am force. Approach. Two blows; neck and gut. Down he go, writhing. I trample spectacles. Remove watch from pocket and smash. Shatter pens. Tear papers. Then I am permitted to get back into elevator and go downstairs again. It was ten-thirty. I was late. Damned inconvenient. Took taxi to 99 Wall Street.

Tipped driver ten dollars. Sealed one thousand in envelope (secretly) and sent driver back to bldg to find and give to clerk.

Routine morning's work in office. Market jumpy; big board hectic; hell to balance and compensate, even though I know the patterns of money. I am behind by the sum of $109,872.43 by eleven-thirty; but, *a pas de géant* the patterns put me ahead $57,075.94 by half-past twelve o'clock noon, Daylight Saving Time, which my father used to call Woodrow Wilson time.

57075 makes nice pattern, but that 94¢. Pfui. Made the whole balance sheet look lopsided, ugly. Symmetry above all else. Only 24¢ in my pocket. Called secretary, borrowed 70¢ from her and threw sum total out window. Felt better as I watched it chime down to the street, but then I caught her looking at me with surprise and delight. Very bad. Very dangerous. Fired girl on the spot.

"But why, Mr. Storm? Why?" she asked, trying not to cry. Darling little thing. Freckled face and saucy, but not so saucy now.

"Because you're beginning to like me."

"What's the harm in that?"

"When I hired you I warned you not to like me."

"I thought you were kidding."

"I wasn't. Out you go. Beat it."

"But why?"

"I'm afraid I might start liking you."

"Is this a new kind of pass?" she asked.

"God forbid."

"Well, you don't have to fire me," she flared. "I hate you."

"Good. Then I can go to bed with you."

She turned crimson and opened her mouth to denounce me, the while her eyes twinkled at the corners. A darling girl. I could not endanger her. I put her into her hat and coat, gave her a year's salary for a bonus, and threw her out. *Punkt.* Made memo: Hire nothing but men, preferably married, misanthropic and murderous. Men who could hate me.

So, lunch. Went to nicely balanced restaurant. Tables attached to floor. No moving them. All chairs filled by patrons. Nice pattern. No need for me to compensate and adjust. Ordered nicely patterned luncheon for self:

Martini   Martini

Martini

Croque M'sieur Roquefort

Salad

Coffee

But so much sugar being consumed in restaurant, I had to take my coffee black, which I dislike. However, still a nice pattern. Balanced.

$X^2 + X + 41 =$ prime number. Excuse, please. Sometimes I'm in control and see what compensating must be done. Other times it's forced on me from God only knows where or why. Then I must do what I'm compelled to do, blindly, like speaking the gibberish I speak; sometimes hating it, like the clerk in the Woolworth Building. Anyway, the equation breaks down when x=40.

The afternoon was quiet. For a moment I thought I might be forced to leave for Rome (Italy), but something adjusted without needing me. The A.S.P.C.A. finally caught up with me for beating my dog to death, but I'd contributed $10,000 to their Shelter. Got off with a shaking of heads. I penciled moustaches on posters, rescued a drowning kitten, saved a woman from a mugging, and had my head shaved. Normal day.

In the evening to the ballet to relax with all the beautiful patterns, balanced, peaceful, soothing. Then I take deep breath, quash my nausea, and force myself to go to *Le Bitnique,* the Beatnik joint. I hate *Le Bitnique,* but I need a woman and I must go where I hate That freckled girl I fire . . . so slender and full of delicious mischief, and making eyes at me. So, *poisson d'avril,* I advance myself to *Le Bitnique.*

Chaos. Blackness. Sounds and smells a cacaphony. One 25 watt bulb in ceiling. One maladroit pianist play Progressive. Against L.

wall sit beatnik boys, wearing berets, black glasses, and pubic beards, playing chess. Against R. wall is bar and beatnik girls with brown paper bags under arms containing toilet articles. They are shuffling and manuevering for a pad for the night.

Those Beatnik girls! All skinny . . . exciting to me tonight because too many American men dream about over-stuffed women, and I must compensate. (In England I like over-stuff because England like women skinny.) All wear tight slack, loose sweater, Brigitte Bardot hair, Italian make-up . . . black eye, white lip . . . and when they walk they make with the gait that flipped that Herrick cat three centuries ago when he split and wrote:

> *Next, when I lift mine eyes and see*
> *That brave vibration each way free;*
> *Oh how that glittering taketh me!*

I pick one who glitter. I talk. She insult. I insult back and bug drinks. She drink and insult[2]. I hope she is lesbian and insult[3]. She snarl and hate, but helpless. No pad for tonight. The pathetic brown paper bag under her arm. I quell sympathy and hate back. She does not bathe. Her thinking patterns are jangles. Safe. No harm can come to her. I take her home to seduce by mutual contempt. And in living room (see diagram) sits slender little freckly-face secretary, recently fired, now waiting for me.

!

I

now

write

part of

s   p

t   a

o   r

r   i

y   in   s

Capital of France

Address: 49b is Avenue Hoche. Paris, 8eme, France.

Forced to go there by what happened in Singapore, you understand. It needed extreme compensation and adjustment. Almost, for a moment, I thought I would have to attack the conductor of the *Opéra Comique,* but fate was kind and let me off with nothing worse than indecent exposure under the *Petite Carousel.* And I was able to found a scholarship at the Sorbonne before I was taken away.

Anyway, she sat there, my little one, in my penthouse now with one (1) bathroom, and $1,997.00 change on top of the refrigerator. Ugh! Throw $6.00 out window and am soothed by lovely 1991 remaining. She sat there, wearing a basic black cocktail dress with tight skirt, sheer black stockings, black opera pumps. The freckly skin gleamed reddish rose from embarrassment. Also red for danger. Her saucy face was very tight from the daring thing she thought she was doing. Dammel I like that.

I also like the nice even curve of the legs, and the bosom. Balanced, you understand? ❋ ❋ Like so; but not too thrusting. Tactful. Also her cleavage.) (Like so; and just as rosy as her face, despite desperate powdering to make her skin milky. That powder; a nuisance. I go to kitchen and rub burnt cork on shirt-front to compensate.

"Oh-so," I say. "Me-fella be ve'y happy ask why you-fella chop-chop invade along my apa'tment. Excep' mus' now speak pidgin-English. Ve'y much embarrass along me. Excuse, please, until change come."

"I bribed Mr. Lundgren," she blurted. "I told him you needed important papers from your office."

"Entschuldigen Sie, bitte. Meine pidgin haben sich geaendert. Sprachen Sie Deutsch?"

"No."

"Dann warte ich."

The beatnik turned on her heel and bounced out, her brave vibration each way freee. I caught up with her in front of the elevator, put 101 (perfect pattern) into her hand and said good night in Spanish. She hated me. I did a naughty thing to her ❋ ❋

(no excuse) and returned to the apartment when my American-English returned to me.

"What's she got?" the Freckle ask.

"What's your name?" I indict.

"My God! I've been working in your office for three months. You don't know my name? You really don't?"

"No, and I don't want to know it now."

"I'm Lizzie Chalmers."

"Go away, Lizzie Chalmers."

"So that's why you always called me 'Miss.' Why did you shave your head?"

"Trouble in Vienna."

"It's chic," she said judgematically, "but I don't know. You remind me of a movie star I loathe. What do you mean, trouble in Vienna?"

"None of your business. What are you doing here? What do you want from me?"

"You," she said, blushing fiery.

"Will you, for God's sake, go away!"

"What did she have that I don't?" Lizzie Chalmers demanded. Then her face crinkled. "Don't? Is that right? What. Did. She. Have. That. I. Do. Not. Yes, right. I'm going to Bennington. They're strong on aggression, but weak on grammar."

"What do you mean, you're going to Bennington?"

"Why, it's a college. I thought everybody knew."

"But *going*?"

"I'm in my junior year. They drive you out with whips to acquire practical experience in your field."

"What's your field?"

"It used to be economics. Now it's you. How old are you?"

"One hundred and nine thousand eight hundred and seventy-two."

"Oh, come on! Forty?"

"Thirty."

"No! Really?" She nodded contentedly. "That makes ten years difference between us. Just right."

"Are you in love with me, Lizzie?"

"Well, I'm trying to get something going."

"Does it have to be me?"

"I know it sounds like a notion." She lowered her eyes. "And I suppose women are always throwing themselves at you."

"Not always."

"What are you, blasé, or something? I mean . . . I know I'm not staggering, but I'm not exactly repulsive."

"You're lovely."

"Then why don't you touch me?"

"I'm trying to protect you."

"I can protect myself when the time comes."

"The time is now, Lizzie."

"The least you could do is offend me the way you did that girl in front of the elevator."

"You snooped?"

"Sure I snooped. You didn't expect me to sit here on my hands, did you? I've got my man to take care of."

"*Your* man?"

"It happens," she said in a low voice. "I never believed it, but it happens. You fall in and out of love, and each time you think it's for real and forever. And then you meet somebody and it isn't a question of love any more. You just know he's your man, and you're stuck. I'm stuck."

She raised her eyes and looked at me . . . violet eyes, full of youth and determination and tenderness, and yet older than twenty years . . . much older. And I knew how lonely I was, never daring to love, always compelled to live with those I hated. I could fall into those violet eyes and never come up.

"I'm going to shock you," I said. I looked at the clock. 1:30 A.M. A quiet time. Please God the American tongue would stay with me a while longer. I took off my jacket and shirt and showed her my back, cross-hatched with scars. Lizzie gasped.

"Self-inflicted," I told her. "Because I permitted myself to like a man and become friendly with him. This is the price I paid, and I was lucky. Now wait here."

I went into the master bedroom where my heart's shame was embalmed in a silver case hidden in the righthand drawer of my desk. I brought it to the living room. Lizzie watched me with great eyes.

"Five years ago a girl fell in love with me," I told her. "A girl like you. I was lonely then, as always. Instead of protecting her from myself, I indulged myself. Now I want to show you the price *she* paid. You'll loathe me for this but I must show you . . ."

A flash caught my eye. Lights in a building down the street going on. I leaped to the window and stared. The lights in the building three down from me went off . . . five seconds eclipse . . . then on. It happened to the building two down, and then to the one next door. The girl came to my side and took my arm. She trembled slightly.

"What is it?" she asked. "What's the matter?"

"Wait," I said.

The lights in my apartment went out for five seconds and then came on again.

"They've located me," I told her.

"They? Located?"

"They've spotted my broadcasts by d/f."

"What's D. F.?"

"Direction-finder. Then they turned off the current in each building in the neighborhood for five seconds . . . building by building . . . until the broadcast stopped. Now they know I'm in this house, but they don't know which apartment." I put on my shirt and jacket. "Good night, Lizzie. I wish I could kiss you."

She clamped her arms around my neck and gave me a smacking kiss; all warmth, all velvet, all giving. I tried to push her away.

"You're a spy," she said. "I'll go to the chair with you."

"I wish to Heaven I were a spy," I said. "Good-by, my dearest love. Remember me."

Soyez ferme. A great mistake letting that slip. It happen, I think, because my American slip, too. Suddenly talk jumble again. As I run out, the little devil kick off opera pumps and rip slit in cocktail skirt up to thigh so she can run. She is alongside me going down the fire stairs to the garage in basement. I hit her to stop, and swear at her. She hit back and swear worse, all the time laughing and crying. I love her for it. Damnation! She is doomed.

We get into car, Aston-Martin, but with left-hand drive, and speed west on Fifty-third Street, east on Fifty-fourth Street, and north on First Avenue. I am making for Fifty-ninth Street bridge to get off Manhattan island. I own plane in Babylon, Long Island, which is always ready for this sort of awkwardness.

"*J'y suis, J'y reste* is not my motto," I tell Elizabeth Chalmers, whose French is as uncertain as her grammar . . . an endearing weakness. "Once they trapped me in London at post office. I received mail at General Delivery. They sent me a blank letter in a red envelope, and that's how they followed me to 139 Piccadilly, London W.1. Telephone Mayfair 7211. Red for danger. Is your skin red all over?"

"It's not red!" she said indignantly.

"I meant rosy."

"Only where the freckles merge," she said. "What is all this escape? Why do you talk so funny, and act so peculiar? Are you sure you're not a spy?"

"Only positive."

"Are you a being from another world who came on an Unidentified Flying Object?"

"Would that horrify you?"

"Yes, if it meant we couldn't make love."

"What about conquering earth?"

"I'm only interested in conquering you."

"I am not and have never been a being from another world who came on an Unidentified Flying Object."

"Then what are you?"

"A compensator."

"What's that?"

"Do you know dictionary of Misters Funk & Wagnalls? Edited by Frank H. Vizetelly, Litt.D., LL.D.? I quote: One who or that which compensates, as a device for neutralizing the influence of local attraction upon a compass-needle or an automatic apparatus for equalizing the pressure of gas in the— Damn!"

Litt.D. Frank H. Vizetelly does not use that bad word. Is my own because roadblock now faces me on Fifty-ninth Street bridge. Should have anticipated. Should have felt patterns, but too swept up with this darling girl. Probably there are roadblocks on all bridges and tunnels leading out of this $24 island. Could drive off bridge but might harm my angelic Elizabeth Chalmers which would make me a *brute figura* as well as sadden me beyond redemption. So. Stop car. Surrender.

"*Kammerade*," I pronounce, and ask: "Who you? Ku Klux Klan?"

Hard-faced mans say no.

"White Supremacists of the World, Inc.?"

No agains. I feel better. Always nasty when captured by lunatic fringes looking for figureheads.

"U.S.S.R.?"

He stare, then speak. "Special Agent Krimms from the FBI," and show his badge. I enthuse and embrace him in gratitude. FBI is salvation. He recoil and wonder if I am fairy. I don't care. I kiss Elizabeth Chalmers and she open mouth under mine to mutter: "Admit nothing; deny everything. I've got a lawyer."

Brilliant lights in the office in Foley Square. The chairs are placed just so; the shadows arranged just so. I have been through this so often before. The anonymous man with the bleak eyes from the subway this morning is questioning me. His name is S. I. Dolan. We exchange a glance. His says: I goofed this morning. Mine says: So did I. We respect each other, and then the grilling starts.

"Your name is Abraham Mason Storm?"

"The nickname is 'Base.' "

"Born December 25?"

"I was a Christmas baby."

"1929?"

"I was a depression baby."

"You seem pretty jaunty."

"Gallows humor, S. I. Dolan. Despair. I know you'll never convict me of anything, and I'm desperate."

"Very funny."

"Very tragic. I want to be convicted . . . but it's hopeless."

"Home town San Francisco?"

"Yes."

"Grand High School. Two years at Berkeley. Four years in the Navy. Finished at Berkeley. Majored in statistics."

"Yes. Hundred per cent American boy."

"Present occupation, financier?"

"Yes."

"Offices in New York, Rome, Paris, London?"

"Also Rio."

"Known assets from bank deposits, stock and bond holdings, three million dollars?"

"No, no, no!" I was agonized. "Three million, three hundred and thirty-three thousand, three hundred and thirty-three dollars and thirty-three cents."

"Three million dollars," Dolan insisted. "In round numbers."

"There are no round numbers; there are only patterns."

"Storm, what the hell are you up to?"

"Convict me," I pleaded. "I want to go to the chair and get this over with."

"What are you talking about?"

"You ask and I'll explain."

"What are you broadcasting from your apartment?"

"Which apartment? I broadcast from all of them."

"In New York. We can't break the code."

"There is no code; only randomness."

"Only what?"

"Only peace, Dolan."

"Peace!"

"I've been through this so often before. In Geneva, Berlin, London, Rio. Will you let me explain it my own way, and for God's sake trap me if you can?"

"Go ahead."

I took a breath. It's always so difficult. You have to do it with metaphore. But it was 3:00 A.M. and my American would hold for a while. "Do you like to dance?"

"What the hell . . . ?"

"Be patient. I'm explaining. Do you like to dance?"

"Yes."

"What's the pleasure of dancing? It's a man and woman making rhythms together . . . patterns. Balancing, anticipating, following, leading, co-operating. Yes?"

"So?"

"And parades. Do you like parades? Masses of men and women co-operating to make patterns. Why is war a time of joy for a country, although nobody admits it? Because it's an entire people co-operating, balancing and sacrificing to make a big pattern. Yes?"

"Now wait a minute, Storm . . ."

"Just listen, Dolan. I'm sensitive to patterns . . . more than dancing or parades or war; far more. More than the 2/4 pattern of day and night, or the 4/4 pattern of the seasons . . . far, far more. I'm sensitive to the patterns of the whole spectrum of the universe . . . sight and sound, gamma rays, groupings of peoples, acts of hostility and benign charity, cruelties and kindnesses, the music of the spheres . . . and I'm forced to compensate. Always."

"Compensate?"

"Yes. If a child falls and hurts itself, the mother kisses it. Agreed? That's compensation. It restores a pattern. If a man beats a horse, you beat him. Yes? Pattern again. If a beggar wrings too much sympathy from you, you want to kick him, don't you? More compensation. The husband unfaithful to the wife is never more kind to her. All wives know that pattern, and dread it. What is sportsmanship but a compensating pattern to off-set the embarrassment of winning or losing? Do not the murderer and murderee seek each other to fulfill their patterns?

"Multiply that by infinity and you have me. I have to kiss and kick. I'm driven. Compelled. I don't know how to name my com-

pulsion. They call Extra Sensory Perception, Psi. What do you call
Extra Pattern Perception? Pi?"

"Pie? What pie?"

"Sixteenth letter of the Greek alphabet. It designates the rela-
tion of the circumference of a circle to its diameter. 3.14159+.
The series goes on endlessly. It is transcendental and can never be
resolved into a finite pattern; and it's agony to me . . . like pi in
printing, which means jumbled and confused type, without order
or pattern."

"What the hell are you talking about?"

"I'm talking about patterns; order in the universe. I'm compelled to keep it and restore it. Sometimes I'm compelled to do
wonderful and generous things; other times I'm forced to do insane things . . . talk garbage languages, go to strange places,
perform abominable acts . . . because patterns which I can't perceive demand adjustment."

"What abominable acts?"

"You can pry and I can confess, but it won't do any good. The
patterns won't permit me to be convicted. They won't let me end.
People refuse to testify. Facts will not give evidence. What is done
becomes undone. Harm is transformed into good."

"Storm, I swear you're crazy."

"Maybe, but you won't be able to get me committed to an asy-
lum. It's been tried before. I even tried committing myself. It
didn't work."

"What about those broadcasts?"

"We're flooded with wave emissions, quanta, particles, and I'm
sensitive to them, too; but they're too garbled to shape into patterns. They have to be neutralized. So I broadcast an anti-pattern
to jam them and get a little peace."

"Are you claiming to be a Superman?"

"No. Never. I'm just the man *Simple Simon* met."

"Don't clown."

"I'm not clowning. Don't you remember the jingle? *Simple
Simon met a pieman, going to the fair* . . . ? For Pee-eye-ee-man,
read Pee-eye-man. I'm the Pi Man."

Dolan scowled. At last he said: "My full name is Simon Ignatius Dolan."

"I'm sorry. I didn't know. Nothing personal implied."

He glared at me, then threw my dossier down. He sighed and slumped into a chair. That made the pattern wrong and I had to shift. He cocked an eye at me.

"Pi Man," I explained.

"All right," he said. "We can't hold you."

"They all try," I said, "but they never can."

"Who try?"

"Governments, thinking I'm in espionage; police, wanting to know why I'm involved with so many people in such cockeyed ways; politicos in exile hoping I'll finance a counterrevolution; fanatics, dreaming I'm their rich messiah; lunatic fringes; religious sects; flat-worlders; Forteans . . . They all track me down, hoping they can use me. Nobody can. I'm part of something much bigger. I think maybe we all are, only I'm the first to be aware of it."

"Off the record, what's this about abominable acts?"

I took a breath. "That's why I can't have friends. Or a girl. Sometimes things get so bad somewhere that I have to make frightful sacrifices to restore the pattern. I must destroy something I love. I—— There was a dog I loved. A Labrador retriever . . . I don't like to think about him. I had a girl once. She loved me. And I— And a guy in the navy with me. He—— I don't want to talk about it."

"Chicken, all of a sudden?"

"No, damn you; I'm accursed! Because some of the patterns I must adjust to are out-world rhythms . . . like nothing you ever felt on earth. 29/51 . . . 108/303 . . . tempi like that. What are you staring at? You don't think that can be terrifying? Beat a 7/5 tempo for me."

"I don't know music."

"This has nothing to do with music. Try to beat five with one hand and seven with the other, and make them come out even. Then you'll understand the complexity and terror of those strange patterns that are coming to me. From where? I don't know. It's

an unknown universe, too big to comprehend; but I have to beat
the tempi of its patterns and make them come out even . . . with
my actions, reactions, emotions, senses, while those giant pres-
sures

push

and reverse me

back

and turn me

forth   inside

and   out

back . . ."

"The other arm now," Elizabeth said firmly. "Lift."

I am on my bed, me. Thinking upheaved again. Half ($\frac{1}{2}$) into
pajamas; other half ($\frac{1}{2}$) being wrestled by freckly girl. I lift. She
yank. Pajamas now on, and it's my turn to blush. They raise me
prudish in San Francisco.

"*Om mani padme hum,*" I said. "Translation follows: Oh, the
jewel in the lotus. Meaning you. What happened?"

"You passed out," she said. "Keeled over. Mr. Dolan had to let
you go. Mr. Lundgren helped carry you into the apartment. How
much should I give him?"

"*Cinque lire. No. Parla Italiano, gentile Signorina?*"

"Mr. Dolan told me what you told him. Is that your patterns
again?"

"*Si.*" I nod and wait. After stop-overs in Greece and Portugal,
American-English finally returns to me. "Why don't you get the
hell out of here while the getting's good, Lizzie Chalmers?"

"I'm still stuck," she said. "Get into bed . . . and make room
for me."

"No."

"Yes. You can marry me later."

"Where's the silver case?"

"Down the incinerator."

"Do you know what was in it?"

"I know what was in it."

"And you're still here?"

"It was monstrous, what you did. Monstrous!" The saucy little face was streaked with mascara. She had been crying. "Where is she now?"

"I don't know. The checks go out every quarter to a number-account in Switzerland. I don't want to know. How much can the heart endure?"

"I think I'm going to find out," she said. She put out the lights. In the darkness came the sound of rustling clothes. Never before have I heard the music of one I love undressing for me . . . for me. I make one last attempt to save this beloved.

"I love you," I said, "and you know what that means. When the patterns demand a sacrifice, I may be even crueler to you, more monstrous . . ."

"No," she said. "You never were in love before. Love creates patterns, too." She kissed me. Her lips were parched, her skin was icy. She was afraid, but her heart beat hot and strong. "Nothing can hurt us now. Believe me."

"I don't know what to believe any more. We're part of a universe that's big beyond knowledge. What if it turns out to be too gigantic for love?"

"All right," she said composedly. "We won't be dogs in the manger. If love is a little thing and has to end, then let it end. Let all the little things like love and honor and mercy and laughter end . . . if there's something bigger beyond."

"But what can be bigger? What can be beyond?"

"If we're too small to survive, how can we know?"

She crept close to me, the tips of her body like frost. And so we huddled together, breast to breast, warming ourselves with our love, frightened creatures in a wonderous world beyond knowing . . . fearful, and yet an tic ccip ppat inggg.

THEODORE STURGEON

The Man Who Lost the Sea

SAY YOU'RE A KID, AND ONE DARK night you're running along the cold sand with this helicopter in your hand, saying very fast *witchy-witchy-witchy*. You pass the sick man and he wants you to shove off with that thing. Maybe he thinks you're too old to play with toys. So you squat next to him in the sand and tell him it isn't a toy, it's a model. You tell him look here, here's something most people don't know about helicopters. You take a blade of the rotor in your fingers and show him how it can move in the hub, up and down a little, back and forth a little, and twist a little, to change pitch. You start to tell him how this flexibility does away with the gyroscopic effect, but he won't listen. He doesn't want to think about flying, about helicopters, or about you, and he most especially does not want explanations about anything by anybody. Not now. Now, he wants to think about the sea. So you go away.

The sick man is buried in the cold sand with only his head and his left arm showing. He is dressed in a pressure suit and looks like a man from Mars. Built into his left sleeve is a combination timepiece and pressure gauge, the gauge with a luminous blue indicator which makes no sense, the clockhands luminous red. He can hear the pounding of surf and the soft swift pulse of his pumps. One time long ago when he was swimming he went too deep and stayed down too long and came up too fast, and when he came to it was like this: they said, "Don't move, boy. You've got the bends. Don't even *try* to move." He had tried anyway. It hurt. So now, this time, he lies in the sand without moving, without trying.

His head isn't working right. But he knows clearly that it isn't working right, which is a strange thing that happens to people in shock sometimes. Say you were that kid, you could say how it was, because once you woke up lying in the gym office in high school and asked what had happened. They explained how you tried something on the parallel bars and fell on your head. You understood exactly, though you couldn't remember falling. Then a minute later you asked again what had happened and they told you. You understood it. And a minute later . . . forty-one times they told you, and you understood. It was just that no matter how many times they pushed it into your head, it wouldn't stick there; but all the while you *knew* that your head would start working again in time. And in time it did. . . . Of course, if you were that kid, always explaining things to people and to yourself, you wouldn't want to bother the sick man with it now.

Look what you've done already, making him send you away with that angry shrug of the mind (which, with the eyes, are the only things which will move just now). The motionless effort costs him a wave of nausea. He has felt seasick before but he has never *been* seasick, and the formula for that is to keep your eyes on the horizon and stay busy. Now! Then he'd better get busy—now; for there's one place especially not to be seasick in, and that's locked up in a pressure suit. Now!

So he busies himself as best he can, with the seascape, landscape, sky. He lies on high ground, his head propped on a vertical wall of black rock. There is another such outcrop before him, whip-topped with white sand and with smooth flat sand. Beyond and down is valley, salt-flat, estuary; he cannot yet be sure. He is sure of the line of footprints, which begin behind him, pass to his left, disappear in the outcrop shadows, and reappear beyond to vanish at last into the shadows of the valley.

Stretched across the sky is old mourning cloth, with starlight burning holes in it, and between the holes the black is absolute— wintertime, mountaintop sky-black.

(Far off on the horizon within himself, he sees the swell and crest of approaching nausea; he counters with an undertow of weakness, which meets and rounds and settles the wave before it can break. Get busier. *Now.*)

Burst in on him, then, with the X-15 model. That'll get him. Hey, how about this for a gimmick? Get too high for the thin air to give you any control, you have these little jets in the wingtips, see? and on the sides of the *empennage:* bank, roll, yaw, whatever, with squirts of compressed air.

But the sick man curls his sick lip: oh, git, kid, git, will you?— that has nothing to do with the sea. So you git.

Out and out the sick man forces his view, etching all he sees with a meticulous intensity, as if it might be his charge, one day, to duplicate all this. To his left is only starlit sea, windless. In front of him across the valley, rounded hills with dim white epaulettes of light. To his right, the jutting corner of the black wall against which his helmet rests. (He thinks the distant moundings of nausea becalmed, but he will not look yet. So he scans the sky, black and bright, calling Sirius, calling Pleiades, Polaris, Ursa Minor, calling that . . . that . . . Why, it *moves.* Watch it: yes, it moves! It is a fleck of light, seeming to be wrinkled, fissured rather like a chip of boiled cauliflower in the sky. (Of course, he knows better than to trust his own eyes just now.) But that movement . . .

As a child he had stood on cold sand in a frosty Cape Cod evening, watching Sputnik's steady spark rise out of the haze (madly, dawning a little north of west); and after that he had sleeplessly wound special coils for his receiver, risked his life restringing high antennas, all for the brief capture of an unreadable *tweetle-eep-tweetle* in his earphones from Vanguard, Explorer, Lunik, Discoverer, Mercury. He knew them all (well, some people collect match covers, stamps) and he knew especially that unmistakable steady sliding in the sky.

This moving fleck was a satellite, and in a moment, motionless, uninstrumented but for his chronometer and his part-brain, he will know which one. (He is grateful beyond expression—without that sliding chip of light, there were only those footprints, those wandering footprints, to tell a man he was not alone in the world.)

Say you were a kid, eager and challengeable and more than a little bright, you might in a day or so work out a way to measure the period of a satellite with nothing but a timepiece and a brain; you might eventually see that the shadow in the rocks ahead had been there from the first only because of the light from the rising satellite. Now if you check the time exactly at the moment when the shadow on the sand is equal to the height of the outcrop, and time it again when the light is at the zenith and the shadow gone, you will multiply this number of minutes by 8—think why, now: horizon to zenith is one-fourth of the orbit, give or take a little, and halfway up the sky is half that quarter—and you will then know this satellite's period. You know all the periods—ninety minutes, two, two-and-a-half hours; with that and the appearance of this bird, you'll find out which one it is.

But if you were that kid, eager or resourceful or whatever, you wouldn't jabber about it to the sick man, for not only does he not want to be bothered with you, he's thought of all that long since and is even now watching the shadows for that triangular split second of measurement. *Now!* His eyes drop to the face of his chronometer: 0400, near as makes no never mind.

He has minutes to wait now—ten? . . . thirty? . . . twenty-three?—while this baby moon eats up its slice of shadowpie; and that's too bad, the waiting, for though the inner sea is calm there are currents below, shadows that shift and swim. Be busy. Be busy. He must not swim near that great invisible amoeba whatever happens: its first cold pseudopod is even now reaching for the vitals.

Being a knowledgeable young fellow, not quite a kid any more, wanting to help the sick man too, you want to tell him everything you know about that cold-in-the-gut, that reaching invisible surrounding implacable amoeba. You know all about it—listen, you want to yell at him, don't let that touch of cold bother you. Just know what it is, that's all. Know what it is that is touching your gut. You want to tell him, listen:

Listen, this is how you met the monster and dissected it. Listen, you were skin-diving in the Grenadines, a hundred tropical shoal-water islands; you had a new blue snorkel mask, the kind with face plate and breathing tube all in one, and new blue flippers on your feet, and a new blue spear gun—all this new because you'd only begun, you see; you were a beginner, aghast with pleasure at your easy intrusion into this underwater otherworld. You'd been out in a boat, you were coming back, you'd just reached the mouth of the little bay, you'd taken the notion to swim the rest of the way. You'd said as much to the boys and slipped into the warm silky water. You brought your gun.

Not far to go at all, but then beginners find wet distances deceiving. For the first five minutes or so it was only delightful, the sun hot on your back and the water so warm it seemed not to have any temperature at all and you were flying. With your face under the water, your mask was not so much attached as part of you, your wide blue flippers trod away yards, your gun rode all but weightless in your hand, the taut rubber sling making an occasional hum as your passage plucked it in the sunlit green. In your ears crooned the breathy monotone of the snorkel tube, and through the invisible disk of plate glass you saw wonders. The bay was shallow—ten, twelve feet or so—and sandy, with great growths of brain-, bone-, and fire-coral, intricate waving sea fans, and fish—such fish! Scarlet and green and aching azure, gold and rose and slate-color studded with sparks of enamel blue, pink and peach and silver. And that *thing* got into you, that . . . monster.

There were enemies in this otherworld: the sand-colored spotted sea snake with his big ugly head and turned-down mouth, who would not retreat but lay watching the intruder pass; and the mottled moray with jaws like bolt cutters; and somewhere around, certainly, the barracuda with his undershot face and teeth turned inward so that he must take away whatever he might strike. There were urchins—the plump white sea egg with its thick fur of sharp quills and the black ones with the long slender spines that would break off in unwary flesh and fester there for weeks; and filefish and stonefish with their poisoned barbs and lethal meat; and the stingaree who could drive his spike through a leg bone. Yet these were not *monsters*, and could not matter to you, the invader churning along above them all. For you were above them in so many ways—armed, rational, comforted by the close shore (ahead the beach, the rocks on each side) and by the presence of the boat not too far behind. Yet you were . . . attacked.

At first it was uneasiness, not pressing, but pervasive, a contact quite as intimate as that of the sea; you were sheathed in it. And also there was the touch—the cold inward contact. Aware of it at last, you laughed: for Pete's sake, what's there to be scared of?

The monster, the amoeba.

You raised your head and looked back in air. The boat had edged in to the cliff at the right; someone was giving a last poke around for lobster. You waved at the boat; it was your gun you waved, and emerging from the water it gained its latent ounces so that you sank a bit, and as if you had no snorkel on, you tipped your head back to get a breath. But tipping your head back plunged the end of the tube under water; the valve closed; you drew in a hard lungful of nothing at all. You dropped your face under; up came the tube; you got your air, and along with it a bullet of seawater which struck you somewhere inside the throat. You coughed it out and floundered, sobbing as you sucked in air, inflating your chest until it hurt, and the air you got seemed no good, no good at all, a worthless devitalized inert gas.

You clenched your teeth and headed for the beach, kicking strongly and knowing it was the right thing to do; and then below and to the right you saw a great bulk mounding up out of the sand floor of the sea. You knew it was only the reef, rocks and coral and weed, but the sight of it made you scream; you didn't care what you knew. You turned hard left to avoid it, fought by as if it would reach for you, and you couldn't get air, couldn't get air, for all the unobstructed hooting of your snorkel tube. You couldn't bear the mask, suddenly, not for another second, so you shoved it upward clear of your mouth and rolled over, floating on your back and opening your mouth to the sky and breathing with a sort of quacking noise.

It was then and there that the monster well and truly engulfed you, mantling you round and about within itself—formless, borderless, the illimitible amoeba. The beach, mere yards away, and the rocky arms of the bay, and the not too distant boat—these you could identify but no longer distinguish, for they were all one and the same thing . . . the thing called unreachable.

You fought that way for a time, on your back, dangling the gun under and behind you and straining to get enough warm sustained air into your chest. And in time some particles of sanity began to swirl in the roil of your mind, and to dissolve and tint it. The air pumping in and out of your square grinned frightened mouth began to be meaningful at last, and the monster relaxed away from you.

You took stock, saw surf, beach, a leaning tree. You felt the new scend of your body as the rollers humped to become breakers. Only a dozen firm kicks brought you to where you could roll over and double up; your shin struck coral with a lovely agony and you stood in foam and waded ashore. You gained the wet sand, hard sand, and ultimately with two more paces powered by bravado, you crossed high-water mark and lay in the dry sand, unable to move.

You lay in the sand, and before you were able to move or to think, you were able to feel a triumph—a triumph because you were alive and knew that much without thinking at all.

When you *were* able to think, your first thought was of the gun, and the first move you were able to make was to let go at last of the thing. You had nearly died because you had not let it go before; without it you would not have been burdened and you would not have panicked. You had (you began to understand) kept it because someone else would have had to retrieve it—easily enough —and you could not have stood the laughter. You had almost died because They might laugh at you.

This was the beginning of the dissection, analysis, study of the

monster. It began then; it had never finished. Some of what you
had learned from it was merely important; some of the rest—vital.

You had learned, for example, never to swim farther with a
snorkel than you could swim back without one. You learned never
to burden yourself with the unnecessary in an emergency: even
a hand or a foot might be as expendable as a gun; pride was expendable, dignity was. You learned never to dive alone, even if
they laugh at you, even if you have to shoot a fish yourself and say
afterwards "we" shot it. Most of all, you learned that fear has many
fingers, and one of them—a simple one, made of two great a con-
centration of carbon dioxide in your blood, as from too rapid
breathing in and out of the same tube—is not really fear at all but
feels like fear, and can turn into panic and kill you.

Listen, you want to say, listen, there isn't anything wrong with
such an experience or with all the study it leads to, because a man
who can learn enough from it could become fit enough, cautious
enough, foresighted, unafraid, modest, teachable enough to be
chosen, to be qualified for——

You lose the thought, or turn it away, because the sick man feels
that cold touch deep inside, feels it right now, feels it beyond ig-
noring, above and beyond anything that you, with all your experience and certainty, could explain to him even if he would listen,
which he won't. Make him, then; tell him the cold touch is some
simple explainable thing like anoxemia, like gladness even: some
triumph that he will be able to appreciate when his head is working right again.

Triumph? Here he's alive after . . . whatever it is, and that
doesn't seem to be triumph enough, though it was in the Grenadines, and that other time, when he got the bends, saved his own
life, saved two other lives. Now, somehow, it's not the same: there
seems to be a reason why just being alive afterwards isn't a triumph.

Why not triumph? Because not twelve, not twenty, not even
thirty minutes is it taking the satellite to complete its eighth-of-
an-orbit: fifty minutes are gone, and still there's a slice of shadow

yonder. It is this, *this* which is placing the cold finger upon his heart, and he doesn't know why, he doesn't know why, he *will* not know why; he is afraid he shall when his head is working again . . .

Oh, where's the kid? Where is any way to busy the mind, apply it to something, anything else but the watch hand which outruns the moon? Here, kid: come over here—what you got there?

If you were the kid, then you'd forgive everything and hunker down with your new model, not a toy, not a helicopter or a rocket-plane, but the big one, the one that looks like an overgrown cartridge. It's so big even as a model that even an angry sick man wouldn't call it a toy. A giant cartridge, but watch: the lower four-fifths is Alpha—all muscle—over a million pounds thrust. (Snap it off, throw it away.) Half the rest is Beta—all brains—it puts you on your way. (Snap it off, throw it away.) And now look at the polished fraction which is left. Touch a control somewhere and see—see? it has wings—wide triangular wings. This is Gamma, the one with wings, and on its back is a small sausage; it is a moth with a sausage on its back. The sausage (click! it comes free) is Delta. Delta is the last, the smallest: Delta is the way home.

What will they think of next? Quite a toy. Quite a toy. Beat it, kid. The satellite is almost overhead, the sliver of shadow going —going—almost gone and . . . gone.

Check: 0459. Fifty-nine minutes?, give or take a few. Time eight . . . 472 . . . is, uh, 7 hours 52 minutes.

Seven hours fifty-two minutes? Why there isn't a satellite round earth with a period like that. In all the solar system there's only . . .

The cold finger turns fierce, implacable.

The east is paling and the sick man turns to it, wanting the light, the sun, an end to questions whose answers couldn't be looked upon. The sea stretches endlessly out to the growing light, and endlessly, somewhere out of sight, the surf roars. The paling east bleaches the sandy hilltops and throws the line of footprints into aching relief. That would be the buddy, the sick man knows, gone for help. He can not at the moment recall who the buddy is, but in time he will, and meanwhile the footprints make him less alone.

The sun's upper rim thrusts itself above the horizon with a flash of green, instantly gone. There is no dawn, just the green flash and then a clear white blast of unequivocal sunup. The sea could not be whiter, more still, if it were frozen and snow-blanketed. In the west, stars still blaze, and overhead the crinkled satellite is scarcely abashed by the growing light. A formless jumble in the valley below begins to resolve itself into a sort of tent-city, or installation of some kind, with tube-like and sail-like buildings. This would have meaning for the sick man if his head were working right. Soon, it would. Will. (Oh . . .)

The sea, out on the horizon just under the rising sun, is behaving strangely, for in that place where properly belongs a pool of unbearable brightness, there is instead a notch of brown. It is as if the white fire of the sun is drinking dry the sea—for look, look! the notch becomes a bow and the bow a crescent, racing ahead of the sunlight, white sea ahead of it and behind it a cocoa-dry stain spreading across and down toward where he watches.

Beside the finger of fear which lies on him, another finger places itself, and another, making ready for that clutch, that grip, that ultimate insane squeeze of panic. Yet beyond that again, past that squeeze when it comes, to be savored if the squeeze is only fear and not panic, lies triumph—triumph, and a glory. It is perhaps this which constitutes his whole battle: to fit himself, prepare himself to bear the utmost that fear could do, for if he can do that, there is a triumph on the other side. But . . . not yet. Please, not yet awhile.

Something flies (or flew, or will fly—he is a little confused on this point) toward him, from the far right where the stars still shine. It is not a bird and it is unlike any aircraft on earth, for the aerodynamics are wrong. Wings so wide and so fragile would be useless, would melt and tear away in any of earth's atmosphere but the outer fringes. He sees then (because he prefers to see it so) that it is the kid's model, or part of it, and for a toy, it does very well indeed.

It is the part called Gamma, and it glides in, balancing, paral-

lels the sand and holds away, holds away slowing, then settles,
all in slow motion, throwing up graceful sheet fountains of fine
sand from its skids. And it runs along the ground for an impossible
distance, letting down its weight by the ounce and stingily the
ounce, until *look out* until a skid *look out* fits itself into a bridged
crevasse *look out, look out!* and still moving on, it settles down to
the struts. Gamma then, tired, digs her wide left wingtip carefully into the racing sand, digs it in hard; and as the wing breaks
off, Gamma slews, sidles, slides slowly, pointing her other triangular tentlike wing at the sky, and broadside crushes into the
rocks at the valley's end.

As she rolls smashing over, there breaks from her broad back
the sausage, the little Delta, which somersaults away to break
its back upon the rocks, and through the broken hull, spill smashed
shards of graphite from the moderator of her power pile. *Look
out! Look out!* and at the same instant from the finally checked
mass of Gamma there explodes a doll, which slides and tumbles
into the sand, into the rocks and smashed hot graphite from the
wreck of Delta.

The sick man numbly watches this toy destroy itself: what will
they think of next?—and with a gelid horror prays at the doll lying in the raging rubble of the atomic pile: *don't stay there, man
—get away! get away! that's hot, you know?* But it seems like a
night and a day and half another night before the doll staggers to
its feet and, clumsy in its pressure-suit, runs away up the valley-
side, climbs a sand-topped outcrop, slips, falls, lies under a slow
cascade of cold ancient sand until, but for an arm and the helmet,
it is buried.

The sun is high now, high enough to show the sea is not a sea,
but brown plain with the frost burned off it, as now it burns away
from the hills, diffusing in air and blurring the edges of the sun's
disk, so that in a very few minutes there is no sun at all, but only
a glare in the east. Then the valley below loses its shadows, and
like an arrangement in a diorama, reveals the form and nature
of the wreckage below: no tent-city this, no installation, but the

true real ruin of Gamma and the eviscerated hulk of Delta. (Alpha was the muscle, Beta the brain; Gamma was a bird, but Delta, Delta was the way home.)

And from it stretches the line of footprints, to and by the sick man, above to the bluff, and gone with the sandslide which had buried him there. Whose footprints?

He knows whose, whether or not he knows that he knows, or wants to or not. He knows what satellite has (give or take a bit) a period like that (want it exactly?—it's 7.66 hours). He knows what world has such a night, and such a frosty glare by day. He knows these things as he knows how spilled radio-actives will pour the crash and mutter of surf into a man's earphones.

Say you were that kid: say, instead, at last, that you are the sick man, for they are the same; surely then you can understand why of all things, even while shattered, shocked, sick with radiation calculated (leaving) radiation computed (arriving) and radiation past all bearing (lying in the wreckage of Delta) you would want to think of the sea. For no farmer who fingers the soil with love and knowledge, no poet who sings of it, artist, contractor, engineer, even child bursting into tears at the inexpressible beauty of a field of daffodils—none of these is as intimate with Earth as those who live on, live with, breathe and drift in its seas. So of these things you must think; with these you must dwell until you are less sick and more ready to face the truth.

The truth, then, is that the satellite fading here is Phobos, that those footprints are your own, that there is no sea here, that you have crashed and are killed and will in a moment be dead. The cold hand ready to squeeze and still your heart is not anoxia or even fear, it is death. Now, if there is something more important than this, now is the time for it to show itself.

The sick man looks at the line of his own footprints, which testify that he is alone, and at the wreckage below, which states that there is no way back, and at the white east and the mottled west and the paling bleek-like satellite above. Surf sounds in his ears. He hears his pumps. He hears what is left of his breathing. The cold clamps down and folds him round past measuring, past all limits.

Then he speaks, cries out: then with joy he takes his triumph at the other side of death, as one takes a great fish, as one completes a skilled and mighty task, rebalances at the end of some great daring leap; and as he used to say "we shot a fish" he uses no "I":

"God," he cries, dying on Mars, "God, we made it!"

THROUGH TIME AND SPACE
WITH FERDINAND FEGHOOT: XV

In 2961, FERDINAND FEGHOOT persuaded the Council of Worlds to admit Little Stravinsky. After Dr. Hassan ben-Sabah had finished denouncing that planet, he said:

"Gentlemen, our learned colleague has accused the Little Stravinskians of 'the utmost barbarity'—even though they have achieved automation and space travel. Why? Because they cling to their old, picturesque customs. They shackle their King to his throne with a Chain of Gold which is their equivalent of the Crown. Every year, they choose fifty singers with seven-stringed harps to serve this Chain, as they put it, entertaining the Monarch with ballads and lays. At the end of each year, they have a great contest in which the singers belabor each other with whips until the last one on his feet gets the Grand Prize. Well, what of it?"

"The Grand Prize is a beautiful virgin!" screamed Dr. ben-Sabah. "She is called Miss Little Stravinsky of, say, 2961. The winner gets her for his concubine. It is shocking! Immoral! Uncivilized! Nothing like this ever happened on Earth!"

"Nonsense!" laughed Ferdinand Feghoot. "Why, we even have an old saying: Bards of a fetter flog to get 'er."

GRENDEL BRIARTON

Duke of Earl

eacial

Buckleys
1701 Church St
Nashville, Tenn